GLITTERBUSH

GLITTERBUSH

Hal Barwood

Planting Paranoia
an astrobotanical adventure

Glitterbush

This is a work of fiction. Southern Arizona, the city of Tucson, national intelligence agencies, robots, crystalline minerals, and Sonoran Desert plants are real, but the communities, enterprises, locations, and oddities depicted herein are either fictional in themselves or fictional in detail. All the characters and incidents in this fictional world are products of the author's imagination. No resemblance to any real person or the operations of any real organization is intended.

for Olin & Lillian

and the future

Table of Contents

PART ONE

1

Ten Years ago . . .

"Whoa, Cookie. See that? What in the name of all four aces do we have here?"

Rancher Ken Olson was mounted up on his favorite roan mare, conducting a leisurely spring survey of the KO Ranch, his property in the hills west of Tucson, Arizona. He had crested a sandy ridge and was squinting down into a little valley. There among the creosote and cholla and buffelgrass, something was reflecting the afternoon sun like a mirror, with dazzling effect.

"That's not a creosote bush, Cookie old gal."

He jammed a knee into the horse's side and coaxed her down the gentle slope. As he worked his way to the bottom he kept a sharp eye on his surroundings. This time of year, the Sonoran Desert was cold at night. Maybe some poor wandering soul lost one of those space blanket things. Or a big water bottle. Or some kind of crinkly food wrap. He stopped and scanned the area for intruders. Human coyotes occasionally led bewildered migrants through his land on their way to a better life in *El Norte*. Most of the coyotes carried weapons, and he did not want to get shot.

When he approached within thirty yards of the glistening object he could make out some detail. It was a bush, all right, about the size of the nearby brittlebush plants, sitting in a shallow depression. Thin stalks thrust upward from the sandy soil, and leaves sprouted from each stalk.

Olson dismounted and led his horse forward for a close look. He felt vaguely uneasy and cast quick glances this way and that, tickled by the sensation of being watched. But no humans or animals were anywhere to be seen. He loosened his old revolver in its holster, just in case a snake was lurking.

The leaves of the bush were copper-colored. As they turned on their stems in a light afternoon breeze they appeared alternately shiny and dull. Olson thought their metallic glint was mighty strange, but their size and shape — square, an inch across, with the stem coming off one corner — was even stranger. He fingered one, plucked it for closer examination. It was hard, with a subtle geometric texture. He thought it looked more like some kind of crystal than any desert plant.

He scanned the area again for intruders, trying to shake off an unaccountable case of the willies.

▼

A few days later Olson was standing in a dimly lit tavern on the south side of Tucson, enjoying a beer at the bar with some of his old cronies. In between snatches of conversation about beef prices, the subject of his strange bush came up.

Playing cards at a nearby table was Jack Beard, a feature reporter for the *Pima County Prospect,* Tucson's penny-saver weekly newspaper. His interest in poker ebbed when he overheard mention of a plant with metal leaves. He folded his hand, stood up, and introduced himself.

"Beard? The *Prospect?* Oh sure, I've seen it. At the grocery store. Nice to meetcha," said Olson.

"You're a rancher?"

"Sure am. Out west, off Kinney Road. Got a pretty good spread where I raise cattle and horses."

Beard signaled the bartender to refill both their glasses.

"I couldn't help overhearing your story about that bush. Metal? Out there in the middle of nowhere?"

"That's about the size of it."

"What do you think? Some college prank? An art project?"

"Didn't look that way. Looked like it was alive . . . growing."

"You know, I do stories about the odd doings around here. Keep the paper colorful, grab those shoppers' interest. Could I take a look?"

Olson studied the man. He was small and old — as old as himself — nattily dressed in a nice shirt and slacks, with a string tie in place. His hair was slicked back and neatly parted.

"Well, I don't know. How are you on a horse? It's a ride."

Beard hesitated. "The truth is, I have never been on a horse."

"I've got an old Jeep, but I hate to put tracks through the desert."

"Of course, I understand." He handed Olson his business card. "I may call you."

▼

Associate Professor of Geology Amos Jurnegan, Ph.D., a trim man in his fifties with a full head of greying hair and a short beard, was staring out of his office window in the Gould-Simpson building on the University of Arizona campus.

Spring break was underway, and his view, framed by bifocals on his nose and palm trees below, revealed not a single student on the grounds. He sighed, imagining himself down in Rocky Point fishing on the Sea of Cortez. Instead he was preparing material for the annual GeoDaze conference. He was bored and glad to be disturbed when a respectful knock came tapping on his office door.

"Ah, hello, am I in the Department of Geosciences?"

"That you are."

"Professor Jurnegan?"

"That's me." He stared at his visitor, a small fellow getting along in years, wearing a neat white shirt and string tie. "And you are?"

"Jack Beard. I'm a reporter."

"Uh-oh, what's the scandal?" He smiled. "You get no comment from me."

"No scandal. I heard an interesting story the other day, and before I write anything up, I thought I ought to check with someone who knows some science."

"What sort of story?"

"Well, sir, a rancher I know, man named Ken Olson, spotted a funny-looking bush out on his property near here. He never saw anything like it, and it kind of bothered him."

"I'm a geologist, not a botanist. Why pick on me?"

"I couldn't find anyone over in Life Sciences."

"Spring break. They're all off living life instead of trying to teach it."

"Can't blame 'em, huh? This bush I heard about, the rancher claimed it was made out of metal. Some kind of shiny metal crystals."

Jurnegan's eyebrows rose.

"It was growing?"

"That's what the man said."

"Really. Is he reliable? How'd he happen to confide this information?"

"Chatter in Bromley's Mexican Pub, southside a ways."

"Was he drunk?"

"No, sir. Olson's a stand-up, no-nonsense kind of fellow. If he says he saw this thing, he saw it."

"Okay."

"My question to you is, what was he looking at? You ever hear of something like this?"

Jurnegan's mental gears started to mesh.

"No, not exactly that description, no."

"I see. It's a mystery. That's my lead."

"Now hold on. Your informant is a rancher, you said, yes? He might not have just the right kind of vocabulary needed to identify a botanical object, no offense."

Jurnegan reached into a book shelf and withdrew a copy of *The Sibley Guide to Trees*. He thumbed through it with knitted brows. Then he pulled down a copy of *Shrubs and Trees of the Desert Southwest* and made a show of examining its contents. After a few moments he lifted his head out of the pages and addressed the reporter.

"Here's my thought," he said, brandishing the book to cover an improvised lie. "Brittlebush mutation. Not common, but it is known in the literature."

"Not a mystery, not to you anyway."

"Not a mystery at all, I'm afraid."

"I could write it up as an unusual freak."

"I wouldn't bother. Kind of dull, really, you ask me. You want to educate your readers? Get their attention? Worry them about tamarisks. They're invasive, and they're stealing our water."

Beard nodded, completely deflated.

"Thank you for your time, Professor."

"Glad to help."

▼

Olson was out in the barnyard feeding his horse an apple when a dust trail boiled up on the long ranch drive, heading his way.

He turned to watch the approaching car. He didn't recognize it.

"What in hell, Cookie . . ."

The car bounced into the ranch house yard, maneuvered around one of Olson's tractors and slowed to a stop, revealing itself as a Land Rover when the dust settled. Out stepped a bearded man in his fifties. He was wearing a safari vest with pockets and rings and loops stitched all over it, and he was carrying a fancy digital camera. He mashed a camping hat down on his head and came forward.

"Hello, there. Mr. Olson?"

"Yup. What can I do for you?"

"Nice place you got here." The man cast his eyes around the buildings, the vehicles, and the animals with evident appreciation. "My name's Amos Jurnegan. I teach over at the University." He gestured back toward Tucson. "I heard an interesting story," he said with a grin. "Something about a bush you might have seen, a bush made out of metal."

"Who told you that?"

"Some old-time reporter for the local paper. He wanted to know what I thought about it . . ."

"That guy Beard. He's a nosy old goat."

". . . but I don't know what to think. Did he have his facts on straight?"

Olson regarded his visitor with cool detachment. The man looked alert, looked serious, looked like he spent time in the great outdoors. "What do you teach?"

"I'm a geologist." Jurnegan paused, then added, "with a special interest in how plants and animals impact the natural world, help shape the land."

"And you're curious about my bush."

Jurnegan nodded. "Very."

Olson thought for a moment, then started toward his barn. He made a come-along sign, and the professor eagerly followed. They trudged around the building, worked their way past a corral full of cattle.

"Small cows," noted Jurnegan.

"*Criollos,*" returned Olson. "Small, good on arid land. A trend that started in New Mexico and spread here. Coronado brought these animals in from New Spain, four hundred years ago."

"I had no idea," said Jurnegan.

"No one does. Here's what you're looking for."

They stopped ten yards past the corral. Standing in front of them was a tall bush, coppery in color. The leaves made a little jangling sound in the light breeze that blew across the ranch.

"Hello!" said Jurnegan. He brought up his camera and started taking pictures.

"I decided to replant. It's half a day's ride out to where I found this thing," explained Olson.

"I didn't really believe that reporter, but you never know. Glad I checked."

Jurnegan bent over the plant. He noted the bronzy shine, fingered the leaves. He was beside himself. Goose bumps were forming on his arms. A feeling of tremendous discovery gripped him. Visions of the Nobel Prize flickered through his head.

"I'd like to buy your plant, Mr. Olson. For research. Name your price."

2

Nine years ago . . .

Samuel Chow was a third generation farmer. His great grandfather emigrated from Guangdong Province in China to work on the railroads. When the last tunnel was blasted and the tracks were all laid, he took up residence in the Sacramento River Delta, where he ran a dry goods store.

He was one of a multitude, and the good white folks of California felt threatened by the flood of immigrants who didn't look like them. In 1879 the state legislature revised the California constitution to restrict Asian property ownership. In 1913 it passed a law to enforce the constitution's provisions.

His son, Samuel's grandfather, chafed under the restrictions, felt himself marginalized, recoiled from the white resentment, and moved himself and his young wife to Arizona. There he found work tending citrus trees. He was good at it. He lived frugally, saved his money.

Just before Arizona passed its own alien land law, he bought a lemon grove from an elderly widow. When he died, ownership devolved upon his only child, Samuel's father, who fared even better. After all the land laws were overturned by the U.S. Supreme Court, he moved to Marana, just north of Tucson, where he bought a small pecan orchard.

Pecans, native to the Midwest and Old South where water was plentiful, were becoming a big commercial crop in the deserts of southern Arizona, thanks to modern irrigation techniques. Samuel's father prospered.

Samuel himself was fascinated by the desert landscape, and he liked to hike out beyond the trees he inherited looking for exotic minerals and semi-precious stones. He was sharp-eyed, and he found a few.

One day, his teenage daughter Holly was outside feeding chickens when Dad came back cradling a strange bush. It had a coppery cast. The exposed root ball was angular and jagged.

She regarded the thing with wary mistrust.

"Where did you find that?"

Her father pointed westward. "Up country. In the hills."

Holly tentatively reached out and touched the glistening leaves. They clattered musically, like a wind chime.

"Cool. Also creepy. What is it?"

Samuel Chow shook his head. "I have no idea." He grinned like a happy schoolboy. "Never know what you'll find out here."

Holly took charge of the bush. "I'll find a spot. We should plant it, let it grow, see what happens. Maybe I can do a report for science class."

3

Eight years ago . . .

Professor Jurnegan had given some consideration to his best plan of action. He didn't trust the university environment. No doubt, if they got wind of his discovery, the boys in Life Sciences would stick their noses in, and they might even take over. Probably would, he decided. Almost certainly. As a journeyman faculty member in the wrong department, who was granted tenure without much enthusiasm, his contributions would be downgraded, possibly dismissed outright by the biologists. He thought he'd be lucky to get his name on the papers that were sure to emerge from his amazing discovery, papers he wanted to write, papers guaranteed to establish the reputation of whatever author submitted them.

So he told no one on campus. Instead, he took out a bank loan and leased a hothouse on South Kolb Road, out near the airplane graveyard on the southern edge of the city. There he proceeded, with great difficulty, to grow offshoots of his strange bush. After more than a year of hard work he had six healthy plants, each one about a foot high.

He had rigged up a lab bench for chemical analysis and, with the help of an arsenal of powerful reagents, had made some progress in deciphering the composition of his extraordinary specimens.

He wasn't satisfied with his progress, however. He needed space, electrical power, lights, X-ray diffraction equipment, DNA sequencers, spectrum analyzers, a long list.

In pursuit of his ambitions, today he was standing at the lab door, happy to be outside in cool spring air. He was waiting for an important visitor. A visitor with money to spend.

Presently a Mercedes sedan drove into his little parking area and a plump older man in a baggy linen suit emerged. He looked around with a dubious scowl as he wobbled toward the hothouse, leaning on a cane.

"Mr. Ingleside?" asked Jurgenson, thrusting out a hand.

"Hubert Ingleside. Call me Hub. You're Jurgenson?"

Jurgenson nodded. They shook hands.

"Welcome to my slightly unorthodox research lab."

"Not much to look at, I'll say that."

"The view is better inside. Let me show you."

Jurgenson led Ingleside into his lab, led the man over to the original bush, which now towered four feet above the clear polypropylene tub in which it was sitting. He threw a switch and a pair of grow lights bathed the plant in artificial sunlight.

"See this? My discovery. Why I called you."

"Mmm. What is it? Looks like a sculpture piece for some damn office building."

"Not at all. It's a plant. Unique. A new species. New genus for that matter. Good God, a whole new family in the tree of life."

Ingleside looked at the bush without much interest, rattled the leaves with his walking stick. He leaned down to the roots, visible through the plastic enclosure. A rhomboid shaped block the size of a potato was attached there.

"I'm not a research and development man, Professor. I make optical sensors for our missiles. I do it because the work turns a profit."

"I know, *Opticon.* Great company."

"I'm also a U of A alumnus, proud of my old school. Why don't you show this to your colleagues at the university?" He turned a quizzical eye on the professor.

Jurgenson clasped his hands together. "It's not hard to explain. My colleagues are academics. They want to write papers. Once they publish, they'll lose all interest."

"How about yourself?"

"Well, I wouldn't mind getting published in the right journal. But I also want to exploit the possibilities."

"Unh-huh, make some money. And what's the potential here? Call me slow, but I don't see it right off the bat."

Jurnegan held up a finger. He turned to the bench beside the plant, picked up a pair of electrodes, and stuck them into the soil holding the bush. He turned off the grow lights, connected the electrode wiring to a digital voltmeter. He handed the instrument to Ingleside.

"Notice the readout? Zero-point-zero-something insignificant, see?"

"I see."

"Now I turn on the lights overhead, like so . . ." He snapped the light switch. ". . . and, tah-dah, what now?"

Ingleside held the voltmeter at arm's length. "Two-point-four-two volts."

"And I didn't even connect the electrodes directly to any of the roots, if those little tendrils are actually roots."

Ingleside puckered his lips. "Solar power."

"Yessir. If nothing else. A breakthrough. But I will need financial backing to develop the possibilities. It takes money to make money. "

"So I've been told."

"Of course, I've read all about you and your very successful company," said Jurnegan, trying not to sound too eager. "I know you're well-heeled, with a penchant for risky investments." He grinned. "I'll be a good one."

Ingleside frowned at the makeshift lab, at the milky Plexiglas ceiling, at the decaying wooden beams barely holding the place together. A sour expression wrinkled his brow.

"The first thing we have to do is get you out of here."

4

Five years ago . . .

James Lockwood, a slim, muscular, dark-haired man in prime physical shape, was hiking along a little-used trail on the north side of the Catalina mountains, not far from the Tucson exurb of Oracle, Arizona, where he was born and grew up thirty years ago.

He had just mustered out of the U.S. Army as a captain in the Military Intelligence Corps, with two deployments to Afghanistan under his belt. He'd had enough of unwinnable foreign wars and declined to re-enlist when his four-year commitment ended.

He was repeating one of the hikes he had made when working toward Eagle Scout, back in high school days. He was using the demanding terrain, with its steep ridges, spiny cactuses, and dense thorny undergrowth as a way to meditate on his future.

Military duty was history, but he realized the experience had given him a taste for unearthing secrets, for getting to know the unknown, for making a mark on life. He considered the possibilities — CIA, NSA, Department of State, private security, Arizona congressional staffer — without coming to a conclusion. In truth he was flummoxed by civilian life, and readily admitted as much to himself and to anyone who asked.

As the day wore on, he found himself on the rim of a steep canyon. A trickle of water was visible coursing down through it. His thoughts were interrupted by a sudden glint down below. The sun was reflecting off something bright and shiny. What the hell?

He walked back and forth, looking for a way to descend for a closer look. He was no mountain climber and wanted an easy route down. Something walkable. But the cliff face was forbidding. His rational self suggested forgetting the whole thing, but the more he looked at the shiny object, the more curious he became. After carefully evaluating the rock face, he selected a narrow chimney with knobs and joints where fingers could grab and toes could fit. He took a deep breath and lowered himself into the vertical channel. His foot felt a ledge, then another. He moved slowly, concentrating on every little move.

He was halfway down and making good progress when an outcrop he was grasping came loose. He clawed at the rock but found no other grip. His right foot slipped from its toehold.

"Oh shit."

He started to slide, picked up speed, and skittered downward, bouncing off rocky protrusions, tumbling head over heels down the canyon wall.

"Ahhhhh — !"

He crashed through the creosote bushes crowding the bottom of the drop and rolled into the trickle of water in the sandy canyon bottom.

"Unnnhhhhh . . ."

He was dazed and barely conscious. Groaning in agony, he dragged himself out of the little streambed and up onto a sandy bank. There, just before he blacked out, he noticed he had almost fallen on the shiny object of his quest. It was some kind of bush. He reached out to touch it.

▼

Twenty-four hours later a trio of bird-watching women found him buried in debris.

"Look here, Ethel."

Lockwood's head and one arm were visible, but the rest of him was covered in a loose layer of sand.

"Oh dear."

One of them took his pulse.

"He's breathing."

"The sand . . ."

"Breezy last night, and" — Ethel tilted a hiking stick up toward the cliff where scratches and damaged plants attested to Lockwood's spectacular fall — "he must have come down that cliff the hard way. And then the wind pushed the sand on top."

"Like a little dune."

"It's a wonder he's alive."

Alive he was. While the women were discussing a glossy black bird that had just landed on a nearby saguaro, Lockwood woke up. He shook himself free of the sand and sat upright.

"Whoa, ladies, he's awake," said Ethel.

"Yeah," he croaked. He looked back up the cliff. "Wow, that is some double-black-diamond ski run."

"Are you all right, young man?"

Lockwood felt himself. No broken bones, no obvious bruises. "I think so."

"That's amazing. You are a very lucky person," said Ethel.

"Truly amazing," affirmed the second bird watcher.

"I would not have believed it," said the third.

"Didn't anyone ever tell you not to hike alone?"

"Yeah, I guess." He winced. "I don't follow all the rules."

"I should say not."

Lockwood raised his right arm. Tangles of blackened crystalline branchlets were entwined around his wrist. Little pointed ends were embedded in the flesh of his forearm. He clawed the things off with his other hand.

He looked around. "Where's the rest of my bush?"

"What?"

"Up on the canyon rim there, I spotted a bush down here shining like a mirror. Metal or crystals."

They all scanned the area. Ethel bent over and picked up a twig. "Could be this? It's black now, but it looks burned. Maybe you saw a fire."

"A burning bush, ha ha." The second bird watcher clapped her hands.

Lockwood was puzzled. "Maybe."

Ethel regarded Lockwood with beady eyes. "You look a little bit confused. Sure you're okay?"

"Seem to be."

Ethel was not convinced. "What's your name?"

Lockwood was stumped. Now that the question was asked, he realized he didn't know. "Um, thinking. I have it. Right here." He pointed at his head. "Tip of the tongue deal."

"Oh sure. You see stars?"

He nodded. "Unh-huh. Planets and comets too."

"Could be you're concussed. Can you walk?"

Lockwood stood up. "I'll be all right."

"Try again. Your name."

Lockwood scowled. The most tightly bound portion of a man's identity was strangely missing. "It'll come, it'll come."

"You march straight down the hill, you hear, and see a doctor," ordered

Ethel. "You've had quite a fall. Think of all those football players. Concussions are serious."

Ethel's companions nodded agreement.

Lockwood smacked the sand off his clothes. "Will do, ma'am."

The hikers moved away up the canyon.

"That bird, I claim phainopepla."

"How do you know it's not a female pyrrhuloxia?"

"The color, the wing patches, the flycatcher jizz."

Lockwood started downhill. Then he stopped and shouted back to the receding bird watchers.

"Hey! It's Lockwood! My name is James Lockwood!"

He laughed, relieved to get his mind back.

▼

He was still feeling scattered when he reached the trail head parking lot and his old Nissan pickup truck. But one source of confusion was now eliminated. The purpose of his hike was accomplished in a roundabout way, and he now knew what he wanted to do with his life — work for that astronaut, General Upshaw, the guy who wrestled with the Hubble telescope. Get a job at NASA!

"You can call me 'Jim,'" he said, aloud and proud.

"Jim has a plan!"

5

Three years ago . . .

Advanced Solar Research LLC, the company created by Professor Jurgenson with Hubert Ingleside's money, was now quietly doing business in the desert outside Tucson's city limits. Operations were housed in a gleaming white pre-fab building assembled from arches of pleated steel, making it look like an overgrown accordion. A fenced-in garden plot was attached to the rear of the building, where a half-dozen gleaming bushes were slowly growing.

Inside, Jurgenson was demonstrating his latest discoveries to his benefactor.

"Look at this, Hub . . ."

Ingleside squinted at the little square leaflets on a small bush.

"No, no — forget the leaves, check the root ball. Here . . ."

Jurnegan lifted the bush out of its container and placed it on a Plexiglas tray.

"Okay, ready? I turn on the grow lights, like so . . ."

He snapped a switch and intense white light filled the lab.

". . . and we see the root ball . . . well, root block is more like it, a solid mass, right?"

Ingleside was concentrating all his attention on the very odd plant, expecting to be fooled by a clever magic trick. "If you say so. Your point?"

"Now, here's the thing — see that metal plate on the bottom of the tray? I flip a switch and charge it electrically with, let me see, about ten volts."

Ingleside caught his breath. The root ball or block instantly dissolved into what looked like a pile of sand.

"Sand . . ?"

"And, when I turn off the power, *voilà,* the sand reassembles into the root ball."

Indeed it did. Ingleside shivered involuntarily. He scratched his head.

"Spooky, huh?" said Jurnegan with a grin. "Gives me the creeps. You too, looks like."

Ingleside nodded. "What the hell kind of plant is this? What are we dealing with?"

Jurnegan shook his head. He grinned again. He was elated by the mystery, by the chance to investigate something completely new. "I have no idea, to tell you the truth. I've written a paper."

"You what?"

"It's speculative, doesn't get into the details. It proposes the mineral *perovskite* as a novel solar power source. The leaves, I did an analysis, and they are a species of perovskite. Titanium crystal lattice, with some calcium in there, classic stuff."

"Don't tell me you published something."

"Oh yeah, of course I did. In *The Journal of Geophysical Processes*, peer-reviewed and all."

Ingleside's face reddened.

"Jesus Christ, Amos, we agreed to keep this secret until we can commercialize. Entrepreneurs will read all about this, this perovskite material, and they'll go to school on us. We'll lose our lead."

"Nonsense. We don't really know what's going on. We need information, we need more specimens. My paper is a lure, it's bait. It will snag anyone who is working on this."

"You better damn well hope so."

"It's a fishing pole, and we'll catch ourselves some fish, you wait."

▼

Holly Chow, now a senior at the University of Arizona with a major in engineering, was hunched over her laptop computer in the Chow family ranch house in Marana. She was finishing up a school assignment when she heard a car pull up outside, heard a door slam and, shortly thereafter, heard a loud knock.

She opened her door to find a bearded man of fifty or so standing there, dressed in casual clothes, with a safari vest on and a camera in his hand.

"Miss Chow?"

Chow nodded. "Yes?"

"Hello, there. I'm Amos Jurnegan, I teach geology over at the University."

"Unh-huh. What do you want?"

Jurnegan was struck by the very pretty young woman confronting him on the step. He registered her chilly response and smiled a disarming smile.

"Well, I recently got a letter. A very interesting letter, I may say, describing metallic bushes."

"Unh-huh."

"The letter was from you, right? You wrote it?"

"Yes . . . you're Jurnegan? The professor?"

"I take it you read my paper."

"In that geophysics journal. All about an exotic mineral in the leaves of plants."

"Perovskite," intoned Jurnegan with professorial authority.

"Yeah, I remember . . . perovskite."

Chow abruptly stuck out a hand. "Nice to meet you."

Jurnegan took it and shook it.

"Likewise."

"I read your report, but I still don't understand what Dad found."

Jurnegan went right for the big question: "May I see what you've got?"

Chow stepped down into the yard and beckoned to the professor.

"Over here."

She led the way toward the family pecan orchard. Jurnegan stopped near the edge. Water was misting into the air under each tree trunk. A trickle worked its way into the gravel at his feet.

Chow opened a box on the side of a shed, turned a valve, and the water stopped flowing.

"Irrigation method?" wondered the professor. "Doesn't look like others I've seen."

"It's original. I designed it for my thesis."

Jurnegan was impressed. "How'd that turn out?"

"Oh, I got an A. We're hydrating with about half the water Dad used last year. Come on, our little bush lives just around the corner."

On the back side of the shed a golden bush was growing. Three feet high, three feet wide, with a crown of metallic little leaves that sparkled in afternoon sunshine. Jurnegan whistled. Although he was already growing several bushes in his lab, a spasm of shivery wonder ran up his spine.

"That's a big one," he said.

"You've seen more of these?"

"Oh yes."

"What is it? Kind of spooky, right? Dad and I have been racking our brains."

Jurnegan hesitated. Then: "It's a mutation. That's what we're studying. The betting is brittlebush, but you can't be sure."

Chow frowned. "No, I guess not."

Jurnegan dropped to a knee, leaned forward and began photographing the plant. "I would like to buy your bush, Miss Chow. This could be a big factor in my research."

Chow thought about the idea. "Okay, why not? Our family contribution to science."

"How much?"

"Hmm, I've never thought about it. I'll have to ask Dad."

A new voice turned them both around. "Don't bother. That bush is not for sale." It was Samuel Chow, Holly's father, walking over from an old tractor he had been working on.

Jurnegan got to his feet. "Sorry to hear that, sir. You have a very valuable item here. Valuable for science, anyway."

"Be that as it may," said the older Chow. "It is part of the ranch now. Not for sale."

"I'm willing to make a very generous offer. Sure I can't change your mind?"

"I am sure. No sale."

Jurnegan shrugged. "Well, I tried. You take good care of this bush. And if you have a change of heart, here's my number."

He attempted to hand Chow a business card. The old man stuck his hands in his pockets. His daughter snatched the card, and Jurnegan turned away.

The Chows watched him drive off in his Land Rover.

"I'll bet we could get a lot of money for this thing, Dad. What's biting you?"

"Don't know. Don't much like our bush, but I like that man even less."

▼

Three weeks later Holly Chow was awakened in the middle of the night by an angry crackling noise. Flickering red light was coming through her window. She eased herself out of bed and looked outside.

"Dad! Dad!" she shouted, running for the door. "The shed is on fire."

The fire department arrived half an hour later, and by then the building was reduced to ashes and embers. Chow's irrigation machinery, much of which was fashioned from PVC plastic, was scorched and melted.

Out beyond the shed's blackened concrete foundation, the Chows' golden bush was gone.

▼

Jurnegan arrived at the Advanced Solar Research facility mid-morning, after an early lecture. A white Mercedes, which he recognized as belonging to his partner Ingleside, was already parked out front. He was irritated to see that most of the remaining parking area was taken up by a huge Pewter Metallic Hummer H2.

The front door to the lab was open, further irritating him. He stepped inside and was surprised to find Ingleside chatting with a couple of rough-looking dudes dressed in what he took to be military fatigues.

"Hub," he said. "To what do I owe the pleasure?"

"Morning, Amos."

Ingleside grinned. He turned to one of the men standing with him. The man lifted a plastic tub from the nearest bench and handed it over. Ingleside turned back to Jurnegan and presented him with a three-foot by three-foot metallic bush, complete with a blocky root ball visible through the transparent walls of the tub.

"What — ?" Jurnegan's eyes went wide.

"Midnight asset acquisition, my friend."

"From the Chow place?"

"Who knows?"

"Come on, Hub, we need discovery coordinates. Research methodology, how we'll know where to look for these things."

Ingleside inclined his head, bowing to the demands of science.

"Okay, then, at the expense of security and deniability, you can take that nut farm as the location of our, uh, discovery."

Jurnegan nodded and set the bush on a bench bristling with lab equipment. In spite of the way the thing arrived, he was thrilled to have it. He rubbed his hands together to brush off any dirt.

"So, tell me, who are these guys?"

Ingleside gestured to his companions. "Business associates. Allow me to introduce the Durango brothers."

The men stepped forward, arms outstretched.

"I'm Earl," said the older one. He was tall and sported a bristly moustache.

"Tyler here. 'Ty' to my friends," said the younger. He was heavier than his brother and balding prematurely.

Jurnegan shook their hands.

"Pardon me, but you two don't look exactly like your average lab technicians."

"We're mercenaries," Earl cheerfully admitted.

"We used to work for *Blackball, Inc.,*" said Ty.

Jurnegan frowned. Ingleside noted his disapproval and quickly intervened.

"Now, Amos, they work for *you.*"

"Really."

"Really. When you deal with the military, as I do, you get to know all kinds of interesting people."

"I'll bet."

"You learn the value of expertise."

"No doubt . . ."

"And you learn how to expedite. These men, the Durango brothers, they know how to get things done."

6

One year ago . . .

Gerrit Darlington Holzgraf III was at loose ends.

With no ready excuse to offer, he accepted the peremptory summons of his stepmother and drove out from his modest condo in Pittsburgh, Pennsylvania, to see her. His destination, a rare one, was the Holzgraf family estate in the exclusive suburb of Mill Forge Heights, whose half-timbered buildings sprawled across a tree-studded hilltop overlooking the Allegheny River.

He parked his Porsche Cayman in the wide circular drive and ambled up to the main entrance, a grand portico that would have made a castle look good. There ancient Benson, a long-time family retainer, greeted him with a smile and a frown.

"Nice to see you, sir. Been a while."

"Thanks, Ben. Where is the queen today?"

"The gazebo. Be respectful, she's got her knickers knotted."

Holzgraf rolled his eyes. The two men bumped elbows in a little trans-generational ritual, and the young visitor strode into the colossal mansion, through an opulent living area the size of a tennis court, through the ballroom, as big as a convention hall, and out through the garden, larger than a football field. The gazebo itself was in fact an enormous house with five bedrooms, done in Tudor style. His stepmother was waiting on the glassed-in patio, drinking tea. She put down a handful of lawyer's letters and newspaper clippings as he sidled up to her.

"Gerrit! Here you are. I don't know what I'm going to do with you."

"Hello, Mavis."

"Sit down, have some tea." She smoothed the wrinkles of her yellow garden dress.

Holzgraf leaned over, planted a perfunctory kiss on the woman's cheek, scraped a wrought iron chair across the slate pavement, sat, and threw a pair of long legs onto the table.

"Don't be rude, Guy."

Holzgraf dropped his feet into the nearest unoccupied chair.

The second Mrs. Holzgraf was a newly widowed trophy wife no more than fifteen years older than her stepson. She was glamorous, fashionable, and nobody's fool. She rustled the papers she was studying.

"What I have here, my dear boy, are reports. Your activities do not go unnoticed."

"I guess not, huh?"

"And they are shocking. Money, the root of all evil, is also the root, in your case, of carelessness, foolishness, and wretched excess."

"And that's just the good part."

"Don't get smart with me. I lived with your father."

"Dad . . ."

"If I could put up with his bullshit buffet, you are merely dessert."

Holzgraf dropped his feet to the floor, placed his elbows on his knees, and rested his chin on his fists. "Okay, I got it. What's the verdict?"

"Let's start with school. You were within three credits of an engineering degree and switched to biology."

"Yup."

"Cutting up frogs."

Holzgraf sat up. "Whoa there. No one cuts up frogs anymore. We study their DNA, analyze their genomes, find out what all those little RNA snippets do."

"The Holzgrafs are engineers. That's the family tradition."

"All except you," he noted with a crooked smile.

"Wellesley didn't offer an engineering degree," sniffed Mrs. Holzgraf. She lifted a letter from the pile at her fingertips.

"Moving on — last year, the car crash."

"Not my fault. Bill Summers was driving."

"His father's Corvette. With a suspended license, I see. Really, Guy."

Holzgraf raised a hand and silently spun a finger around in the air to acknowledge his guilt.

Mrs. Holzgraf looked at him coolly over the rims of bejeweled reading glasses. "Yes, you're right, one mustn't dwell upon misfortune. Next — the hang gliding accident. You missed an entire semester."

"Hard landing. My back is fine now. Look at me." He wiggled around in his chair, rotated his shoulders dramatically.

Mrs. Holzgraf waved an emergency rescue bill at him.

"Helicopter skiing in Canada? You broke your leg."

"Cracked a femur. It didn't come apart."

"Then there was that stunt in Yosemite. My God, less than six months after surgery. With screws in your leg."

"We scaled El Capitan in three days."

"A cliff! Thousands of feet high! You could have been killed."

"We had ropes and pitons and climbers' friends. Only two nights on the face, and the weather was ideal."

"You want to live a long life, I hope? No more of that stuff."

Holzgraf pointed to the pile of paper. "This is about my inheritance, right?"

Mrs. Holzgraf pursed her lips. "Of course. You're reaching the appointed age, but I have to give the okay."

"I know."

"And I'm not going to open the treasury unless you agree to calm down and find a purpose in life. Good God, Guy — you're almost thirty years old."

Holzgraf squirmed uncomfortably. His expression hardened. "What could I have for a hundred million that I can't have for ten?" he asked defiantly.

"You are being impertinent. The real question is, how are you going to take your place in the family business?"

"What if I don't want any part of the family business?"

"Don't be childish. I won't hear such talk. Darlington Industries hangs in the balance."

"Whatever."

Mrs. Holzgraf turned a page while clocking the reproach. "Oh dear, the poor young prince, struggling against the shackles of wealth." She sighed. "You're a good actor, Guy, I'll give you that. Now pay attention. There's one more item we need to discuss." She gave her stepson a hard look.

"Uh-oh."

"Uh-oh, indeed — an accusation of sexual assault." Her voice took on an icy tone. "I had to write a check."

Holzgraf gritted his teeth. "Hang on, Mavis — Mother — you know that was nothing but blackmail. A poor kid chasing deep pockets. I never touched that woman, never dated her, wasn't at her sorority when she alleges the incident took place, and I have witnesses for everything."

"Yes, they swore you were drunk and disorderly at a bar downtown, where no one should ever be seen."

She rapped her fingernails on the tabletop.

"And now you've given up on the Ph.D."

"Hey, I have my masters, and I don't think academic life suits me. I need action, more of a challenge."

Mrs. Holzgraf let out a disdainful snort.

"Imagine if your father heard that! They say life teaches humility. Learning from you, I should graduate with honors. *Summa cum laude.*"

Holzgraf couldn't help himself. He grinned idiotically. His stepmother seemed to soften. She patted his hand.

"Go see Uncle Rudi. And behave yourself. Rudi doesn't share my famous sense of humor."

"I will, soon as I figure anything out. Life, what a puzzle."

7

Six months ago . . .

Professor Jurnegan was in his well-appointed lab, replanting Advanced Solar Research's collection of glistening bushes. He was disappointed by the slow growth rates he had observed over the years, and which he had scrupulously documented in copious notes.

He had tried various lighting regimes, and growth varied, but not dramatically. New soil, he thought, might well be the answer. Especially new soil rich in titanium. Titanium was one of the primary constituents of perovskite, and he knew that the crystalline leaves of his plants were composed of perovskite. Titanium, that's the ticket, thought he.

As he was shuffling plants from one bench to another he accidentally placed two of the larger ones beside each other.

Thump.

Jurnegan looked toward the noise and was surprised to see the two bushes rocking back and forth. He moved closer, eyes wide. Inside the plastic tubs, something was moving around, plowing up soil. He reached out and yanked the bushes apart. The movement stopped.

"What in hell . . ?"

He pushed the bushes back together. The movement resumed. Something was writhing around in each of the tubs. A cold shiver ran up his spine. He pulled them apart again and picked up his telephone.

"Hub? Get over here. Something's happening. You've got to see it."

Ingleside had financed Jurnegan's operation long enough to expect a return on investment. A return which, so far, was not forthcoming. He was not enthusiastic.

"Well look, Amos, I'm tied up with sensor specs for the new Shiva missile. Big contract. Take some pictures and send 'em over, why don't you?"

"No no no, Hub. You need to be here. We've got an unexpected development on our hands."

"Is there money in it?"

"Money? I don't know. How about a Nobel prize?"

By the time Ingleside arrived at the lab, Jurnegan had removed all the soil from the suspicious bushes. They were now sitting in clear plastic containers five feet apart, roots and jagged root balls exposed. Jurnegan finished positioning a video camera, turned on a pair of movie lights, and started recording.

"It is now five PM on August twenty, and I have placed both of ASR's largest bushes in see-through vessels, soil removed. Watch closely, Hub. Now I'm going to rearrange them, like so . . ."

He took hold of one of the bushes and shoved.

Thump!

When the containers came together the root balls dissolved into what looked like sand. In an instant the piles of sand reconstituted as a pair of wormlike things. They wiggled around and around the plastic cases.

Jurnegan separated the bushes, and the wormlike things turned back into root balls. Fibrous roots coiled around them.

"Shall we go again?"

"Uno mas," said Ingleside.

Jurnegan repeated the procedure. Once again the root balls turned into restless worms, and then back into root balls.

"Seen enough?"

Ingleside nodded thoughtfully. Jurnegan turned off the lights and the video camera.

Ingleside peered cautiously into one of the containers, stuck his cane inside, and probed the root ball, now inert. He retreated to a chair and plunked himself down.

"What have we got here, Amos?"

Jurnegan's head was bobbing up and down.

"Behavior," he said.

Ingleside pondered the matter. "Have you checked the DNA? Done an analysis? Any actual relation to brittlebush, like you've mentioned now and then?"

Jurnegan was excited, but grim. "There is no DNA, Hub. That was just a bedtime story."

"No DNA . . ."

"None whatsoever."

Ingleside shook his head. "In that case . . . my God . . . maybe . . . maybe we ought to let the right people in on our secret, know what I mean?"

"Not yet. Not until we know more. If there's a news flash coming, it's got to be our news flash."

Ingleside stood up with a cautious grunt. "Keep me posted. And don't write any papers unless we talk about it, okay?"

Jurnegan nodded assent.

"As for you — don't tell your military buddies any tall tales."

Ingleside waved his cane in the air as he limped to the exit.

"Mum's the word."

8

Three months ago . . .

The corporate headquarters of Darlington Industries was located in a suite of offices looking out on the Monongahela River from 11 Stanwix Street in downtown Pittsburgh. But Rudolf Holzgraf, the CEO, liked to work from the original grimy factory out on Neville Island, even though Darlington's industrial products were now manufactured in fourteen modern factories spread across six midwestern states and the Republic of Korea.

One fine day in November, his nephew Gerrit aimed his Porsche at the Neville Road bridge and drove across the Ohio River to pay a long-deferred visit.

"Uncle Rudi?"

The CEO was a middle-aged man with prematurely grey hair. He smiled and welcomed his nephew with a cordial wave.

His executive desk sat in front of a wide window that offered a panoramic view of the factory floor. Holzgraf crossed the room and peered through it. There, far below, industrial robots were assembling high-pressure hydraulic couplings, the only items still being manufactured in Pittsburgh.

"What are you doing here?" asked Holzgraf. "This place runs itself."

"Hello, Guy. I'm sentimental. Sit down, let's talk."

Holzgraf dropped into a chair facing the desk.

"Your mother —" Uncle Rudi began.

"— stepmother," corrected Holzgraf.

"Yes, yes, stepmother. Good grief. Whatever she is, she is at wit's end with you."

"I know. I'm not trying to make her crazy. It's just the way she is."

Uncle Rudi stared at the ceiling. "The ways she is . . ."

Holzgraf toed the privacy screen on his uncle's desk. "It's weird. Half the time she makes me feel like a child of ten, and the other half . . ."

Uncle Rudi's eyebrows lifted. "What?"

"Well, she's only like fifteen years older than me, right?"

Uncle Rudi groaned. "She flirts with you. It makes you uncomfortable."

"You can say that again. I'm no Oedipus."

The older man laughed. "Easy, Guy. She flirts with everyone. She is, however, your legal guardian, and she holds the keys to your inheritance and future with our company."

"Right, I'm hip, I know what's at stake."

"Do you? Without an engineering degree, I don't see how you can ever run Darlington Industries." He spread his hands. "I suppose we'll have to improvise. Set you up at Stanford, get you an MBA . . ."

"You don't understand. I don't want to run Darlington Industries."

"No?" Uncle Rudi paused to take a deep stay-calm breath. "Too bad, that's a big disappointment." He scratched his head. "Well, Mavis warned me. And I was hoping to play a lot more golf as the years wear on."

"You'll find someone."

"Who? The cousins? The idea makes me sick. We'll have to bring in an executive, a gunslinger, always a gamble. Maybe even go public, and that — that's the doomsday road."

"Sorry, Uncle. I guess you guys should have had more kids."

"We all have our faults. Tell me, what is your lofty goal if not the family business? Mavis said you've settled on a career in biology."

"That's right. I have."

"Where will you be teaching?"

"No teaching. Industry."

"Pharmaceuticals? There's big money there."

Holzgraf shook his head. "Did you know that there is more than one kind of photosynthesis in the plant world?"

"I did not."

"A lot of the monocots — grasses and their relatives — use photosynthesis four, it's more efficient. Roses? They don't compete. And sugar cane is the most efficient plant of all. It converts around eleven percent of the sunlight falling on it."

"Do tell."

"Not much competition for solar cells, which are up around twenty-five percent efficiency these days."

"Is there a moral to this tale . . ?"

Holzgraf nodded. "You bet. I've been reading an interesting academic paper. Some prof down in Arizona thinks perovskite, as seen in a few bizarre plant mutations, might, with the right kind of development, improve photosynthetic efficiency a hundredfold — biologically."

"Perovskite?"

"It's a mineral. I'm not qualified to run Darlington, but I want to set up a research arm. 'Holzgraf Energetix.' It will put us in the power business. No matter what those oil and coal guys say, it's the future. I can get us there."

Uncle Rudi sat back in his chair. A grudging smile of approval slowly spread across his face.

"All right, but first, let's remember our branding. Call it 'Darlington Energetics,' if you don't mind. Stay away from the Holzgraf name, we never use it."

"Why not?"

"Too German. What's the business plan? How will you organize? Staff up?"

"No org, no staff. Just me and my curiosity for now. I'll be the Darlington in the energetics department."

9

Two months ago . . .

Dr. Roman Garibaldi, Ph.D., a ruddy-faced man in his forties with rumpled hair and a rumpled suit, was roaming Albuquerque International Sunport, waiting for a flight out of New Mexico.

He was a senior analyst at *The Institute for Research on Integrated Systems,* otherwise known as *The IRIS Corporation,* a government think tank. He had just spent a long week in Los Alamos advising bomb designers. The assignment was tiring, and he was eager to return home.

While he restlessly paced the shopping arcade, he was reporting on his activities to an officer in the U.S. Air Force via an encrypted mobile phone.

". . . it's new, it's clever. Minimal fissile material. They want to fit their warheads on your air-launched boosters. You guys."

Pause.

"Is it promising? Yes, General, I like the ignition geometry. Looks like they cracked the nut."

Pause.

"As you know, we at IRIS don't design, we just consult. We ran their math, and it checks out on our computers, but we'll need time on the big machine in order to get a really reliable simulation."

Pause.

"I understand your concern. I share it. But I can't discuss details, I'm in a public space here. Suffice it to say we want to scare people, not bomb them. My worry — pardon me — we should be flying Minutemen from their actual locations. Not sure how many North Koreans will read up on weapon optimization, but they sure as hell will notice a missile from Wyoming that lands in the Sea of Japan. And, hey, maybe send another one into the Persian Gulf while you're at it, just for sport."

Pause. Garibaldi moved the phone away from his ear, wincing at the fierce and negative response.

"Radical, I know. Just kidding, General. Personally, I wouldn't hurt a fly, but being nice doesn't deter squat in this crazy world."

He put the phone away and started paying attention to the shops. An offering for his loyal and patient wife would be in order, he thought, considering how often he was absent on classified missions.

The *Sandia Spirit* gift shop looked promising. Turquoise earrings, necklaces, and brooches were on view in the window. Amusing refrigerator magnets and Georgia O'Keefe art postcards as well. He was mentally dismissing the ostentatious turquoise baubles when his eye fastened on something unusual, an exquisite glittering plant in a ceramic vase.

He stepped into the shop.

"May I see that plant in the window?"

The clerk, a cheerful Hispanic woman, fetched it to the sales counter, where Garibaldi examined the metallic stems and the sparkling little diamond-shaped leaves.

"This, uh, this object is very beautiful."

"Why thank you."

"What is it, art glass? The shine, some sort of glaze?"

"Oh no, sir, it is a plant."

"Really. You mean, a model of a plant, right? What kind?"

"It is a real plant. It is growing."

Garibaldi was about to voice his doubts, then stopped to think.

"Growing . . . huh . . . do you get many of these 'plants' in your shop?"

"No sir, this is the only one I have seen."

"Know where it came from?"

"The owner. He is, how you say, a desert rat. He found it."

"Here in New Mexico?"

"Yes, sir. He is old. He does not travel far."

Garibaldi fingered the leaves. "It looks dead. It looks like a sculpture piece or something. How do you know it's growing?"

"These leaves — here and here" — she pointed — "they are bigger now. I watch every day. Growing."

Garibaldi stroked his chin. He brought a finger up, touched his nose, coming to a decision.

"I would like to buy this plant, but I don't see a price tag."

"For something unique and collectible like this — don't be shocked, it is high — twelve hundred dollars."

Garibaldi nearly choked.

"Or, perhaps something that just looks like a plant would be better. Over here we have these very nice cactus-shaped ceramic spoon rests."

Garibaldi dug out his wallet.

"No thanks. I'll take the plant."

10

One month ago . . .

Holly Chow was returning to the pecan ranch in Marana from a somber ceremony in Oro Valley. She was carrying a small stone jar.

Her father had sold the orchard behind her house to a larger Marana operation years ago, while she was still in college, when his health began to fail. Liver cancer, unexpected, terrible, and now deadly.

The jar contained his ashes. She was there to scatter them among the tall pecan trees, leafless and funereally black in mid-January. He had scattered the ashes of her mother in the same orchard when she was still a child. Now, fulfilling a solemn promise, Holly was mixing his ashes with hers.

She walked slowly in the lanes between the trees, dusting the ground with what she hoped and believed was Dad's spirit, forming an eternal bond between man, woman, the life-force, and the Earth itself.

Her eyes were dry. Tears, when they fell, had poured out when she first heard the awful news of her father's illness. She might have felt guilty about the lack of apparent grief upon his passing, but instead she was proud of her stoic resolve. She told herself she was self-reliant, a comforting idea which happened to be true. Growing up in the Southwest, with very few Asian Americans around, she was also a lonely outsider. She believed she had to be self-reliant. A cool customer, on her own, happy that way.

When the stone jar was empty, she continued to walk back and forth among the trees. Here and there an early leaf bud showed on a dark grey branchlet. Pecans always leafed out late, but the faintest prospect of the coming spring renewal cheered her up. She decided to have a look at the irrigation pump the new owners had installed.

Where the old shed had burned, a new one was in place. Aluminum and fiberglass, painted white. She flipped the latch and opened the door. Three gleaming yellow industrial pumps were housed inside, centered in a well-engineered tangle of PVC pipes. A gasoline-powered generator was in there too, ready for emergency service. She smiled. The system design was hers, even if the pumps themselves were bigger, more powerful, and way beyond her college budget.

On a nostalgic impulse, she walked around to the rear of the shed, remembering the odd bush Dad had found up in the hills, and which she had replanted. Gone now, stolen, just a memory.

But wait. She leaned close to be sure. There, half-hidden among the brittlebush and desert mallow was a glassy plant, shining like crystal. Growing, apparently, from roots left behind when the parent was taken. It was about eighteen inches high, beautiful in its profound otherness.

"Well well well," she murmured. "Dad, you would have loved this."

PART TWO

11

Now . . .

Dr. Garibaldi drove up to the gates of NASA Ames Research Center in Mountain View, California, in a cheap rental car. A guard at the gate asked for his clearance, which an assistant had printed out before he left his home office in suburban Virginia.

He handed the paper over, along with his government photo ID, and was waved onto the sprawling campus. He had never been there before. Beige stucco buildings flanked wide green lawns edged with sycamore trees. Somewhere in the background a gigantic hangar left over from the heyday of dirigibles loomed above the red tile roofs. Somewhere else the enormous grey bulk of the world's largest wind tunnel loomed as well, advertising serious research heft. He thought the Spanish Colonial architecture and the spacious layout of Shenandoah Plaza looked a lot like nearby Stanford, where he had sometimes lectured.

He was in California for an appointment with the center's director. A nice young woman in the administration building pointed him to an elevator and, with many small gestures, told him how to navigate to the right office.

He knocked on an open door and stuck his head in.

"General Upshaw?"

Major General Maurice Upshaw, a large black man of sixty years, stood up from his desk and the various research proposals he was considering.

"Roman! Come on in. Save me from the boredom of worthless projects to reject."

Garibaldi hiked across a wide expanse of carpet to shake the director's hand. "Thanks for meeting me, sir."

"Glad to do it. You tracked me down."

"Yes I did. Congratulations on your appointment."

"I don't think you've seen me in my priestly robes."

"Nope. The last time we got together I was advising you on the center of mass of the big scope, down in Houston."

"I remember."

Upshaw was a former A-10 pilot in the Air Force who went on to a distinguished career as an astronaut commanding the space shuttle, most prominently on two Hubble Space Telescope repair missions.

"Okay, before I drag you off to a commissary lunch, what's up? Your people sounded mighty mysterious. What's bugging IRIS these days that isn't a classified military secret?"

Garibaldi opened his briefcase.

"Oh, it's classified all right. You better believe it." He produced a sheaf of color photographs and handed them over. "Take a look."

Upshaw sat down, adjusted a pair of reading glasses, and leafed through the pictures.

"This." He tapped a print. "This is a bush, yes?"

"Right, it's a bush. About ten inches high."

"The color — is it right? Looks funny."

"I'll say. Notice the little square leaves, the specular reflections, the crystalline structure."

Upshaw dropped the pictures onto his desk. He pushed them around, reviewing the details. "I see, but I don't understand. What am I looking at?"

Garibaldi cracked a sour smile. "Well, General —"

"Call me 'Mo' these days," said the director, interrupting. "Military service is lost in my jet exhaust."

"Well, Mo, the lady in the gift shop where I found this bad boy thought she had a bonsai tree. The shop owner discovered the thing a little ways south of Albuquerque. But it's no tree. It's not a plant of any kind."

"An art object? Some knick-knack?"

"Not a chance. It's growing. I showed one of the 'leaves' to a good botanist at George Mason. Told him nothing. He made an analysis. The little squares that look like leaves are made out of perovskite, a rare titanium mineral that forms in the Earth's mantle, and once in a while gets thrown up to the surface by volcanoes."

Upshaw spread the pictures across his desk and inspected them all over again. At length he slumped back in his chair. "I take it you don't think this thing came from deep inside Earth's mantle."

Garibaldi shook his head. "No indeed. I also made an attempt to extract DNA — an obvious thing to do. There are undiscovered flora on Earth, after all. People still find entirely new species of real trees now and then. And? No dice. There is no DNA in this object."

Upshaw looked up at his visitor. "No DNA. And it's growing. So, the reason you're here is . . ."

His voice trailed off, silenced by a flood of crazy thoughts.

Garibaldi nodded. "Yup, exactly."

Upshaw shifted uncomfortably in his executive chair. "Why pick on me? I'm just a NASA bureaucrat."

"You're aware. You're the only person I know who's in position to make a move, shake other bureaucrats. You've got contacts in intelligence. Supported SETI in that hoohah with Congress last year."

Upshaw aimed a finger at the ceiling and outer space beyond. "You know, unlike some of my more imaginative colleagues, I never saw anything strange — anything *extraterrestrial* — up there."

"Of course not."

"You're sure about this? No mistake? Willing to fall on your sword if you're wrong?"

"Absolutely. The case is bulletproof."

Upshaw ran a hand over his closely cropped grey hair.

"What do you want me to do? I'm guessing there might be more of these things."

12

"What's new, Amos? Say something to cheer me up."

Hubert Ingleside was in the raw desert outside Tucson, reluctantly making a visit to the secret location of Advanced Solar Research after blowing off two meetings in a row. These days he had to force himself to pay attention to the money-draining startup operation. A true venture capitalist would have called a halt long ago, but Ingleside thought of himself as a romantic soul.

"You're worried about progress. I know it's slow," confessed his partner. "I'm starting to think we should abandon the pure solar power concept — even though getting nineteen percent efficiency isn't bad for a lonely research droid like me — and concentrate on *reverse photosynthesis* instead."

"We've been at this forever. Quit now, I want my money back."

"Don't talk like that, Hub. Solar power produces electricity. What you call reverse synth produces some electricity, but it also turns out fuel. Pure hydrogen and environmentally neutral methane and ethanol. Depending on the recipe. Give me a while, both are within reach."

Ingleside grimaced. "I'm not as patient as I once was. Your stories are wearing thin, my friend."

Jurnegan, as enthusiastic as ever, was slow to grasp the meaning of Ingleside's negative attitude: the end of his project. That's what Ingleside was telling him. A surge of adrenaline caused his academic heart to race. Suddenly he understood the peril, and just as suddenly he knew how to delay the fateful day of reckoning.

"Here, look at this."

He reached into a desk drawer and extracted a letter. He dangled it in front of his business associate.

"What?" said Ingleside, unmoved by the performance.

"I'll tell you what — it's a letter from a man in Turkey. A school teacher. He read my paper. He lives out in the sticks near Karabük, wherever that is. He found one of our bushes in his back yard. He is willing to sell."

"Let me see that."

Ingleside read the letter. Then he read it again.

"Turkey. The other side of the world."

"Not quite, but certainly not local, heh heh. Now think — it is possible we need to pollinate these things. Most plants work like that — male and female, sexual reproduction, even though plants can't actually mate like animals."

"I know all about the birds and the bees."

Jurnegan bobbed his head. "Of course you do. Maybe — just maybe — a bush from some distance is just what we need. Maybe ours are all the same damn sex, or whatever the hell."

Ingleside seemed to consider the idea. He was silent for a while, evidently weighing costs and benefits.

"All right," he said, making up his mind. "Give this to the Durangos. I know they've operated over there in the past — Syria, the civil war, Islamic State, et cetera, et cetera. — they'd love to buy your bush."

13

"Where the fuck are we, Ty?"

The Durango brothers were speeding along a Turkish superhighway in a Fiat van, heading north out of Ankara.

The younger Durango consulted the iPad in his lap. He scrolled through the map app, checking route numbers.

"E-89, looks like. Stay on this until we see signs for Karabük, then we exit onto E-80."

"Jesus, all these names. What does 'oğlu' mean?"

"It's a prefix, I think. 'Son-something-or-other.'"

"You looked it up."

"Prepping for the mission, bro."

"What about all those little marks on the letters? How is anybody supposed to pronounce anything?"

"They used to write Arabic letters —"

"— looks like they still do."

"No, that guy, what's-his-name, Atatürk, he switched them over."

"Except they fucked it all up with those dots and danglers. Christ alive."

"Drive on, we don't have to live here."

"Just pick up a plant, I know. It better not be a scam."

Earl Durango tightened his grip on the wheel.

"What's the speed limit anyway?"

"No idea. Just stay with traffic, we'll be fine."

An hour later they passed through Karabük, a surprisingly modern small city. A half-hour after that they were driving through Safranbolu. They wound their way through the town center, turned up a narrow hillside road, and climbed into the outskirts. Earl brought the van to a halt at a problematic intersection.

"Eflani or Bartin?" he asked.

Ty consulted his map. "Bartin, up that way." He pointed to the left fork.

Soon the road narrowed further, and the pavement ended. Dry grass and shrubs covered most of the hillsides they were passing through, but here and there outcrops of limestone demonstrated the hard land underneath.

"Good luck any plants growing here."

The school teacher's house was perched on a steep embankment overlooking a line of treeless hills. Below them the wide open landscape was dotted with houses and farms. Neatly whitewashed stucco under red tile roofs. Sunlight dappled wide fields shadowed by puffy clouds gliding by.

Earl parked the van in a crooked driveway behind a tiny Hyundai sedan. Ty put away his iPad, felt instinctively behind his back for a Beretta pistol he always carried. Not there, of course; forbidden on commercial airplanes. He swore.

"What are you doing?" asked Earl.

"I miss my piece. Like to have it, you know, if the mission goes south."

"Nothing goes south. Come on."

Earl led his brother around the building. On the far side a young boy was dribbling a basketball and draining jumpers. When he saw the Americans he dropped the ball and ran into the house, yelling for his father.

The Durangos followed him to the door. Before they could knock, a thin man in an ill-fitting suit jacket and a three-day stubble of beard greeted them.

"Hello. I am expecting Jurnegan. One of you, yes?"

"We're the Durangos, his representatives."

"Ahh, so it is. I was hoping to meet the man who wrote that extraordinary paper. He has great insight." The man's English was good, a small surprise to the Americans.

"Well, uhh, he's a teacher. Like you, we heard. And he's too busy at the university to come all the way from Tucson."

"Of course. I understand."

"You have an unusual plant for sale? We're here to buy it."

"Yes, yes. I was out in the hills on holiday, not so long ago. I came to a grove of trees, and in the middle the leaves were all gone, like a tunnel. There was a small hollow — um, a depression? — in the ground. And, most unusual, in the middle of the hollow was a bush. I had no idea what it could be, so I began to do research. It matched the speculations in Jurnegan's monograph."

"You have it?"

The man turned into the house. "Nazim!" he shouted.

The young boy came forward carrying a plastic tub. A glistening bush about two feet high and wide was nestled in the tub.

"Jesus Christ," said Earl.

"We are glad to sell. The plant is strange, and it makes us feel strange to have it."

"How much are we talking about?" asked Ty.

"Two thousand. Cash. I believe I wrote this price to the professor, and he agreed."

"Right, that's what we were told. Two thousand — dollars or euros? We have both."

"Euros. It must be euros."

"Pay the man, Ty," said Earl.

Ty Durango reached into a side pocket on his pants and produced a wad of bills. He thrust them toward the eager school teacher, who took them with shaking hands.

"Excuse me, I must count." Twenty hundred-euro bills later the man gestured to his young son. "It is well, Nazim. They may take the bush."

The boy handed the thing to Earl.

"Give my respect to Professor Jurnegan. He is a smart fellow, he will do well to discover the true nature of this plant, I believe."

"You're doing pretty well yourself," said Earl, tipping an elbow toward the sheaf of bills clutched tightly in the teacher's grip.

The Durangos gave father and son a casual salute and returned to their van.

On the way out of town they met a Range Rover going in the other direction. Passing the SUV, a big one, required some careful maneuvering on the narrow gravel track, but they didn't give the encounter a second thought.

▼

The Range Rover pulled into the driveway the Durangos had just vacated. A young man with curly dark hair emerged. He was wearing aviator sunglasses, and although he was clad in a plain grey T-shirt and faded jeans, something in his bearing suggested a military background.

He knocked on the school teacher's door. After a moment, the same thin man who met the Durangos appeared.

"Yes? How may I help you?"

"Tayyar Sedik?"

The man nodded. "My name."

"I'm Captain Lockwood."

"American?"

"Yup." He grinned. "How can you tell?"

He stuck out a hand, and the school teacher gave it a cautious shake.

"I understand you have a plant for sale. Something unusual, something of scientific interest. You got my letter? I'd like to buy it."

The school teacher flung his arms out wide to indicate an apology.

"Very sorry, no, I have no letter. So I did not know of your interest, Captain. It is sold. I sold it already."

"Sold it," repeated Lockwood, unpleasantly surprised to hear the news.

"I am afraid so. Just now, not an hour ago."

Lockwood glanced over his shoulder, as if expecting to see the buyer still hovering nearby. "May I ask who bought it?"

"Americans like you."

Lockwood nodded thoughtfully. "Two guys? Were they driving a big grey van?"

"I believe so, yes."

"Well damn. I think I just met them on the road."

14

The *Tucson Gem and Mineral Show,* held every February in the Tucson Convention Center, was the oldest, biggest, and best exhibition of its kind in the world. Vendors from more than a dozen countries were offering their exotic wares in hundreds of well-lit booths spread out over more than three acres of exhibition space. Its tremendous popularity generated an overflow that poured into dozens of lesser venues spread across the city. People gathered annually from all over the country to see, buy, and sell the spectacular examples of finely wrought jewelry and mineralogical treasures on display.

This year's theme was *Red, White & Blue,* and to carry it out rubies, diamonds, and sapphires in all shapes and sizes were on view in bulletproof glass cases.

In the lecture halls, rockhounds were discussing streak plates, hardness numbers, and regaling audiences with tales of the discoveries that made their fortunes.

Wandering among the exhibits, rubbing elbows with the casual show-goers and canny buyers alike, was Gerrit Darlington Holzgraf III. His eyes were roving this way and that as he strolled along under the decorative umbrellas hanging from the high ceiling, taking in one outrageous exhibit after another. Here a case full of plump gold nuggets; there a diamond the size of a quail egg; down the row a column of pure tourmaline a foot high; and beyond that a quartz sphere a yard in diameter spinning on a stand like a little planet. Over by the food carts a he noted a pair of stunning dinosaur fossils, a weighty iron meteorite, and a large map of Arizona composed of polished granite, feldspar, and marble with a $35,000 price tag.

He paused at a booth to admire exquisitely prepared specimens of minerals with names only experts could decipher, such as azurite, kunzite, okenite, sphalerite, and wulfenite. He wondered about the especially obscure rhodochrosite and hydroxylapophylite.

"You look like serious collector," said the man behind the table in a heavily accented voice. Holzgraf looked up at the sign pinned to the curtain behind the exhibit:

BASIL TEMKHIN
Moscow

"You buy or sell?" asked the man, evidently Gospodin Temkhin himself. A short black beard compensated for thinning black hair. He was round and stout, clad in a purple dress shirt and white tie under a brown suit, on which lunch crumbs were visible.

"Nahh, just curious," said Holzgraf. "Unless . . . unless . . . hmm, I don't see any perovskite."

"No perovskite," said Temkhin. "Why ask?"

"Um, well, I'm interested in solar power. Doing research."

Temkhin smiled. "Aha, making useful of trinkets. *Khorosho!*"

"Trying, anyway," said Holzgraf with a tight smile.

The Russian made no attempt to conceal his broken English. He cocked his head. "You read paper, *da?*"

"What paper?" asked Holzgraf casually, although he knew the answer.

"Jurnegan. Perovskite, solar, we all read, I think."

"I guess so. It's the shizz." Holzgraf shrugged. He began to doubt the Russian was much of a mineral man. "Here's a question: I don't know what 'kyanite' is. What's in there anyway?"

It was the Russian's turn to shrug. "No idea. Am salesman only. My experts, no visa. You Americans, so particular, ha ha."

"Right," said Holzgraf and moved away.

In the next aisle over, while marveling at a football-sized blob of orange calcite, he accidentally bumped into a bearded man in his fifties negligently dressed in a faded polo shirt and safari vest. He made no connection with the Jurnegan paper, and the author, for that's who it was, had no idea of Holzgraf's interest.

Holzgraf pointed to the price. "Ninety-nine thousand bucks! You see that? Wow."

Jurnegan waggled his head sympathetically. "Nice if you can get it."

"You've been to the show before?"

"Never miss."

"Stuff like this sells? The price is right?"

"Oh sure. You can't tell by the clothes people are wearing, but there's some serious money walking the floor."

Holzgraf was feeling awfully naïve. "How many shows has this, this glob of stuff, been too? How many more before someone carts it away?"

"Quite a few, but I'm just guessing. Sellers put stuff like this on display to put a stake in the ground, show they've got the chops, beef up the value of their other rocks."

"I get it. You buying?"

Jurnegan shook his head. "Heavens no. I'm just another tourist. You need special knowledge to trade, just like the stock market — or you'll get fleeced."

"Thanks for the warning."

Holzgraf continued on, booth after booth. More gems, minerals, rocks, jewelry, each exhibit as dazzling as the last. He noted the glass cases, the locked boxes, the spiky crystals and sculpture pieces. He began to wonder how anyone could safely pack delicate amethyst, aquamarine, and fluorite crystals for transportation.

At last, nearly exhausted by hours on the floor, he found himself in the far reaches of the hall where lesser vendors held sway, offering cheap rings and necklaces, lapis samples for a dollar, tiny cast-metal fairies, glass bong pipes, and Rolex watches of dubious provenance. There, tucked into a corner, he stumbled upon an intriguing collection of small coppery crystals spread out on a plain white table cloth.

Sitting in the tiny booth, looking very bored, was a young woman of obvious Asian heritage. Her arms were crossed over a grey blouse sparkling with shiny black sequins. A pink jacket covered her shoulders to ward off a downdraft from the air conditioning. Pinned to the backing curtain was a modest printed sign:

HARRIET CHOW
perovskite pendants

"These things are perovskite?"

"Yes."

"You're sure?"

"Of course. Perfect for very stylish necklaces."

He regarded the seller with as much interest as the minerals. She wasn't classically beautiful, but very attractive in a cool sort of way. Round face, flat nose, narrow dark eyes that he thought looked wintery, a full mouth, and coarse black hair cut at the shoulder with a knotted hank springing from one side of her head.

He picked up a little tented sign naming the price: *$50.*

"I would like to buy them."

Chow studied the man in front of her. He was about her own age. Tall, gangly, sharp features, wavy blond hair. A soul patch under his lower lip. Bright blue eyes. He was wearing a dark green T-shirt with a circular diagram of photosynthesis chemistry silk-screened on the front under the words, *One Ring To Rule Them All.* She occasionally fantasized about an anglo boyfriend. The idea was a pathetic cliché, that she knew, the stuff of West Coast culture, social media chatter, and celebrity couples. And yet here was a guy standing right in front of her, Mr. Anglo-Saxon himself.

"How many?"

He grinned. The radiant effect made her heart do a little flip-flop.

"All of them."

She stopped her mouth from sagging open. "Uhh, I don't have my credit card processor working right now. Square glitch, phone went dead, the usual hassle. So it has to be cash."

He started counting the little crystals. "You've got a hundred of these things sitting here."

"Yup. One hundred and four, actually."

"Five thousand bucks?"

"That's right. Five thousand two hundred to be exact." She said, adopting a detached professional air.

"Is your price firm? Doesn't look like you've sold anything."

"Yes, firm. Don't haggle. It's the first day of the show."

He nodded. "Okay, but I don't have that much cash with me."

She pointed toward the wall behind her. "There are ATMs just down the street. Bank of America, Chase, Wells Fargo, all the locals, your choice."

"Right. I will hit the bank and return with legal tender. Do not sell these to anyone else, I won't be ten minutes."

"I'll give you half an hour," she said. A shy little smile escaped from her all-business façade.

Five minutes later another customer cruised by and stopped.

"Whoa," he said. "Look what I see."

Chow leaned toward him. "Yes?"

The man, a slim but muscular guy with curly dark hair, swept a finger back and forth over her display. "Perovskite? The real thing?"

"Yes and yes," she said. My God, another young anglo, and this one as cute as the other.

"I would like to buy . . . well, the whole lot. What do you say?"

"Oops. Already sold, I'm afraid."

"What do you mean? Here they are."

"My customer is off rounding up cash. I don't take credit cards today."

The man considered the situation. He turned bright brown eyes on Chow, well aware of his charm, it seemed. "Unh-huh. What if you sell me just one? Your customer won't care, he'll still have dozens of these things." He smiled. Her heart melted.

"Well . . . okay. But just one. I made a promise."

"Here's fifty bucks, cash. And here's my business card, just in case your customer never returns."

"He'll be back."

"That's what they all say."

She took the card, a blue rectangle with the name, *Captain James Lockwood,* emblazoned in the middle.

"Captain Lockwood?"

"Not on active duty these days, it's my old army rank."

Chow fingered the card. It was hard plastic, an understated declaration of serious intent. She indicated the array of little square crystals. "Pick your poison. They all look pretty much the same to me, but you get to choose."

Lockwood spent some time looking over the display, then picked up one of the crystals. "This one looks good. Thanks for your consideration."

"My pleasure," said Chow and meant it. "Have a nice day."

He gave her an informal salute. "You too."

Basil Temkhin was standing nearby, pretending to appraise opal rings in a booth across the aisle. He waited for Lockwood to depart, then sidled over to Chow's station.

"Perovskite? Very rare. I buy."

Chow looked him over. Her immediate thought, unalloyed with any doubt, was, wow, a Russian spy. He seemed friendly.

"Sorry, all sold."

"But you just sell to young man."

"A single crystal."

"Sell same to me, then."

Chow was taken aback by the sudden interest in her wares. Not something she anticipated, and it made her wish she had set her price higher.

"Okay, fair enough. Take your pick, fifty dollars."

Temkhin dropped two twenties and a ten on the table. He picked out a crystal, polished it on a lapel of his suit, squinted at it.

"Perovskite, *da.* I like."

"There you go," said Chow.

"*Spasiba*," said the Russian. "*Proshchay.*"

He turned and walked away.

No one else expressed the slightest interest in her little crystals, and Chow was daydreaming when Holzgraf returned with the promised cash payment for the rest of her stock. She snapped to attention when the pile of fifty dollar bills flopped down before her.

"You're back, you made it."

Holzgraf started scooping up crystals. As he collected them, several got loose and dropped back onto the display table.

"Here," said Chow, offering a plastic baggie.

"Thanks."

She peeled off two of the bills and handed them back.

"What's this?" he asked.

"While you were gone, two other customers wanted to buy everything. Just like you. I couldn't turn them away, so I sold them one crystal each."

"Oh. Broke your promise, huh?"

"Whoa, I'm being upfront . . . what are we talking? Less than two percent? And you get the rest."

Holzgraf pocketed the bills. "Can't really complain. And, hey, if you have any more of these things, I'll buy them too."

Chow looked unhappy. "They're very rare. Crystals, right? Want to know what they really are?"

"You bet I do."

"Leaves. Leaves from the weirdest plant you ever heard of."

"I haven't heard of anything. Where did you find them?"

Chow hesitated. Not a good idea to get too specific. "In the hills."

Holzgraf swung an arm around to take in the territory. "Somewhere near Tucson?"

"Sorry, that would be telling. It's my, what do you call it? Trade secret."

"Fine. I understand — you rockhounds." He handed her a nicely printed card citing *Darlington Energetix.*

"Gerrit Holzgraf? *The Third?* That's you?"

"Yes indeed."

"And the company? Oh, I get it, you're hot on solar power." A statement, not a question. Her intuition surprised Holzgraf.

"You have guessed *my* secret. Rumplestiltskin is my name. And you are" — he glanced at her sign — "Harriet?"

"On my driver's license. But it's really just 'Holly.' Take good care of those things. Hope your project works out."

Holzgraf closed up the plastic bag containing one hundred and two little coppery shards of perovskite, waved goodbye, and walked away.

Chow watched until he was out of sight, then, stock gone, grabbed her purse, shoved her chair against the table, and vacated her booth.

▼

Outside, Chow crossed the street and threaded her way through parked cars to a dusty Subaru Impreza Crosstrek. She threw her bag in the back seat, dropped behind the wheel, and drove off.

Holzgraf was leaning against a tall column supporting the Convention Center porte-cochère, not quite out in the open, but not bothering to conceal himself either. He watched Chow leave, then crossed the parking lot. Waiting for him was a four-door Jeep Wrangler in Mojave Sand colors that sparkled like it just came off the showroom floor, which it did. He had owned the machine for all of three days, having made the purchase on impulse with his Chase Ultraviolet Visa Card, a financial instrument average consumers never heard of.

He jumped in and got on Chow's tail.

▼

Not long thereafter, Professor Jurnegan happened to stroll by Chow's booth. He stopped when the placard on the wall caught his eye. Perovskite pendants? He stared at the bare table top, idly fingered the price tag, and resumed his tour with a shrug.

15

Holly Chow drove up Granada Avenue and stopped at the light controlling the Congress Street intersection. By the time the left turn arrow blinked green, Holzgraf's new Jeep was right behind her.

She shot up the on-ramp to Interstate 10 and accelerated north. Holzgraf let a couple of cars get in between him and her Subaru, then sat back to see what she was doing. His plan was simple, and part of it already seemed to be working: buy her out, hand over enough money to make her wish for more, and see if that brought him any nearer to the source of her perovskite crystals. Leaves, she said. From the weirdest plant he never heard of. That he had to see.

The Impreza rolled along, leaving the speed limit and Holzgraf's Jeep far behind. He let her pull away, staying within eyesight, an easy task on the long straightaways. When the industrial sprawl of northern Tucson thinned out he began to wonder about her destination.

"Not all the way to Phoenix, please," he muttered aloud.

Nope. After fifteen minutes her right turn signal started blinking, and she veered down an off-ramp just south of Marana. She ducked under the highway and turned west on Paloma Valley Road. Holzgraf followed.

"Now we're getting somewhere," he mused as the two cars passed the Paloma Valley airport.

Chow drove steadily for another mile through open country. Holzgraf could see a line of barren hills in the distance, and beyond them the blocky mesas and sharp peaks of the Silver Bell Mountains.

"Down these mean streets a man must go . . ." he mumbled, quoting Raymond Chandler. He was enjoying the chase. Pretty good work for an amateur sleuth, he thought. He doubted Philip Marlowe himself could do a better job tailing anyone.

Chow's Subaru turned north, and then, after a few blocks lined with sprawling suburban homes as brown as the surrounding desert, it turned west again. There was no traffic, so Holzgraf dropped farther back, suddenly nervous about being discovered.

He trailed the Subaru north onto yet another back road. Almost immediately Chow brought her car to a halt.

"Uh-oh, busted." Holzgraf slowed to a crawl.

But Chow was merely stopping to pick up mail from a box on the corner. After a brief pause to sort through the flyers and catalogs, she started up again and exited onto a narrow gravel track leading further west toward a stand of leafless trees. Big ones. A vortex of dust trailed behind her.

Holzgraf slowly crept along in Chow's wake. Pretty soon he was driving into the parking area of an impressive pecan ranch. A wide stucco house with a flat gravel roof was sitting directly in front of him. He could see other smaller buildings just beyond. But no Subaru, and no Chow. He maneuvered his Jeep behind a propane tank sitting up on concrete blocks and stopped to think. He wasn't sure what to do next. After a few minutes his curiosity got the better of his nerves, and he left the Jeep, walked forward, and peered around to the rear of the house. Chow was nowhere in sight, but her car was parked near one of the outbuildings.

Suddenly a door banged open and Chow was striding away under the tall pecan trees. Gone was the sequined blouse and pink jacket. She was dressed in a khaki T-shirt over cargo shorts. Her feet were laced into tall hiking boots. She had a wide-brimmed straw hat pulled down over her brow and a pack slung over her shoulder. Tied to the pack was an orange plastic bucket. She was moving at a good pace with the aid of a pair of aluminum walking sticks.

Holzgraf watched her go, then retreated to his Jeep. Chow's pack looked full. Obviously she was outbound on a serious hike. He opened the tailgate, shook out a pack of his own and, ruefully aware that he knew nothing about hiking in the wintertime Arizona desert, crammed all the gear he could think of into the thing. A jacket, sweaters, sleeping bag, ultra-lightweight tent, propane stove, food packets, water bottles, snake-bite kit. He slathered sun block all over his face, neck, and arms, donned a well-worn Pittsburgh Pirates cap, and set out to follow her on foot.

▼

On the far side of the pecan orchard, Holzgraf located a faint trail running into the desert. It led across the Agua Negro Wash and up into low hills. After half a mile it wound into a shallow arroyo. Holzgraf's long legs got him in between its gently sloping walls in quick time. While he moved he kept his eyes peeled for Chow, but she was nowhere to be seen. He was pretty sure he was moving faster than she was, and it made him fret about picking the wrong route, but now and then a diminutive footprint scuffed into the hard ground or a hole where a walking stick had penetrated told him he was on the right track.

Before he knew it an hour had passed. It was now late afternoon, and the westering sun was throwing long shadows. A chilly breeze sprang up. Holzgraf shivered. He paused to throw on his jacket.

Looking ahead, he noticed that the arroyo narrowed sharply. The side walls were angling inward, rising up, getting steeper. He decided to climb out and continue along the rim, hoping for a glimpse of his quarry. But when he crested the ridge she was still out of sight. Probably hidden among the creosote, mesquite, and palo verde trees, he guessed.

He was trudging along, looking for more evidence of Chow's passage when a distant thumping noise intruded on his thoughts. He turned around and spotted a helicopter flying low over the landscape, heading in his direction.

"Hello there, who are you, buddy?"

He surmised that whoever was in the chopper might share his goal, and he didn't like the idea of helping anyone, so he quickly worked his way back down into the arroyo. A moment later the machine roared overhead, just above the ridgeline. The downdraft from its rotor blades blew his cap off.

Once it passed he collected his cap and continued onward into what was becoming a narrow canyon. The high walls muffled the noise of the helicopter, but he could still hear it moving back and forth somewhere up ahead, evidently searching for something.

As the canyon deepened it began to twist and turn. Once upon a wetter time, a seasonal stream had carved it out of fractured bedrock. Holzgraf thought an aquifer might still be present, a source of water capable of nourishing whatever oddball plant Chow had found. As he plodded along, the bushes and trees captured his attention. He focused on the scraggly twigs and branches, hoping to spot something shiny, wondering what it might prove to be. The sound of the helicopter had faded away. He turned a corner.

"You!"

Holzgraf stopped short. Standing right in front of him was Holly Chow. Her right arm was thrust forward. Her hand was gripping a can of pepper spray. Her thumb was on the valve.

"Stay right where you are, big guy."

"Don't shoot. I'm not moving."

Chow scowled. "You set this up. That's why you bought everything, to see where I found my little treasure."

"I confess," said Holzgraf. He took a step backward.

"Well, Mr. Solar Power Fake, those leaves came from a bush in my back yard. You're on a wild goose chase."

Holzgraf knew better.

"It wasn't always there, or you wouldn't be risking snakes and bugs on a long hike."

"Dad . . ."

"He found it. You don't know where."

She tilted her head. "Not exactly."

Holzgraf pointed toward the sky. "That helicopter? I don't think we're the only ones looking."

"Maybe not. Whatever. Go back where you came from. This is my territory."

"Uh, I read the map, and I believe we're actually standing in the north end of a national park. Or if not, BLM land. Owned by all us taxpayers."

"Screw you."

She turned, hiked away uphill, and disappeared around the next bend. Holzgraf watched her go. Then he turned aside, gave the canyon wall a quick survey, and scrambled up with technical climber's expertise.

Up on top of the rim he could see the helicopter hovering over a knoll a quarter of a mile or so away. He noted the paint scheme: all white. He crouched down, extracted a pair of binoculars from his pack, and trained them on the chopper. Thus magnified, he noted that the machine was a Bell Jet Ranger. It bore a red NASA worm logo on its fuselage.

"Our space program, exploring Planet Earth," he muttered.

While he was watching, the helicopter landed. Two men jumped out. One of them was wearing army camo. The other, in jeans and T-shirt, was unfolding an entrenching tool. He had dark glasses on. There was a gun on his hip.

The entrenching tool bit into the hard desert crust. Dirt and pebbles flew up. In a few short minutes the two men were lifting some sort of plant from the ground. Its leaves were glittering in the late afternoon sun.

"Damn," said Holzgraf.

The two men bagged the plant in black plastic and hoisted it aboard their helicopter. In another minute the machine was roaring over Holzgraf again. He watched in frustration as it disappeared into a spectacular desert sunset.

16

The winter sun went down in a hurry.

Twilight was brief and fading while Holzgraf considered his options. He was at least a couple of miles from his Jeep. Probably three. He remembered the rocky trail he had taken and its faint markings. He doubted his ability to retrace his steps in the dark.

Not far away, he spied a shelf of bedrock elevated above the local terrain. It looked like perfect shelter. He carried his pack through a tangle of chaparral, selected a nice flat spot in a cozy corner, and set about erecting his little tent.

By the time he got his propane camp stove blazing, it was full dark. He prepared dinner — powdered soup stirred lazily in a stainless steel pot — by the light of a small headlight strapped to his forehead. While he waited for his food to cook he opened a pint bottle of Jack Daniel's Tennessee Whiskey and poured a measure into a plastic cup.

"Here's to fucking perovskite," he said.

"Amen," came a voice.

Holzgraf nearly spilled his drink. He tore off his headlight and aimed it at the sound. The beam picked up Holly Chow sitting on a boulder not ten feet away. She raised a hand to shield her eyes from the glare.

"Ouch, turn that off, I can't see a thing."

"Holly Chow," he said, recovering. He directed the light around his spartan campsite. *"Mi casa es tu casa."*

Chow stood up, came forward, and settled cross-legged in front of the camp stove.

"Gerrit Holzgraf *The Third*. A man at home in the desert," she observed. "Got any more of that stuff?" She presented a plastic cup of her own.

"Sure."

He poured her a drink. They clicked cups together and drained them.

"What you said — to perovskite." She wiped her mouth. "I brought some ramen, if you want to share."

"Okay. What happened to the hostility?"

"Nothing. I still think you're a shit. But I'm hungry. It's dark, and I forgot my propane tank."

Holzgraf rummaged around in his pack and came up with another cooking pot. "Ever see that helicopter before?"

Chow opened her ramen baggie and shook the freeze-dried contents into the pot. "I was going to ask you the same thing."

Holzgraf poured some water over the ramen. "Those guys found one of your plants, looks like. We know how I got onto you, my sleuthing skills . . ."

"Ha ha."

". . . right, but what about them? They figured it out too."

Chow nodded. She lifted a small plastic card from a pocket on her shorts and handed it over. Holzgraf fingered it experimentally.

"Captain Lockwood, huh? Man has good taste in business accessories. Heavy duty, nicely printed. I can't even bend it."

Chow gave him a quizzical look. "And . . ?"

He weighed the card experimentally, measured the thickness with his thumb and forefinger. "Oh Christ, it's a tracker."

"Bing bong."

The soup began to bubble. He removed it from the stove and poured it into little bowls. "Have a spork," he said.

She grabbed the card and held it over the now open flame. It crackled and popped, giving off a toxic odor.

"Woof, ugh, I am an idiot," she said.

Holzgraf grinned. "I'm not arguing. I was watching that chopper through binocs. It was painted white, and there was a NASA logo on it. Two guys were digging up a bush. The leaves were shiny."

"Was one of them young and good-looking?"

"I dunno, could be. Your brave captain?"

"Probably. The bastard."

Holzgraf refilled their cups with another jolt of whiskey.

"What do you think is going on? What is NASA doing here?"

"No idea. Why are you so interested?"

"Perovskite really does promise a solar energy breakthrough."

Chow pointed a finger. "You read Jurnegan's paper too."

Holzgraf chuckled. "Yes I did."

"Maybe it's some kind of mutation. Our bush was kind of slow, but it was growing for sure."

"I'm a biologist, and I don't think those things are plants at all," he declared. "But who knows?"

They clicked cups together.

"Tell you what, though," he vowed, "I am going to find out."

"Here's to the mystery," she said. She was shivering.

"I've got a bivvy sack you could cover up with."

She nodded acceptance. He fished a nylon bag out of his pack. She pulled it up over her legs.

They sipped their whiskey, regarding each other warily. After a while Holzgraf offered a suggestion.

"We should team up."

Chow gave him half a nod.

17

Hubert Ingleside was in a mellow mood. The optical sensor contract for the Air Force's latest air-to-air weapon system, the overdue, overbudget, and overhyped Shiva missile, had finally come through, and his company, Opticon, more formally chartered as the Optical Controls Corporation, now stood to reap scandalous profits.

He was driving south on the old Mineral Highway, leaving Tucson. He whistled tunelessly as he motored along the obscure back road, turning here, then there, working his way into the far suburbs and open desert to Amos Jurnegan's expensive solar research operation.

All thought of killing the project had melted away in light of his good fortune with the military. Jurnegan had called him, all excited, the fool, about some damn thing going on. He could hardly remember, but he was happy to take a look, and afterward treat the poor man to a gentlemen's lunch.

Jurnegan was busy with a line of grow-lights when Ingleside arrived. He had arranged a collection of portable tables into a rectangular pattern covering half the shop. On them he had constructed a maze made out of clear plastic tubes strapped together with duct tape. The resulting enclosed tunnel complex resembled a generous habitat for pet rodents.

"Look here, Hub, this you gotta see."

Ingleside shuffled to the maze and peered inside.

"Ready? I've got one of our bushes here at the end, see? Minus the soil. I'm placing the one we got from Turkey right beside it, like so."

When the two 'plants' touched in the plastic bin, their root balls instantly turned to what seemed like sand. The two piles vibrated energetically, and coalesced into a very shiny, wormy-looking thing. It thrashed around in a little circle.

Not what Ingleside expected. The hairs rose on his forearms.

"Sweet Jesus, what is that?"

"We don't know, do we? Isn't it wonderful?"

Ingleside hissed dissent.

"Well, from a scientific point of view. But it is spooky, I feel the same way. Now watch this."

Jurnegan walked alongside the maze turning on his powerful grow lights.

The wormy thing followed him from light to light. When all the lights were shining, it sped up. Soon it was racing around the track, rattling through it over and over, first taking one route, then another.

Ingleside hobbled back from the demonstration. "How do you stop it?"

Jurnegan grinned. "It will stop by itself after a while. It's using energy, doing work, like anything else, and after a while it will run out."

Ingleside licked his lips. "When? When will it run out?"

Jurnegan glanced at his watch. "Oh, say an hour, hour and a half? If I turn off the lights, it poops out faster. Couple of minutes."

"Turn off the lights."

▼

The two entrepreneurs tucked themselves into a back corner of the El Charro Café in downtown Tucson for a strategizing session. They were sipping margaritas in a room full of sturdy old wooden tables, most of them empty at the tail end of the lunch hour. Garishly illustrated posters of heroic Hispanic men and their admiring women shared the butter-colored walls with a collection of Mexican sombreros.

Jurnegan raised his glass. "Here's to Opticon!"

Ingleside nodded absently. "The contract is signed. That Air Force bird will have the best eyes money can buy."

Jurnegan smiled. "Congratulations, you'll be rich all over again."

Ingleside ignored the remark.

"Amos — we don't know what we've got in those tubes of yours. It makes me nervous."

Jurnegan lost his smile. "Me too, if you want to know. I can't keep any help. People stay a week, then don't show up next Monday morning."

"Not only that, but we've got some competition. The Durangos were just barely a step ahead of someone else over there in Turkey. Last week, I heard some talk among my military friends. There's a NASA helicopter over on the air base, as unusual here as a penguin. It's been seen searching in the hills around town. Up in the Silver Bells, over in the Rincons. What do you suppose it was looking for?"

Jurnegan bit into his chili relleno. "My guess is your guess. Look, we've come this far . . ."

Ingleside held up a hand to interrupt. "Put that demo of yours on video.

Write something up. For once I'm on your side — publish, establish priority. What about it?"

"I've considered the idea. We would make a splash. But I've changed my mind on the whole question. Others may have discovered these plants — we know there's more than one. And they may have an inkling about them, but I'm betting we're the only ones with real knowledge. What we're doing, it's leading somewhere. We need to find out where . . . exactly."

"Think about it, Amos," Ingleside grumbled. "We're dealing with the unknown. We tell ourselves we're growing plants, but we both know that's not really true."

The old man hoisted his cocktail. "I shouldn't be drinking, especially at lunch, but these margaritas are *estupendo.*" He emptied the glass and set it down on the table. He pushed his plate away.

"Look, I've said my piece. ASR is your show. You're the one on the firing line. I couldn't handle it."

Jurnegan stared up at the turquoise ceiling. It took him some time to gather his thoughts. "You just won a big contract, Hub. I'm not as rich as you. My intuition tells me there's a pot of gold at the end of the renewable energy rainbow."

18

At Ames Research Center, Director Maurice Upshaw was gathering the troops for a briefing. Ever since his old friend Roman Garibaldi came to him with photos of a very strange plant, he could hardly sleep at night.

Now Garibaldi was back in town, in the middle of a heavy winter storm. A line of clouds stretching all the way from Hawaii was flooding local roads and melting the Sierra snow pack.

Just as Upshaw began to think that the meeting would have to be postponed, an assistant appeared in his doorway to announce the man's arrival.

"Dr. Garibaldi made it after all, sir."

"Send him in."

"And there's someone with him . . ."

Garibaldi appeared behind the assistant, shaking water from an umbrella.

"Hey, Mo, it's wet out there. We still on?"

"Come on in, Roman. Who's your friend?"

Garibaldi stood aside to let a middle-aged woman enter the room.

"Mo, meet Nancy Weatherall. Nancy, General Upshaw. He's our fearless leader."

The woman, a dumpy figure in a tweed jacket and rough slacks, disdainful of personal grooming, walked boldly forward and shook Upshaw's hand.

"Hello, General. Before we get going, I just want to say thanks for saving the Hubble. I would never have gotten tenure without it."

Upshaw was taken aback, but pleased by the flattery. "Why thank you. And what is your line of work, if I may ask, that made the Hubble so valuable?"

"I'm an astronomer. I teach across the bay." She jerked a thumb northwards.

"Aha," said Upshaw.

"Nancy is not just an 'astronomer,'" amended Garibaldi. "She's the Otto Struve Distinguished Professor of Astronomy at Cal. The Hubble gave her the data for her Near Star Sky Survey. The N-triple-S is a definitive landmark of modern cosmology."

"You tell her what's going on?"

"I did."

"In spite of our solemn agreement." Upshaw pretended to be wounded by the breach.

"Guilty as charged. We need expertise, Mo. You know it as well as I do." Upshaw spread his arms in welcome.

"Okay, then. Have a seat you two. He pressed a button on his intercom. "Hey, Jim, you ready? Bring in the maguffin."

Captain James Lockwood entered a moment later with a potted plant in his protectively gloved hands. The little square leaves gleamed, even in the dull grey light from Upshaw's rain-spattered windows. He placed it on the director's desk and stood aside.

"Say hello to Captain Lockwood."

Nods and waves all around.

"This young man has been working with me for a couple of years now. His latest exploit is this plant — well, whatever it is — I'm using the term loosely. Tell us about it, Jim . . ."

Garibaldi and Weatherall turned their attention to the captain, whose handsome face was darkened by a pretty good sun tan. Lockwood ran his fingers through the leaves. They clattered noisily.

"These leaves — I'd guess you'd call them that — are in fact not leaves at all. They are perovskite crystals. I think Dr. Garibaldi, here, already figured that part out. I've been down in Tucson at the gem show. The general and I discussed the situation, and it seemed like a good place to start our search. People from all over the world who collect minerals make it a point to set up shop there." He gestured toward the window. "And, full disclosure, I grew up down there. Nice to go home to some decent weather.

"Anyway, a woman was selling these things at the show as jewelry. I bought one, handed her a tracking device disguised as my business card and, using our helicopter, followed her into the Silver Bell Mountains. She was looking for this" — he gestured to the little bush — "but I beat her to it."

Weatherall bounced out of her chair and bustled forward for a close look. "So," she said. "This is the real thing?"

"Yes, ma'am."

Weatherall oohed and ahhed. She tentatively reached toward the little leaf-like squares, then drew back. "What a humbling experience. We're the first ones to, to, uh . . ." She fell silent while inspecting the glassy crystals.

"To what, ma'am?" prompted Upshaw.

"Well, this is a big deal. Historic discovery. Proof of . . . proof of something . . . whatever."

Upshaw grunted. "Hard to talk about, I know."

Garibaldi stepped close as well. "Looks like the bush I bought. Same thing."

Lockwood resumed his account of events. "That's not all. Someone up the line at NASA got a letter from a man in Turkey. That letter was relayed to the director here. This Turkish guy, a school teacher, said he had a bush like this and wanted to sell it. But when I got there, it was already gone. So, be aware, we're not the only ones interested."

Upshaw waved his visitors back to their seats. "What's going on, Roman? What have we got here?"

Garibaldi gestured to his companion. "Let's hear what Nancy has to say."

Weatherall pointed at a lectern in front of a large flat TV screen in a corner of the office. She removed a laptop from her briefcase, walked over, and snapped an HDMI cable into place with the easy skill of a professional lecturer. She pressed a button and PowerPoint slides appeared on the big screen.

"All right, gentlemen, here's the scoop. If I was briefed properly, if NASA's intelligence connections are to be trusted, we have discovered several plants growing that appear to be truly exotic. In Turkey, New Mexico, and now southern Arizona. Furthermore, if the old newspaper accounts I was given are correct, it's the second one known from the vicinity of Tucson."

Tear-drop-shaped markers appeared in each location on a map. She pressed a key and a bright red line popped into view, passing through the first three points.

"Notice the straight line here, notice how the eastern locations are far apart, then how the last two are much closer together. This pattern is consistent with a meteor of some substantial size entering the earth's atmosphere at high speed, fragmenting, dropping bits as it decelerates. We get a few pieces scattered on this trajectory, while it's still moving fast, and then a whole cluster when the energy of entry is burned off, and the remaining pieces drop to the ground."

She advanced the slideshow with another keypress. The following image showed a dotted circle many miles in diameter centered on the city of Tucson.

"I expect we'll find more of these things. Not many back eastward — although you never know — and quite a few in southern Arizona."

Upshaw grunted. "Southern Arizona. That covers a lot of territory."

Garibaldi cleared his throat. "If we don't act, some rockhound will get there first."

Upshaw circled his desk and handed sheets of paper to his guests.

"As you might guess, I've had conversations with some senior people in U.S. intelligence. They in turn have had conversations with other senior people."

Garibaldi folded his arms. "Senior people?"

Upshaw frowned. "I don't want to get into it, Roman. Let's leave it at this — other *very* senior people have crafted an order establishing *The Joint Powers Immigration Task Force*."

Weatherall looked troubled. "That's quite a mouthful, General."

Upshaw emitted a dry chuckle. "You mean cover-up. That's about the size of it, especially if what we're after is somehow . . . *problematic*. It will be our job to investigate these plants and what produced them."

He snapped a finger against the papers the astronomer was holding. "Read and sign. Once you're in, it's a career-ending breach to say anything about our little operation."

Eyes dropped onto the order pages. After anxious study, the group seemed to relax.

"I guess Uncle Sam doesn't expect to collect my first-born son," said Garibaldi. He grinned as he signed his name. "I wouldn't miss this for anything less."

"Who's got a pen?" asked Weatherall.

Upshaw handed her a fancy space pen.

"Perfect," she said and signed with a flourish.

Lockwood also signed. They all handed their papers back to Upshaw.

"Okay, fellow agents, we're in business," said the director, stacking the papers and stuffing them into a folder.

"In case you're wondering, I'm not going to watch the battle from afar through binoculars. Frank Balderian, my assistant director, will sit in for me here at Ames while we go to work.

"If you're right, Ms. Weatherall, and there's a cluster down in Arizona, I think we need to saddle up. Hello, Tucson. We are going to document these undocumented immigrants. I doubt they hiked up from Mexico."

19

Over the years, Professor Jurnegan's research operation endured heavy employee turnover, the subject of many a complaint to his partner Hubert Ingleside. Those superstitious Mexicans! An exception was Chester Boggs, a crusty old prospector. Jurnegan heard of him through his contacts at the Tucson Gem and Mineral Society, and he proved to be a valuable asset. Possibly because he spent most of his time out in the desert hunting up glassy plants and little of it within Jurnegan's shop, his morale was unwavering.

Today, however, he was long overdue at ASR's desert facility.

"Where is that guy?" grumbled Ingleside. "Dammit, Amos, I've got serious work piling up back at Opticon."

"I know, I know. I don't set a schedule, really. He's an independent old soul. Have patience, he'll show up."

An hour later he did. Ingleside had never previously met the man, and he was appalled. Boggs was wearing ragged brown overalls, a grimy wool shirt, a crackly sheepskin coat, and tall leather boots. His wild white hair hadn't been cut in quite a while. A grey beard grew down onto his chest. He was filthy. He smelled.

"At last, here you are," exclaimed Jurnegan. "What have you got for us?"

Boggs stared vacantly at the two men.

"Hello? Chester? You okay?"

Boggs shivered. "Well, Professor, I got a tale to tell."

Ingleside could not contain his impatience. "So tell."

"Yes, please," added Jurnegan with some sympathy.

Boggs stared some more, then abruptly seemed to get hold of himself. "I was up in the hills, rightabouts a ways, into the Rincons, I guess you'd say."

He stopped.

"Go on," urged Jurnegan.

"Huh? Oh, right. Up in the Rincons I was. Yup. Looking for one of your bushes. And I found one, like I thought I might . . ."

He trailed off.

"He's a terrific prospector, Hub," said Jurnegan, embarrassed by the old codger's vacant behavior.

"But then," continued Boggs, "I stumbled, kind of. Hit my head on a rock. That was, let me see" — he counted on his fingers — "three days ago or more. I only woke up this morning. And when I did I could hardly think a thought."

He held up a handful of blackened twigs and leaves.

"That bush I was looking at — a big one — why, it was all tangled around me. But when I moved to get up it withered and blowed away. This is all what's left."

Jurnegan took the pieces. They crackled and snapped as he sorted through them.

"Need a bath," said Boggs.

Ingleside did his best to conceal his disgust. "You know, Amos, there's competition out there. I hear NASA is setting up shop here in town."

"What?"

"That's the story. We have quite a few of these little bushes now, but I don't think the opposition is up to speed. Why doesn't Mr. Boggs, here, take this stuff off to the air base, give those boys the benefit of his expertise?"

Boggs seemed wounded. "Mr. Jurnegan?"

Jurnegan turned to his partner. "What's the idea, Hub?"

Ingleside favored Boggs with a sly smile.

"What would you say — Chester is it? — if you were to go off and help our astronaut friends, and report back to us on what they're up to?"

"Be a spy?" Boggs sounded confused.

"That's it, that's it exactly. NASA might hire you, and I hear they pay well considering they're nothing but government bureaucrats. But of course, we'd pay you too."

"We would?" protested Jurnegan.

"Of course," affirmed Ingleside. "We'll double your salary."

Boggs thought for a while.

"Double pay doesn't sound too bad," he allowed.

"Didn't think it would. Now off you go, and you don't need to mention us or anything about our company here."

"Keep my mouth shut," said Boggs.

"That's right. You're quick, old man."

Ingleside picked up a small bush, one of several lined up on a nearby bench and pressed it into Boggs' grasp.

"Say you saw the NASA helicopter. Here's your calling card."

After Boggs had departed, Jurnegan threw up his hands.

"Have you lost your mind, Hub? You just gave away a valuable sample. Every one of these bushes is precious."

"Oh come on, Professor. Of course they're precious. And the one I just gave away is going to prove just how precious it is by opening the door to a ton of information."

"Jesus Fucking Christ," groaned Jurnegan.

Ingleside was unfazed. He jingled the change in his pocket and leaned on his cane.

"I don't think Mr. Boggs is much of a researcher. Not a Ph.D."

"Not too bright, you mean. He's razor sharp in the desert."

Ingleside waved away his partner's objections.

"He'll be better placed where I sent him. We need intelligence, Amos. Need it badly."

PART THREE

.

20

On a clear day in late winter, the temperature in Tucson was almost ninety degrees when Professor Weatherall's flight arrived from San Francisco. Dr. Garibaldi's own flight from Dulles had arrived an hour earlier, and he already had a rental car checked out.

He found Weatherall standing at the arrivals curb smoking a cigarette. She stubbed it out as he drove up in a tiny Ford Fiesta and waved hello.

"Get ready for heat, Nan," he said, leaning across and opening the passenger door

"Can't wait," she replied, seating herself. "It's still pelting down rain out west. El Niño be damned, drought or no drought."

Once they were underway, he gave her his smartphone. The map app was running, and a little marker was hovering over their destination, Davis-Monthan Air Force Base, right in the middle of Tucson, a mile or so east of the commercial airport.

"Air base, Golf Links Road. Can you navigate?" he asked.

"Oh sure. I've been here many times. Love the place . . . well, not so much in summer."

They drove out of the airport, under the Interstate, and across the Union Pacific railroad tracks. They were chatting as they moved slowly through heavy afternoon traffic.

"What brings you out this way? I'm new here," asked Garibaldi.

"Astronomy, what do you think? The town is a sprawling dustbin, but it's a 'dark city,' the university's mirror lab makes the best telescope optics in the world, and I've done some work out at Kitt Peak, the National Observatory. That whole mountain top is covered with scopes. You should see it."

"Unh-huh, probably not this trip." Garibaldi winced. "I think those faraway objects you study are coming to us. We won't need telescopes."

▼

In his second story office on the north end of the air base, General Upshaw could just see part of Runway 30, the only airstrip, which ran for two miles in a southeast-northwest direction. He watched with nostalgic fascination as an old A-10 Warthog lifted off, its engines thundering. An aerial tank. His old ride. The Air Force no longer flew A-10s, but the Air National Guard still did. While he watched, three more followed the first. The incredible noise shook the window pane he was looking through. He placed a palm against the glass to get a feel for the warplanes' power and smiled with pride at their loud authority.

His reverie was interrupted by a knock on the door.

"Come in."

The door swung aside, and Garibaldi and Weatherall stood in the opening. They took a few seconds to orient themselves before moving uncertainly into the new field offices of The Joint Powers Immigration Task Force, trailing their roll-around bags.

"So we guessed right — here you are," said Garibaldi, eyeing the austere room doubtfully.

Upshaw nodded. "Two weeks. We're all set up, I think. Let's get started. Let me just call Jim and our new guy, Chester. You've met Lockwood. You'll love old Chet."

He pressed a switch on an intercom. *"Hola,* Jim. Get in here. Bring our desert rat."

Lockwood and Chester Boggs appeared in short order. Lockwood with muscles rippling under his T-shirt, Boggs in new work pants with his beard trimmed short and his halo of white hair tamed by an aggressive haircut.

"Chester Boggs, meet our team. Dr. Garibaldi here is a physicist, Ms. Weatherall is a famous astronomer."

Weatherall coughed. "Famous in a very small circle of friends."

Boggs touched his brow in a clumsy salute. "Howdy."

Upshaw grabbed a lanyard and closed the blinds on his office window.

"Let's get down to business. Chet, here, came to us last week with a bush, if we may still call these damn things 'bushes.' Saw our helicopter, figured out who we are. He knows the country around here like no one else. We decided to tap into his field experience, so he's on the team now too."

The old prospector was carrying his introductory gift, a small coppery colored bush, which he deposited on Upshaw's desk. He and Lockwood were both wearing heavy rubber gloves.

Weatherall approached the glittering plant and examined it with a hint of foreboding.

"Doctor Weatherall? You don't look happy," noticed the general.

"These things give me goose bumps," she said. She seemed to be mesmerized by the thing. She hesitated, then sucked in her breath and reached out.

"Don't touch!" warned Lockwood.

Weatherall pulled her hand away. "Right. We don't know what these things might be up to, do we? And I always thought, if alien life arrived on our doorstep it would be — the greys. Little people with big eyes. Roswell stuff. But all we've got instead are some faraway world's idea of plants."

"Yeah, spooky plants," said Garibaldi, keeping his distance. "They should be quarantined."

"Already done, Roman. We've got the rest of them in a secure lab here on the base." said Upshaw. "Now, before you folks tell me whether we actually have anything to worry about, I need to say a few words."

The rest of the group came to ragged attention, puzzled by Upshaw's formality.

"This operation is disrupting our lives and will continue to do so for the duration," he said. "Can't be helped. For now and the foreseeable future, we're a team dedicated to the purpose of discovery. Whatever was going on before you signed the pledge is of no account. Unhappy wives and husbands? Spare me. Financial difficulties? I don't want to know. Relatives who need special care? Hire someone. I'm not interested in your personal troubles. We're a team, and I'm focused on teamwork. You with me?"

His listeners stood up straighter, braced and confused all at once. Garibaldi wondered how some poor underling back at Ames might react to the usually affable general's unexpected severity.

"Well?" queried Upshaw. "I need a show of hands. Like the musketeers, all for one, one for all. Got it?"

Hands were slowly raised.

Upshaw nodded approval. "All right then. Remember what I said. I don't make speeches very often and never on a whim. One's enough for intelligent adults, so . . . what have you got, Doctor — it's Nancy, right?"

Weatherall shook herself to break the spell. "Are you sure we're the right group for this job, General? In the movies this kind of thing is always a big army deal. Guns, tanks, hazmat suits, strict protocols."

Upshaw stuffed his hands in his pockets. "I don't think the powers that be think plants, no matter how odd, constitute 'first contact.' That may change, depending on what we pull out of our hats. But for now, it's all up to us."

Weatherall nodded skeptically. "Okay then. Marching orders heard and understood."

She placed her laptop on a slender credenza, connected it up to the TV on the wall, and opened her latest stack of PowerPoint slides. A map of Europe and North America appeared onscreen.

"As previously noted, if we plot a line through the various discoveries, better defined now with Mr. Boggs' latest work, we see a trajectory angled east-northeast to west-southwest, ending pretty much where we sit today. That much is a given."

She pressed a key and markers blinked at the locations of the items so far recovered. Another keypress placed a bright red line over them, connecting the dots.

"Now that I've had time to sort things out and make some tests, I can tell you a lot more. How long these things were in space, when they arrived on Earth."

"How? How can you tell? I'm sketchy on this." admitted Upshaw in an obviously skeptical tone.

"You're a good straight man, General. Any object floating through outer space is constantly bombarded by cosmic rays. They alter isotopes of several different elements . . . sodium and krypton, among others. Then, once inside Earth's magnetic field and atmosphere, those rays no longer penetrate. With funding from our newly commissioned outfit, I measured the final isotopic ratios, plotted them against cosmic abundance, and the difference gives us a picture."

"The picture?"

"These things have been traveling for a hundred years, give or take."

"Good God."

There was silence while the rest of the group absorbed the information. Finally, Garibaldi found his voice. "Coming our way for a century. Is that a long time or what?"

"Not that long."

"Could they be local — from Mars or Europa maybe?"

"I doubt it. The famous Allan Hills meteorite left Mars seventeen *million* years before it landed in Antarctica. I would expect any natural object to be thousands or millions of years old, like all the asteroids randomly whizzing by Earth that we read about."

"So the relatively short exposure is a clue," said Upshaw.

"It is. It is indeed. I think it confirms our assumptions." Weatherall was in her element, and her personal misgivings were overridden by professional enthusiasm. She was talking fast.

"And, folks, that's not all we can deduce. Once on Earth, other processes go to work, radioactive decay of potassium, carbon-14, et cetera. We look at the argon and nitrogen, and they tell us how long the materials in these so-called bushes have been here. The answer is pretty interesting — just about fifteen years — at most."

Another silence.

"What I can't tell you is what season they arrived in," she continued. "All we know is the angle between the trajectory and earth's spin axis. It points east and just a tad northward from the equatorial plane."

"Why do we care about the season?" wondered Lockwood.

"Good question, Captain. These days we have excellent sky surveys. I'm not too humble to say I made some of them. We can check them for possible origins. I'm guessing some star not too awfully far away."

"Seems reasonable, unless you believe in teleportation," offered Garibaldi.

"I don't," said Upshaw. "And I'd like to know who's planting our plants. Can you tell us that?"

Weatherall shook her head. "Sorry, no. The best I can do is make a guess or two . . ."

She pressed a key and the slide changed. Now the group was looking at a map of the night sky with a sprinkling of bright dots arranged on a graph.

"Here are the fifty nearest stars that are known to have planets. When I look where the trajectory points in winter I see nothing."

She clicked to the next slide.

"In spring, nothing."

Next slide.

"In summer, nothing."

Each slide showed a line that stretched across the sky map, where it failed to intersect with any of the other little dots.

"On the other hand, in fall . . . take a look . . ."

She brought up the next slide.

"Here we have a solar system with at least one planet in the Goldilocks zone sitting out there at just about eleven lightyears. A good bet."

The rest of the group stared at the diagram. The trajectory pointed right at the star Weatherall was talking about.

"Does this star have a name?"

"Ahh, no, no name. Hold on, let me see" — she consulted a note — "it's called PCNSO-621371-K, a designation from the survey catalog."

Upshaw raised a hand. "Explain? This old astronaut is confused."

Garibaldi guessed the canny general understood everything well enough, but wanted the facts stated explicitly.

"Public Catalog of Nearby Stellar Objects," recited Weatherall. "It's a K-type star, smaller than the sun and about one billion years older."

"Not very romantic," mused Garibaldi.

Upshaw did some rough math in his head. "If these bushes crossed eleven lightyears in a century . . . they were moving damn fast."

Garibaldi leaned forward. "More than ten percent of the speed of light. That's what?" His brow wrinkled as he did the division.

"How many miles in a lightyear?" asked Boggs.

The rest of the group was startled by the question, coming as it did from an old man whose formal education might have ended in grade school.

"About six trillion miles," said Weatherall.

"It was going seventy-five million miles an hour," declared Boggs.

"Is that right?" wondered Upshaw.

Garibaldi thought some more. Then he and Weatherall chimed in together: "Pretty close."

Upshaw whistled.

"How did you figure that out so quick, Chet?" asked Lockwood.

"I dunno, to tell you the truth. Since I got knocked out, my mind works better than it did."

"Unh-huh . . . right . . . amazing," mumbled the group. No one knew what to make of Boggs' remark.

Upshaw pointed a finger at the screen. "Any object going that fast when it arrived would never survive contact with Earth's atmosphere. We would have recorded a titanic explosion. Hey, maybe we did."

Weatherall shook her head. "The same thought crossed my mind. I've looked at the records, and there's nothing on that score. No explosions."

"You think the thing slowed itself down," said Upshaw.

"Must have," said Weatherall. "We can rule out a meteor. It wasn't some asteroid tumbling through the sky, accidentally sowing seeds like we first thought."

"I'm disappointed," said Garibaldi. "Here we have an advanced civilization, way beyond ours, and it took them a hundred years to get here? I was hoping for *Star Wars* technology. I always wondered — and now we know — there are no wormholes, no hyperspace, no *jump to lightspeed.*"

21

The twenty-first century economy was not kind to Grant Road in the dusty industrial north end of Tucson. Even after the worst of the recession was over, buildings lay vacant where commercial enterprises once flourished. Grimy auto shops did business where retail outlets once stood. The cheerfully confident signs of an earlier era were painted over, and plastic letters half-heartedly applied announced guns, tobacco, used furniture, and payday loans. Most of the signs were in Spanish.

Holly Chow motored briskly along the wide thoroughfare, filled with commuters in cars that never stopped unless forced to do so by traffic lights.

While she drove she kept one eye on her smartphone map, risking a charge of distracted driving. At Caliente Avenue she slowed and turned into the parking lot of a long low building set at right angles to the street.

It was once a respectable motel. Now the room walls had been knocked out and roll-up garage doors fifteen feet wide had been inserted in their place. The units had been turned into semi-industrial bays, and instead of beds, each contained a small business. She parked her Impreza and hiked along the walkway.

First up, an upholstery shop, smelling of leather and plastic that some cutting knife overheated. Next, a used appliance store, where she had to dodge a forest of ancient vacuum cleaners. Next door, possibly run by the same owner, an electronics recycling facility, overflowing with metal computer cases and keyboards. Beyond that she noted a document shredding operation, a sculpture studio bristling with junked auto parts welded into incomprehensible abstract forms, and a taco stand with little metal chairs outside and a sign: *Cerveza Aqui.*

She was heading for the far end of the building, but as she passed the tiny lunch counter, deliberately ignoring the Hispanic men who were ogling her, she failed to notice a tall blond fellow sitting with them, swapping stories. He reached out and tugged at her sleeve.

"Buy you a beer, miss?"

Chow jumped back, then brought a hand up over her mouth.

"Oh God, it's you. Holzgraf. You're supposed to be working." She waved a hand toward his enterprise, a few more doors down the line.

He held up his glass. "I am. I'm working on this."

He smiled. In Chow's eyes it was more of a smirk, but she savored it anyway. She folded her arms defensively, embarrassed by her small mistake.

"You called. The message said you made a breakthrough."

"Kind of." He shrugged a modest shrug.

"Come on then, show me."

Holzgraf put down his glass. *"Hasta, señores."*

He started away, sweeping his arm in a follow-me arc. She skipped along behind his rolling strides.

"You speak Spanish?"

"That's *sí, señorita* . . . with a terrible accent. How about you?"

"Not a word."

"Demasiado. Here we are." He halted at a double-wide bay and gestured proudly toward a little sign:

DARLINGTON ENERGETIX

He clicked a fob and one of the doors rolled up revealing a large, plain, nearly empty interior. Chow could see a table with electronic equipment on it surrounding a square of foam board covered with shiny square crystals. She started inside.

Holzgraf jumped in front and held up his hand to stop her.

"Whoops, hang on, you can't come in yet."

"Huh?"

He crossed the shop to a battered old desk rescued from Goodwill and consulted a computer. A quick keypress revealed the targets of his television surveillance cameras, live video. Each image was slotted into a rectangular array on the screen.

"Damn," he said. He grabbed a stepladder, carried it into a corner, opened it, and climbed up to adjust one of the cameras' point of view.

"What are you doing?" asked his visitor, looking sulky and confused.

"Uh, gotta make sure every square inch is covered." He returned to the computer display. There was Holly Chow in grainy black-and-white, standing just outside his shop. She was checking her smartphone and tapping an annoyed foot.

"Okay, that's better. You can come in. I've got you on camera."

"What is that supposed to mean?"

"Oh nothing. I'm here alone. With, um, a young woman, that's all."

Chow looked Holzgraf up and down. "I googled you. Holzgraf *The Third*. You and your family. Your family business."

"Unh-huh. Good news, I hope."

"You're rolling in dough. That's the surveillance thing. You're worried about . . ." she waved her arms to take in the world.

". . . lawsuits," he finished for her.

"Not just lawsuits . . ."

". . . sexual harassment charges? Yup. My family is wealthy, you heard it here. I and my little company, we have what lawyers call 'deep pockets.' There are no independent witnesses present to back me up, so I have this video system. The feed goes directly to the security company and their servers. I can't touch the output."

"You're a rich kid." Chow was disturbed by the thought.

"Can't deny it."

"Paranoid Pete."

"Well, there's a saying . . ."

"I know," interrupted Chow, "'of course I'm paranoid. The question is, am I paranoid enough?'"

"That's it. I have to be careful."

"Because you suspect poor little me of a raid on your bank account?"

"Nothing to do with you personally. Hey, can we jump past this?"

Chow strolled over to the table and the crystal array.

"For now, anyway. Tell me, who uses Darlington's hydraulic motors? That's what your family makes, right?"

"Among other products."

"So what good are they?"

"They power big earthmoving trucks, heavy-duty tractors, monster diggers. In South America and parts of Africa, we've got them in railroad locomotives."

"So, what have you got here?" She touched one of the crystals, traced a wire to an electrical meter.

"My first solar array, made out of the crystal leaves you sold me. I thought you'd like to see it."

"I should have doubled the price. You could afford it."

"Business is business. Anyway, I'm getting seventeen percent, nineteen under orange light."

"Is that good?"

"For an initial hookup, you bet. Against commercial state-o-the-art? Not competitive, not yet. But I will be."

"What's the ooze here under each little leaf, or whatever these things are?"

"Good question. Photosynthesis? That's my guess."

"Mmm."

"Not only do these things generate some juice, they produce it. Some sort of metallic goo. I'm hoping it's worth something as a fuel."

"Mmm."

"My big problem is volume. I need more of these things."

"And you think I know where to find them."

"I was hoping."

"Sorry to disappoint you. Disappoint myself, I could use the money."

She gave herself a little tour of the shop, noting the electronic equipment, the power tools, the sheets of plastic stacked in vertical holders, the microwave oven. She paused at the small refrigerator and opened it.

"Oof. Salami and string cheese? Frozen pizza? Mountain Dew?" She wiggled her eyebrows at Holzgraf. "I would have thought caviar."

"Ohh . . . you are tough."

She grimaced. "Sorry, that just popped out. Do you have Wi-Fi?"

"Not yet. But I do have a hotspot on my ultra-fast diamond-encrusted smartphone."

She plunked herself down on a chair at the far end of Holzgraf's workbench and opened up a tiny laptop.

"Password?"

"Solario. Capital 'S.'"

"That's two 'o's, weak encryption, you know that, right?"

He shook his head. "You must be in software."

"No."

"An engineer though, right? On the spectrum somewhere."

"Spectrum?" repeated Chow in an icy tone.

"Asperger's, right . . ?"

"I am a perfectly — *normal* — civil engineer. Hydraulics."

"Whoops, apologies, what do I know? Like Darlington Industries?"

"More like big reservoirs and pumping equipment. Getting water to the masses in the middle of a desert."

He nodded vaguely, intrigued by this cool inward woman.

"But I did notice the parallel wiring you rigged up on your array here," she continued. "Might want to take another look at that. I don't think you've got the optimum configuration."

"Not the optimum configuration," he repeated, struck by her blunt no-nonsense manner.

"Okay, then, I'm googling around," said Chow, pointing at her screen. "Back issues of newspapers. Maybe someone has seen these things and thought they were newsworthy. Where's your machine? Help me out here."

Holzgraf meandered over to his computer, slid into his chair, and opened up a web browser.

"I'm curious," he ventured. "You're an engineer, but you were selling stuff at the show. How does that work?"

"Lost my job. City of Tucson is automating, they face budget cuts, I was last in, first out."

"What's with the ranch, those tall trees?"

"Pecans. Big deal around here. Dad sold the orchard, but I still own the house. I rent it out and live in the cottage behind it."

"So you're set. What's the problem?"

"There's a mortgage."

Holzgraf fell silent, lost in thought. After a little while he looked her way. She was leaning into her laptop, intent on chasing down some lead, oblivious to his presence. Her brow was furrowed, her lips compressed. He decided she had beautiful lips.

"So what now? What's next?"

Chow looked up. "I applied to the Mirror Lab at the university. That would be fun. There might be an opening, but it's a long shot."

Holzgraf thought some more. Now she was looking at him through dark and narrow eyes. The intensity of her gaze made him uncomfortable. He blinked.

"Here's an idea — go to work for me. I need help." He managed a wry grin. "Pay will be good, great benefits, what do you say?"

Chow ignored the job offer.

"Don't you wonder about that guy, Jurnegan?" she asked.

"Yeah, I guess. Think he had one of these bushes?"

"I'd bet on it. What else would get him going on perovskite? But his paper is so vague. It's weird."

"Okay, weird. Did I offend you? You didn't answer my question."

But Chow continued down her own track.

"And wait, here's an article in the *Pima Prospect.* Some guy named Beard did a Halloween piece and mentioned metal bushes."

"Lemme see that."

Holzgraf got up, rounded the table, and peered over Chow's shoulder.

HALLOWEEN HEX

Hello, it's Hell-o-ween again, ladies and germs. Forget about ghosts and goblins this year. Now I'm told we have metal bushes in our backyards. Watch out if you see something shiny where your ocotillo used to be. Who knows where it came from? Remember Roswell? Better shake out those Space Cadet costumes. Maybe these things will grow up to be robots from Mars . . .

"Jack Beard. This write-up is ten years old."

"Where is he now?"

"Yeah, where? Let's find out."

Chow nodded. She looked around the room. "Okay, rich kid. I'll join your little company. But if the Mirror Lab job comes through . . ."

Holzgraf was oddly elated. To disguise feelings he didn't quite understand, he focused on the business significance.

"Hey, look, I just doubled Darlington Energetix's employees. We're growing fast, sailing into the future."

After Chow left, Holzgraf got on the phone to his stepmother.

"Hi, Mavis. Thought I'd bring you up to date on my little company."

"Yes, how exciting," said the widow Holzgraf in a neutral tone.

"I just built my first solar array. Seventeen percent conversion to electricity."

"Should I be impressed, dear?"

Holzgraf noted the indifference, the unstated critique.

"And, also, I just hired my first employee. You'll be pleased — she's sharp."

"She?"

"Yes, a woman named Holly Chow."

"Chow? She's Asian?"

"Right. Is that a problem?" Holzgraf was irked by what he thought was a dismissive tone.

"Problem? Of course not," said his stepmother smoothly. "This is the twenty-first century, where we all live now. Perfect equality, isn't it wonderful? But, a cautionary word, if you're willing to hear it — think of your checkered history with women, Guy. No fraternization with employees. You hear me?"

Holzgraf rolled his eyes.

"Loud and clear, madam."

22

The white NASA helicopter rose up out of Davis-Monthan Air Force Base and flew eastward. It passed over the Tanque Verde Ranch resort and up along Redington Road into the Rincon mountain foothills. There it zigzagged back and forth over the steep slopes, searching among the ordinary scrubby desert plants for something extraordinary.

On board were Jim Lockwood and Chester Boggs. Lockwood had a map of the local terrain in his lap. Three circles in red with twenty, thirty, and forty mile diameters were drawn around the city of Tucson. Another three, in blue, were centered east and slightly south of downtown. The circles intersected in several places, among them over the Rincons, their present position.

"We're on the outer rim, both sets," said Lockwood into his microphone.

Boggs clamped his headset over his ears. "What?"

"We're on target," said Lockwood. "Weatherall's cluster pattern."

Boggs nodded. He pointed out the window. "There. Down there."

The helicopter flew on. Boggs became agitated.

"No, no, turn around. Back there."

"You sure?"

"Oh yeah, sure. Old Chester, sure as Shinola."

Lockwood directed the pilot back the way they came. They flew along for perhaps a half mile. Then Lockwood saw it too — down below, a yard or so across. Easy to miss if it were not gleaming like a collection of tiny mirrors in the morning sunshine.

They found a rounded hillock a quarter of a mile away where the chopper could land without smacking a rotor into the tall saguaros that grew everywhere. Lockwood and Boggs climbed out with bags and shovels.

Lockwood was immediately confused by the change in perspective. What seemed clear from above looked puzzling on the ground.

"Where the hell?"

Boggs was already hiking through the chaparral.

"Over thisaway."

The old prospector led Lockwood down one hillside and up another.

"Watch out for snakes, Captain."

After what seemed like a long walk, they came upon the gleaming bush.

"Don't touch it till I get pictures," ordered Lockwood. He placed a ruler beside the bush pointing north, set up a gnomon beside it. Then he hefted a little pocket camera and snapped digital photos from several angles.

"What's that for?" asked Boggs, pointing at the gnomon.

"Ruler shows size and direction. Shadow from that pin shows the sun angle, time of day. "

"Sundial. A science toy . . ."

Being careful not to do any damage, they went about freeing the plant from the hard ground with delicate probes and careful scrapes with their shovels.

"Does this thing make you nervous, Chet?" asked Lockwood.

Boggs stopped digging and stared at the thing before them.

"My first one, it did. Looks strange, don't it? Made me feel strange."

"Unh-huh. I know what you mean."

"Got over it. Don't bother me none no more."

Pretty soon they had the object out of the ground, bagged, and wrapped in plastic.

As they prepared to return to the helicopter, Boggs leaned over and scooped up a handful of the crumbling soil they had plowed up with their shovels. He lifted it to his nose, sniffed, took a bite, chewed, swallowed.

Lockwood stepped away from the old man, looked him over.

"You eat dirt?"

Boggs' face broke into a sloppy grin. "Sometimes. Now and then."

Lockwood's lip curled. "Taste good?"

"Pretty good." He popped a pebble into his mouth, like eating a peanut.

"Jesus Lord."

Boggs carried their find back to the chopper. Lockwood leaned down, brought up a pinch of soil. He stared at it, touched his tongue to the stuff experimentally.

▼

In the Joint Powers Immigration Task Force office at Davis-Monthan, Weatherall pored over her maps. She used a Sharpie to mark the spot where Lockwood and Boggs made their latest discovery, which was now sitting on a foldable table in the middle of the room.

"This one is almost right on the middle blue circle. Well, within the margin of error," she said. "A little more searching, we should find more of these things, confirm my hypothesis."

Garibaldi carefully donned rubber gloves and picked the plant up. He pushed at the roots, feeling for some sort of root ball. He turned to Upshaw. "Nancy thinks she's got it, but we need a better fix. We need to nail down the early trajectory. We need more data points."

General Upshaw stood up from his desk waving a sheaf of telex papers.

"American TV & Appliance — that's the cover name for our main intelligence liaison — think they have a possibility. Someone in Spain wrote a letter to the local paper. Worried about contaminating an olive grove, apparently."

Garibaldi read the intelligence report. "Send Jim to Spain?"

"Yes indeed. Where did he go, anyway?"

If another plant had established itself overseas, Garibaldi wanted it. He went looking for Lockwood, but gave up after poking his head into the various rooms the ITF group had commandeered.

On his way back to Upshaw's office he stopped off in the bathroom. While he was relieving himself at the urinal he thought he heard mumbling in one of the booths. He couldn't understand the words, but the effect was odd. Curiosity aroused, he zipped up and sidled over to the door, bent an ear toward the sound.

"Is that me or *mumble?* Stop *mumble.* Talk, talk, *mumble.* Stop. I don't want to *mumble.* Stop thinking. No more flashes."

Garibaldi's skin went cold. The voice was Lockwood's.

▼

Upshaw beckoned Lockwood into his office and closed the door behind him. He subjected his chief lieutenant to a long and silent visual examination. Lockwood's skin was pale. His eyes were red. It looked like tears might have been flowing. Upshaw motioned him to a chair.

"Roman tells me he heard you talking to yourself in the men's. Is that right?"

Lockwood lowered himself into the seat. "I'm okay. I'm fine."

Upshaw wasn't buying. "How long were you in Afghanistan?"

"Long enough."

"You saw combat?"

"No. MI office in Kabul. You already know all about me."

"Apparently not. You saw something. What?"

Lockwood hesitated. With a visible effort he slowly summoned the fragment of a war story. "There was an attack. In the market when some of us were walking by. Body parts everywhere."

Upshaw nodded sympathetically. "Jim — have you had yourself checked out?"

"No. No need."

"What Garibaldi heard, what you're describing — it's classic PTSD."

"No way. I'm good. The moods come and go."

"Unh-huh. I need you on a mission. A bush in Spain."

Lockwood straightened up. "Want me to take a look?"

"Are you up to it?"

"Sure. Don't worry about me. I won't let the team down."

Upshaw rubbed his balding head. "When you come back, I want you to see someone."

"What's the point?"

"I need people I can trust."

"You can trust me."

"I'm not sure you can trust yourself."

23

The distance south from Madrid to Lucena was just under three hundred kilometers, a four hour trip on the E-5 *Autovia de Andalucia.* The Durangos were halfway there, driving along in a small sedan they rented at the airport.

"SEAT? What kind of a car is that?" asked Earl, shaking his head. He was bored.

"It's pronounced *SAY-AT.* It's Spanish," said Ty.

"They make cars here?"

"Yeah, but they're owned by VW now. VW owns everything."

"I thought, you look around" — Earl indicated the landscape blurring past their windows — "all they made was fucking olive oil."

Indeed, not long after leaving Madrid, it seemed that every square hectare they saw was planted in low, cleanly trimmed olive trees.

"And this thing isn't even a diesel. You could run a diesel on the fucking olive oil, and the hell with fucking OPEC."

"Hey, bro, we're coming up on Bailen, I just saw the sign. We exit to E-902."

"Got it."

They made the turn.

"Here we are driving all over God's creation. For what? For a dollar a day."

"Well, more than that. Pay is pretty good, I'd say."

"But it's just wages. We are wage slaves."

"What are you talking about?"

"For tracking down these damn bushes, I think we should get a percentage, don't you?"

"I dunno. Come on, life is good."

"Life with olive oil."

"Hey, so it's a long trip. Beats whacking ragheads in Syria, bro."

"Yeah, but when we get back, we hold out, see? And we say, we turn over the plant, but we double our pay after this."

"You really want to do that?"

"Why not? Jurnegan's a hopeless academic, he'll do anything we tell him to."

110

"Maybe, as long as it's Ingleside's money."

"That guy? That guy is loaded. The Defense Department funds his operation. And the government doesn't know how to save a dime. Eyes for missiles. Fucking Opticon."

Nearing Jaen they looped around a long flyover, transitioning to A-316. At Alcaudete they transitioned again. Now they were traveling west on A-432. Knobby mountains rose up south of the road. They were skirting the *Parque Natural de las Sierras Subbéticas*.

When the peaks receded in their rear-view mirror, they turned onto A-318. Gas stations, roadside restaurants, agricultural equipment dealers, and yes, commercial facilities to process olives became frequent sights. Lucena dead ahead.

"Got your map? Got your note?"

"Yup. Almost there. Before we get into town, it's off to the left. Some tiny thread of a country road. I think it's called CP-132."

"You think?"

"It's CP-132. Definitely." Ty hauled out his iPad, checked their location with the built-in GPS receiver. "We may not get a sign, so eyes wide, it's coming up."

They turned off the highway onto a narrow dirt track that wound in between endless olive trees.

"My God, what if you're allergic to these damn trees?"

"I'm not."

"Me neither, but my ex-wife's sister couldn't go near one. They had them outside her dorm room at school, and she had to move."

Ty checked his notes.

"Okay, listen up. Should see a house up left, stucco, tile roof."

"That describes every building in this country," groused Earl.

"But it's all alone, nothing else around for half a klik."

"You kidding?"

"That's what the note says."

"Hey, I think I see it. Look for the driveway."

▼

Two days later, Jim Lockwood drove the same highways, byways, and farm-to-market roads, arriving at the same isolated house. He parked and knocked on a heavy oak door. After an uncertain interval the door cracked open and a middle-aged woman in a pale green top over faded jeans peered out.

"*Hola, señora.* Sorry to bother you, ma'am. I'm here from NATO."

He opened his wallet and showed her an impressive ID. The woman stared at it.

"We lost an experimental plant in your area not long ago. A bush about yay big, like so."

He sized the thing with outspread arms.

"We wouldn't want to contaminate your beautiful olives with a dangerous weed, and —"

"*¿Peligro?*" queried the woman.

"Yes, ma'am, I'm afraid so. We noticed your letter to the *periódico,* and I'm here to collect it."

The woman frowned. She pointed at Lockwood.

"*¿Americano?*"

"*Sí, señora.*"

"*Esta cosa*" — she struggled to find some English — "this thing . . ."

"Yes?"

"This mens . . . *Dos* . . . two . . . from *Naciones Unidas* . . ."

"United Nations?" prompted Lockwood, twirling his hand to speed her up.

"*Sí,, sí, sí.* They collect *ya, hace dos días.* Already two days ago."

Lockwood was thunderstruck.

"Two men?"

"*Sí.*"

"Two days ago?"

"*Sí.*"

"Well, shit."

"How you say such dirty talk?!" scolded the woman. She slammed the door.

24

Lockwood caught a military flight from Morón Air Base outside Seville, and was back on the ground in Tucson, empty-handed, in less than forty-eight hours.

Upshaw greeted him with a slip of paper.

"What's this?"

"Your appointment. Dr. Nyberg, 355th Medical Group. He's right here on the base."

"Do I have to do this?" The man was jet-lagged and exhausted.

"We agreed. Team integrity, Jim. It's important."

"How confidential is this?" was Lockwood's first question as he sat down in Dr. Nyberg's little office.

"Absolute."

"My boss won't hear of anything I say?"

"Never."

"Good. That's good."

Dr. Nyberg toyed with a pad and pencil. "You do sound somewhat stressed. Tell me, it won't matter, is there a crime involved?"

Lockwood chuckled absently. "No, no crime."

"Well then, the ethics are simple. The reference I was given noted a tour in Afghanistan. Bad reaction. PTSD was mentioned."

"I don't have PTSD, Doc."

"You know, it's not usually obvious. But these days, I can tell you we'll see strong positive results within six weeks."

"See, I told General Upshaw I had witnessed a horrific bombing."

"That in itself might trigger the syndrome," affirmed Dr. Nyberg with a little nod.

"But I didn't. Didn't see any bombing. I spent all my time in a perfectly secure office."

"I see. That's . . . something, isn't it? Let's talk about it,"

"What's going on is much stranger," confessed Lockwood. "Memory loss. Strange images flashing now and then, like a vivid dream. Losing interest in things." He shrugged sheepishly. "Hard to sleep."

"Memory deficits, dreams, loss of affect," noted the doctor.

"All of the above," said Lockwood ruefully.

"Go on. What else?"

"I'm wondering if it's schizophrenia, really mental."

"Any voices?"

"No voices."

"How's your inner sense of identity?"

Lockwood raised a finger and shook it. "That's kind of the heart of the matter. I feel confused about myself."

Dr. Nyberg nodded again. He stood and stared out his window at the nearby Air Force Boneyard, at all the airplane hulks rotting there. He thought for a while, then returned to his desk and wrote a prescription.

"I'm not worried about you," he declared. He handed a small square of paper to the captain. "Fill this at our pharmacy, a very mild stimulant, keep you on an even keel while we sort this out."

Lockwood sensed the session was over. He rose from his chair.

"Thanks, Doc."

"See you in ten days. You may just be clinically depressed. Mildly depressed, okay? Very treatable."

"Okay . . ."

"Drink a lot of coffee. Can't hurt."

▼

The Durangos needed an extra day to package up their prize as an art object. After a long commercial flight, they passed through American immigration at Tucson International Airport without incident and were waiting for their cargo to clear customs.

"Here we go," said Ty.

A plastic crate came scooting along a rubberized conveyor belt. The customs agent read the attached labels, accepted an authorization form from Earl, made marks on both items with a fluorescent orange marker, and waved them onward.

"Welcome home, gentlemen. Have a good day."

They placed the crate on a hand truck they had rented down the hall, and trundled the thing toward the parking garage.

As they neared their Hummer on the second floor a man appeared beside it. He held up a hand to greet them. He was wearing a suit, a trim black beard, and a wide smile. Not very tall, not very thin. Something in his dress and posture told them he was a foreigner, even before he opened his mouth.

"*Privet, gospoda!* Hello, hello."

The Durangos stopped cold. Ty instinctively let a hand creep around to the small of his back, but there was no insurance there due to the usual air travel restrictions on firearms.

"Christ, Earl, my piece is in the truck."

The man raised his hands in mock surrender.

"No harm, no problem. Here, my card . . ."

He held up a small slip of cardboard and waved it around. Ty reached out and grabbed it.

"Basil Temkhin?"

"*Da.* That's me, *k vashim uslugam.*"

The Durangos' jaws dropped.

"A Russian spy, Earl," said Ty. "Swear to squirrel."

Temkhin grinned.

"No spy. I am *delovoy chelovek,* a businessman."

"Oh, right," said Earl with sardonic emphasis. The two brothers eyed each other. They were wondering if some serious physical moves were going to be needed to reach their vehicle.

"Businessman?" probed Ty, eyes darting into the shadows in case the man had hidden allies ready to jump.

"*Da.* My interest — fine minerals."

"I guess that could be true," allowed Ty after a moment's thought. No one else was lurking anywhere nearby. He started to relax.

Temkhin laughed. "See, you know the truth. I am just me. So, I have a *biznes-predlozheniye* — business proposal."

". . . unh-huh, business," murmured Earl cautiously.

"Tell us," said Ty.

"That crate. A bush inside, *da?* Very strange bush, metal. Exotic minerals. You are working hard to get it. I say, work for me."

"We've already got jobs."

"Yes, yes, but for essential work you do, you are not well paid. Not so?"

Earl shifted his weight. He was reconsidering his rebellious plans versus Jurnegan and Ingleside. "We do okay," he said.

"We're happy in our work," added Ty.

Temkhin seemed to sense that his proposal was falling on deaf ears. He shrugged.

"Keep card. Change minds, pay double. Bring bush, pay triple." He tapped the side of his head. "Think."

He waved cheerily, turned, and moved away between the cars and trucks.

The Durangos opened up the Hummer's tailgate and loaded the crate.

"We just met a fucking *spy,*" said Earl. "A real one. Can you believe?"

"Man, what balls," said Ty.

They climbed into the Hummer.

"Keep the card," said Earl. "Just in case."

Ty patted his shirt pocket.

"Got it. Like you say . . . just in case."

Jurnegan took charge of the bush with a burst of thank-yous. He invited the Durangos to hang around and watch while he processed the find, so they did.

The professor donned rubber gloves, lifted the thing out of the cardboard box it was packed in, and removed the plastic liner. Thick clods of dirt clung to what looked like roots. He dug at them, peeling away the soil to expose the root ball.

"Whoa, there, Matilda. Look at that!" he exclaimed.

The root ball, when exposed, was unlike others he had already seen. This one was an almost perfect cube, hanging from a root at one corner. Little crystals grew out of the cube's faces.

"What the fuck — pardon me," said Earl. Both Durangos were mildly upset by the odd sight.

"Hard to tell what it is, guys. Here, I'll place it in this tub . . ."

He lowered the bush into a five-gallon plastic bucket.

". . . and I'll just bring its cousin — something else you found, remember? — over here and set it down close by . . ."

He did so. The cubical root ball instantly dissolved into a sandy substance.

Earl steadied himself, puffed out his chest. "Listen, Doc, this stuff looks, um, real *unpredictable.* Me and Ty, we had a conference. We're taking risks, and we decided we should ask you for a big . . ."

He stopped talking, all thoughts of money forgotten. His eyes were drawn to the little pile of sand, which suddenly and spontaneously refashioned itself into an ellipsoidal ball. The ball thrashed noisily around the bucket.

"Whoa, Doc," said Ty, backing away. "What is that thing, anyway?"

Jurnegan chuckled. He was in research heaven.

"I dunno, Ty. No one knows. That's what I'm trying to find out."

"I wouldn't go to bed and close my eyes anywhere near it," said Earl. "And I'm no pussy."

"Well, boys, I'm a careful sort of guy myself, so you can be sure I take every precaution."

"You know," said Ty, wiggling a finger at the rolling ball, "I never heard of anything like this before. Where do you think it comes from?"

Jurnegan exhaled. His smile faded. "Can't be sure, but . . ." He cocked his head and pointed up toward the ceiling. The Durangos took another step backward.

"Fucking Mars," said Earl.

"God Almighty on a tumbleweed," said Ty.

25

The Pantano Villas Assisted Living Facility, on Speedway Boulevard near the lumber store, wasn't Tucson's most modern up-to-date institution, but it didn't look like a prison either. At least Chow didn't notice filth or odors or any of the residents walking around naked. Holzgraf wasn't so sure.

"This is it?"

"That's what my search results say. He retired and moved here about three years ago, after his wife died." Chow had spent hours on her laptop to come up with the address, and she resented any doubts.

"Okay, then. Here we go."

The aluminum frame door sensed them coming and slid open on its own.

"Mr. Beard's unit?" asked Chow at the desk.

The clerk brought forth a paper map and a highlighting pen. He drew a fluorescent line from the desk down a long hallway, around a corner, down another hallway, through a patio, and into yet another hallway.

"Number seven-four-three."

"Quite a hike," noted Holzgraf. "Do the residents have electric carts?"

"Some do," growled the clerk. "We're big. You get the walking tour."

"Thanks."

"Be nice to Jack, he's frail."

They nodded and started off down the hall. Chow consulted the map as they walked.

A knock on unit 743 produced an unintelligible grunt from inside. Chow tried the door, an old wooden one with scrollwork decorating the little peep hole. She stuck her eye up to the lens and looked inside. Pretty soon she spotted a man in a wheelchair rolling down the corridor to greet them. They heard some fumbling with the latch. It took a while before the door groaned open.

"Mr. Beard?"

"Hello, young lady."

"Uh, this is Guy Holzgraf, and I'm Holly Chow. We called . . ?"

"Yes, I remember. Come in, come in."

They settled themselves on worn Danish modern chairs. Holzgraf sniffed at the medicinal odor permeating the apartment. Beard rolled back from a trip to his refrigerator with bottles of soda water. The old man seemed glad of any company.

"You mentioned a bush made out of metal. If you found out I knew of one, you must have read that old Halloween column in the *Prospect.*"

"Yup, we did," said Chow, sipping her drink.

"Hell-o-ween, heh heh. I like that little invention." He savored the term: "That's what I called it, *Hell-o-ween.*"

Chow locked eyes with Holzgraf. The old man's body was failing, but his memory seemed reasonably intact. More or less.

"We were wondering how you learned of that bush, Mr. Beard," prompted Holzgraf.

"Call me Jack. I never saw it, you understand. A rancher I was acquainted with mentioned it to me. Found it on his spread."

"Rancher?"

"Ken Olson. Good man."

"Do you know where we can find him? We think there might be more of those things."

"Ahh, now that's the problem. A *con-un-drum.* Old Ken passed on a few years back. We had some snow here. I know, hard to believe, and Ken was out there tending his little Spanish cows in the worst damn weather in a Tucson lifetime. He caught a cold, turned into pneumonia" — he snapped his fingers — "*Spifft!* — gone just like that."

"Gee, that's too bad. Where was the bush? His ranch?"

"Well, young lady, that's another problem. It's gone too."

"Oh no."

"'Fraid so. Ken didn't have children. His cousin's son inherited the ranch, if I remember right, and he turned around and sold it to developers. It's just another collection of faux adobe now, a hundred houses or more, like little brown biscuits. The KO Estates."

"Tucson is growing," said Holzgraf. "Can't stop it."

"That's right, young feller. And I don't belittle the construction. No sir. Three-car garages, Whirlpool appliances, central air. I couldn't afford 'em."

"So where — ?"

"— out off Kinney Road, west of town. You know, I don't think Ken ever had any idea about what he found. We come, we go, we don't learn much, do we?"

"Not without a lot of work," grumbled Holzgraf.

"You got a map? Got the Google?"

"Of course we do, Mr. Beard," said Chow.

"Of course you do. Everyone has the Google. It's the GSA we live in now, The Google States of America."

Holzgraf and Chow drove out to the KO Estates in his brand new Jeep. They wound their way through the slickly paved streets, past low square houses with flat roofs in beige, red, and mustard tones. They all looked as new as his car. Beard had described the development pretty well: the houses were built out of conventional materials imitating the shape of traditional adobe. Here and there bristling ocotillos and immature saguaros had been planted to add character, but for the most part everything seemed raw and sterile.

"At least these things won't melt in the rain," noted Holzgraf.

"What rain?" snorted Chow. "You haven't been here very long, have you, mister?"

Holzgraf made a wry face. "Not too long. I like what I see, though. I may move here. Man, with your sunshine, it's the land of solar power."

"I have an old map of Olson's ranch, and we're already near the western edge of his property," said Chow, burying her face in folds of paper. "He had to ride a horse to get this far out of town."

The two had not actually agreed to become detectives and spend their time searching for peculiar plants. But that's what they were doing. Neither of them wanted to jinx their casual alliance by talking about it.

The street they were on dead-ended at a steel barrier on the border of the development. A narrow trail lead from the street into the desert beyond. Holzgraf parked. He hoisted a light pack, handed Chow her walking sticks, adjusted his Pittsburgh Pirates cap, and led the way into the wild.

The trail guided them up a gradual slope to a long north-south angled ridge, which they crested in less than ten minutes. From there they had a panoramic view of a wide and shallow valley. A light breeze stirred the bushes, their clothing, their hair. As they surveyed the arid prospect, Holzgraf spotted an occasional flicker of light in the sea of shrubs and cactuses.

"There. See that?"

"Where?"

"Just north of west. Uh, line up with that peak in the distance, and bring your eye down . . ."

"Got it."

They set off into the valley.

"Always it's snakes, coyotes, gila monsters, javelinas. Keep your eyes open," warned Chow.

"Oh yeah," said Holzgraf. "Can't wait to see a gila monster."

"They're not some fantasy creature. They bite you, it's straight to ER."

"Okay, okay, I'm watching, I'll be careful."

Within minutes they were standing beside a coppery metallic bush. Its little square leaves were turning in the wind. Every now and then they reflected a flash of sunlight.

Holzgraf dropped his pack and extracted a folding shovel. Chow snapped open a plastic bag.

▼

The two bush-hunters unwrapped their find at Darlington Energetix, placed it on a workbench, and stood back to admire it with a sense of reverence that was almost religious.

"Hey now, energetic employees, we got one!" said Holzgraf.

"I don't understand," mused Chow. "If these things grow all over the place around here — this one was miles from Dad's — why aren't they better known? Better studied? Classified? In the literature?"

"Beats me," said Holzgraf.

"I searched and searched. If our guy Beard did the only write-up aside from Jurnegan's paper, they have to be new, a mutation or something."

Holzgraf was hooking up wires. "Bring that lamp over here."

Chow dragged the lamp across the room. Holzgraf jammed the leads of a digital voltmeter into the root ball.

"Watch this."

He switched the lamp on.

"What have we got?"

Chow read the display.

"Two-point-four volts."

"And I'm not even connected to the plant directly, just to the dirt here."

He twisted the knob on the Variac supplying power to the lamp. The color of the light faded from blue-white to yellow-orange.

"Now check."

"Two-point-nine volts."

"That is weird."

"Huh? Why?"

Holzgraf waved his hands, creating an imaginary biological entity in the space between them.

"Most photosynthesis relies on absorbing red and blue light, reflecting green, hence green plants. This thing likes yellow and orange preferentially. Almost the opposite of what we're used to."

"Let's compare."

Chow had previously transferred the remains of her own discovery to her new place of employment.

"Old versus new. My guy still has a few leaves, I didn't completely destroy it."

She lifted her raggedy bush from a bench in the back of the shop and placed it next to their new find.

Thump.

"What was that?"

"Dunno. Do it again."

Chow picked up her bush, turned around in a circle and put it back beside the larger one.

Thump.

"Whoa."

The pot holding the new bush was wobbling, as if somebody had jostled it. The soil was heaving.

Chow inched forward for a closer look.

"Well, crap, we caught a gopher."

Holzgraf moved up to check.

"That's no gopher. Gila monster?"

"Ha ha," said Chow. She was nervous. "What are we gonna do?"

Holzgraf strode away and came back with a clear plastic tub.

"You hold it, I'll pull."

Chow reluctantly grasped the tub. Holzgraf lifted their find out of its pot and shook it over the tub. Roots unfurled, and a blob of mud fell into the tub. They stared at in wonder. Then it started to move.

Chow leaped back.

"Oh my God!"

Holzgraf dropped the bush he was holding. They both retreated a few paces.

"Okayyyy . . . so it's an animal, not a plant."

"What kind of animal?"

"Not a gopher, that's for sure. You ever read anything about this?"

"Nothing."

They watched while the blob roamed around the tub. Chow noticed a pattern. She took a few experimental steps to her right. The blob moved to follow. Then she moved left. The blob followed again.

"Look at that."

Chow stopped. The blob resumed roaming around.

"I wonder . . ."

She timidly approached the tub.

"Hey, little animal thing."

The blob bulged in her direction.

"It senses my presence."

"Try not to get bitten," said Holzgraf, trying for levity. "Workman's comp insurance is expensive, I don't want any claims."

"What are you?" inquired Chow.

The blob quivered.

"And what about the other bushes? Any more blobs like you?"

The thing rushed around the tub, jarring it, and stopped in front of her again.

"You hear me talking, don't you?"

A wrinkle spread across the blob.

Chow looked around. Holzgraf was standing by the lamp. His hand was on the Variac knob.

"Hey, are you watching — ?" Chow shook a nervous finger at the blob. "This thing, this gloop, is thinking. It's like a naked little brain."

Holzgraf twisted the Variac control, killing the lamp light. The blob dissolved into a layer of sand in the bottom of the tub. He picked up the bush he had dropped and placed it on top of the sand. Immediately, the sand formed into a cubical root ball. Roots crawled around and over the shape, cradling it.

"Enough. I won't sleep a wink tonight," said Holzgraf.

"I am officially creeped out," agreed Chow. "We need to talk to that guy Jurnegan. Does he know about this?"

26

Holzgraf dropped Chow on the University of Arizona campus, miraculously found an empty parking spot for his Jeep at a nearby convenience store, and followed Chow into the Department of GeoSciences.

He caught up with her at the main reception desk, where a young woman was trying to be helpful.

"I'm so sorry, but Professor Jurnegan is on a long sabbatical."

"Do you have an email address? I found something that will really interest him," pleaded Chow.

"I can't give you any information, I'm afraid. He left strict instructions not to be contacted."

"That's terrible," moaned Holzgraf. "He's the leading authority on the use of perovskite, a rare mineral, for solar power."

The receptionist allowed herself a smile.

"Advanced Solar Research, that's his private company. I get letters and bills all the time."

Chow and Holzgraf exchanged glances. A glimmer of hope.

"Have an address?"

The receptionist shook her head. "If I did, I could forward his mail instead of stacking it in his office."

Holzgraf displayed his radiant grin. "An absent-minded professor, would you say?"

The receptionist laughed. "That man, he defines the term. He never checks."

Chow tapped the desk. "Well, thanks anyway."

Holzgraf gave the receptionist his card. "Look, if you hear from him, say we made a discovery that dovetails with his own research."

The receptionist gazed at the card. "I can't promise a thing. I've got a million messages lined up already."

Chow was already heading for the door. Holzgraf turned to follow.

The receptionist had a parting thought. She called after him. "He has a business partner, if you didn't know."

Holzgraf stopped walking. "I didn't."

"The guy who runs Opticon here in town, big military contractor, he's the money man. You could try him."

▼

The Optical Controls Corporation occupied a city block's worth of featureless concrete tilt-up buildings over near the air base.

There was a guard at the gate checking cars, so Holzgraf stopped in the street, handed the Jeep keys to Chow, and headed toward the main entrance on foot.

Holzgraf timed his approach to coincide with the arrival of a delivery van. While the guard was busy explaining something to the driver, Holzgraf passed by on the far side of the vehicle. By the time the van glided forward into the parking lot he was already inside the headquarters building.

A tall fence with locked doors stretched across the hall, barring access to outsiders. Holzgraf pushed his card through a slot in the window of a glassed-in cage. The armed guard inside was unsympathetic. "I'm sorry, sir, but I can't take any messages for Mr. Ingleside."

"Right, of course not. Busy man. Look, I understand that, in addition to Opticon, he is part owner of a company called Advanced Solar Research. I'm wondering if you have an address. Maybe I can reach him there."

"I do not have an address. I have no knowledge of Advanced Whatever. If you want to contact us, the best way — the only way — is through our website. Here's the link, on this page . . ."

The guard pushed a flyer through his window slot. Holzgraf looked it over. A dramatic illustration above the text showed the new Shiva missile coming right at him.

Holzgraf waved the flyer as he departed.

"Congratulations on Shiva."

"Thank you, sir, have a nice day."

▼

Holly Chow opened a folding chair outside her cottage in Marana, plunked herself down with a tall glass of lemonade and her laptop. She pulled her hiking hat down tight against the morning sun and concentrated on cooking up elaborate search terms to feed into Google. She was determined to check every reference that existed on Amos Jurnegan, professor and entrepreneur. Her only clue was the name of his company, and an hour's dull work yielded negative results. She sighed, closed her computer up, and strolled off through the pecan orchard to shake off her frustration.

▼

At the same time in the sparsely furnished offices of Darlington Energetix, Guy Holzgraf was busy with his own computer and his smartphone. Solar power researchers needed lab equipment, he reasoned. His operation certainly did, and he guessed Professor Jurnegan's did too. On his computer he pinpointed every laboratory supply company in Tucson. On his smartphone he made inquiries about Advanced Solar Research. Until he spoke to Crown Technologies, his own supplier, all his requests were denied and dismissed. But the Crown sales rep, Ed Sherman, was willing to listen.

"Ed, buddy," said Holzgraf in a casual tone. "You ever sell to Advanced Solar Research?"

"They a competitor?"

"Nahh, but we're both hot on renewable energy. I want to talk to those guys."

"What's up? We don't usually discuss our customers."

Holzgraf had prepared a small lie for this ethical obstacle.

"Possible merger, if you really want to know," said he.

"Oh-ho, throwing in the towel, huh? Smart move, my friend — Solar? It's all heading for China, or Vietnam, or some damn place in fricking Africa before it's over."

"Ed .. ?"

"Lemme check."

Dull orchestral renditions of old Beatles tunes filled Holzgraf's ear. After a long pause, the salesman came back on the line.

"Here's what I've got. We do in fact sell to Advanced Solar. Quite a lot of stuff."

"Great," said Holzgraf, much relieved. "Give me a number, their location."

He poised a ballpoint pen over a notepad.

"Big problem-o, Guy, no can do."

"Uh-oh, why not?"

"Because we have no idea. We've never made a delivery, never run a credit check. Those dudes are a secretive bunch. They pay cash, and they pick up at will call. I don't know where they are, or how to reach them."

"Damn, Ed. That sucks."

"Sorry, pal."

27

"Where are we headed?" asked Chow.

"We're going to find Jurnegan's company."

"Given our brilliant record so far, what makes you think so?"

"Resourcefulness."

Holzgraf had arranged to meet Chow in the parking lot of the El Con Center, an open air mall in the middle of the city. Now he was driving her to the airport in his Jeep. Chow slouched down in the passenger seat, convinced they were chasing a will-o-the-wisp.

He steered south, then turned into the executive terminal. Chow sat up, began to show some interest.

"Hey, this isn't the airport, where are you taking me?"

"You'll see."

"Did the rich kid charter a private jet?"

"You'll see."

He threaded the Jeep between private hangars, warehouses, and administration buildings, arriving at last at Horton Heliservice. There he parked, got out, opened the passenger door for Chow, and handed her a covered plastic box with the lumpy root ball from their KO Estates find inside.

"Why do we need this? I feel like I'm holding a tarantula."

"Your 'naked brain,' remember? I want Jurnegan to take a look."

"Mmm."

"Grab your pack."

"Pack?"

"I put one together for you."

He handed her a lightweight backpack stuffed with gear. She looked around. Three helicopters were sitting inside painted circles on nearby landing pads.

"You hired a helicopter."

"I did."

"Why would I need a pack in a helicopter?" She was being obstinate.

"Safety precaution." He shrugged. "We'll be out in the desert. My stepmother thinks I'm accident prone."

"Accident prone . . ?"

He hoisted a pack of his own and led the way across the wide asphalt landing zone to a tiny Robinson R22 helicopter done up in bright red paint.

"Cute," she said.

The door was locked. Holzgraf looked around, started pressing buttons on his smartphone. Before he could complete a call, Chow nudged him.

"Here comes our pilot."

A man in a golf shirt with the company logo emblazoned on his chest strode rapidly toward them. He held out a set of keys. Holzgraf took them.

"Thanks, Bob," he said. The man waved and returned to his office.

Holzgraf unlocked the cabin door. He gestured for Chow to mount up.

"Wait a minute. Where's our pilot?"

Holzgraf removed a pair of aviator sunglasses from a shirt pocket and put them on. He turned a bug-like gaze on Chow.

"Oh no," she groaned. *"You're* the pilot???"

He nodded.

"No way. Where's your license?"

Holzgraf opened his wallet and showed her. She examined it closely.

"Looks real," she conceded. "How many hours do you have flying one of these things?"

"Just about one hundred."

"That a good number? It better be," she mumbled.

"Yes it is. Believe it or not, I'm the real thing." He regarded her unhappily, detecting a mild case of class envy.

"Learning to fly? One of the perks of the privileged," he said, determined to slice through the almost taboo subject of unequal wealth.

"Money and time on your hands," she imagined.

"I was bored in school."

Chow rolled her eyes.

"Maybe we ought to forget the whole thing," she said.

"Give up?"

"I don't want to die looking for crazy plants."

Holzgraf's affable demeanor hardened. "You think I'm crazy?"

Chow thought about the notion long enough to make Holzgraf uneasy.

"I guess not . . . not actually crazy. But . . . I don't know. You're reckless."

"Self-confident," he amended.

"And your life of privilege as you call it — well, you're willing to take big chances. I'm not."

Holzgraf felt the knife of truth stab into his brain. He paced around in a little circle beside the helicopter, thinking hard.

"Hey, everything okay?" The Horton representative was striding toward them again, concerned that some problem with the helicopter had surfaced. Holzgraf waved him away.

"It's okay, Bob. We're fine, the ship is fine. We're . . . uhh . . . we're discussing our flight plan."

He stopped pacing and faced Chow. "Your worries are legit, okay? But I'm not giving up. Where's your curiosity, your drive?"

"I've flown exactly twice. Back and forth on a trip to Disneyland when I was nine."

"But you're tough. You're smart. You don't really want to give up?"

"Promise not to kill me?"

Holzgraf puffed out his cheeks and popped his lips. This is when, he later realized, that he started falling for her.

"Promise," he said.

Chow waggled her head in resignation and climbed into the passenger seat. Holzgraf walked around the machine, giving it a careful check, then climbed in beside her.

"Put your headset on, this baby is going make a lot of noise in a minute."

28

Early that morning Hubert Ingleside received a telephone call from an upbeat Amos Jurnegan that greatly disturbed him. *Come on down, Hub, get in on the action. Unparalleled breakthrough. History in the making.*

He shook his head as he thought about the conversation. He was driving faster than he should on Tucson's two-lane thoroughfares, working his way east and south from Opticon's headquarters. He gambled his safety through three yellow lights in a row speeding across the city. He was anxious to get to Advanced Solar Research in time to prevent a disaster.

Over the past few weeks worries about his partner had been slowly growing. The plodding scientist he knew was fading, and an alternately morose and excitable salesman was emerging. The kind of salesman seen on TV pitching vegetable slicers. Ingleside drummed his fingers on the steering wheel. He was entertaining thoughts about bipolar disorder. Maybe the guy was just frustrated by failing, so far, to revolutionize solar power. That was possible. But Ingleside suspected it was worse than that. The abstract and colorless word *stability* was floating through his mind. The lack thereof.

When Ingleside arrived at Advanced Solar Research, he found Professor Jurnegan in an experimental mood. The man seemed sane, if not quite cautious enough to suit his business partner.

"Look here, Hub, glad you could make it for the big event. I've rigged up an experiment."

Ingleside noted the same plastic tubes he had seen on a previous visit. Now they were arranged in a series of connected ovals, with entrances at the far ends.

"We have already witnessed behavior, as you know," explained the professor. "Now I want to find out how the behavioral modules interact, and I've devised a way of doing it. See, we introduce a root ball at each end. Do they move randomly? Do they interact? They start out at some distance. Can they sense each other?"

"Amos . . ."

"Yup, yup, hang on — you're wondering about a control, how does a single module perform?"

"Yes, that, and . . ."

"Right, reproducibility. The whole thing will be recorded by three different cameras. The files are automatically dated, time-coded, synched together. It will be a cinch to study the results."

"Mmm," grunted Ingleside, mulling his doubts. "Let's think this over. What we've got here might be dangerous. I think it is. What about a third party evaluation? Check your methodology? Who do you trust at the university?"

Jurnegan bounced impatiently on the balls of his feet. "No one. My fellow teachers are all hopeless drones. We've got an opportunity here."

Ingleside expressed his continuing doubts by irritably tapping his cane on the concrete floor. "We have no backup . . ."

"Right, so first, a single module," said Jurnegan, getting back to business.

He dumped a root ball into one end of his apparatus, and activated a line of powerful halogen lamps.

"It is three PM on March ninth," he announced to the cameras. "I have opened the experimental grid to one module, lit by seven 1800-lumen halogen lamps at 4100 K."

The root ball sat inert for a minute and a half. Then it slowly dissolved into a pile of sandy material.

"As in previous experiments we see the transition to small particles," intoned Jurnegan.

Shortly thereafter the particles reconstituted themselves as a worm-shaped object.

"Now, at two minutes into the exercise, we observe the bolus," he continued.

The wormy thing slithered along through the tubes.

"We see the bolus moving through the grid. The movement appears random."

He snapped off all the lights except the one nearest the originating bush and its cluster of fibrous roots.

"And now, as expected, we see the bolus return to its starting position."

He turned off all the lights.

"Well, Hub? Behavior. Simplistic, but certainly not plantlike."

Ingleside swayed back and forth. "Not plantlike," he agreed.

Jurnegan closed a plastic gate to sequester the first root ball, opened the far end of his apparatus, and plopped a second root ball inside. He turned the lights back on and addressed the cameras again.

"Now, to continue, we introduce a second subject module, allow it to acquire the same familiarity with the experimental environment."

The second root ball metamorphosed into a worm-shaped object. Like the first one, it scooted through the tubes, exploring the oval maze.

"And we observe that the behavior is essentially the same."

He turned off the lights in a sequence that led the wormy thing back to its home base. He slammed a plastic gate into place, trapping it there.

"Ready, Hub? This is it. Interactivity."

"I don't know, Amos, we should stop here. Stop until we can get some experts in to take a look."

"Experts?" sneered Jurnegan. "We're the experts."

He turned on all the lights for the third time, and removed both gates.

"Both objects have taken shape," he announced. "They are moving."

Two wormy things were now coursing around the interlocking ovals.

"As we have seen before, the movement appears to be random."

The two objects continued moving, apparently unaware of each other. Then, by chance, they both found the same tube, entering from opposite ends.

"Now we observe the boluses approaching each other."

The two objects came within a few inches of touching and stopped.

"They have dissolved," reported Jurnegan.

Two piles of sandy particles sat in the tube for a moment. Jurnegan held his breath. Ingleside instinctively backed away from them.

Little by little, the particles began migrating toward each other.

"The particles are moving. Uhh, looks like they're joining up. We are now five minutes into the run. Here we go, definitely joining. The two little piles are gone. We now see a single larger pile."

The particles began churning, vibrating the tube. Jurnegan leaned forward eagerly.

"At five minutes thirty seconds we see particles moving autonomously."

Pause.

"And now, at six minutes, there appears to be a transformation underway. Transformation, without a doubt."

Pause.

"Six minutes, thirty seconds. The transformed material has acquired a shape. Not as elongated. Ball-like. Possible pseudopods erupting."

Pause.

"Seven minutes. Object is perturbing the containment tube. Object is — holy shit!"

Whether by brute force or through the production of some sort of solvent, the strange ball burst through the side of the tube and rolled off the experimental workbench onto the lab floor. Jurnegan bent to grab it, but it rolled away out of reach.

"Fuck!"

Jurnegan chased the ball to the far end of the lab, where a half-dozen other bushes were lined up on a shelf. Just when he thought he had it in his grasp the ball contracted, then expanded explosively, bouncing high into the air and down among its relatives.

"Jesus Christ, Amos!" squawked Ingleside.

Before Jurnegan could stop it, the ball knocked all the bushes onto the floor, where they spilled out of their containers. The ball dropped beside them, began nuzzling the exposed roots.

"You little horror!" growled Jurnegan, reaching out to pull it away from his precious collection. But he jumped back shaking his hand, which bled as if bitten.

"Shit and damnation!" he exclaimed.

The thing suddenly merged with one of the root balls, doubling in size. It rolled into another, doubled again. Jurnegan turned his attention to his supply of plastic containers, picked up a big one, and slammed it down over the growing object.

Boom!

The container flew up into the air, and the object quickly merged with the remaining root balls.

"Oh no!" gasped Jurnegan.

Now the thing was the size of a big dog, and it had acquired stubby legs. Six of them. It was no longer a thing, an object, but a creature instead. A hostile creature, apparently. Jurnegan retreated.

"Holy crap, Hub. Lock the door!"

Ingleside shuffled toward the entrance.

Jurnegan ran to the side of the lab, where three more bushes were being incubated in a makeshift hothouse. The creature followed. Jurnegan backed against the hothouse door, blocking it. The creature lifted its front legs. The round footpads on the ends morphed into sharp claws. They slashed at Jurnegan, ripping open his shirt.

Ingleside jiggled the main entrance door bolt, frantically attempting to lock it.

Jurnegan stumbled away from the hothouse, and the creature bulled its way inside. It tore away the containers holding the bushes and merged with their root balls, growing and transforming as it absorbed each one.

Jurnegan was on the floor. He was bleeding.

Ingleside was stupefied. The creature, now tall and lean, skittered toward him, moving like an insect. It didn't seem to have eyes, or even a head, but it sensed his presence somehow. The old man pawed at the door, now desperate to open it. He was halfway through and out into the parking lot when the creature reached him. It raised its front legs and drove sharp claws into his back, throwing him to the pavement.

The creature crawled over Ingleside's prone form and stopped. It turned around and around, dancing on six legs. Then it scuttled across the parking lot, clambered up and over the enclosing fence, and scurried off into the desert.

29

The little Robinson helicopter cruised slowly over the industrial outskirts of Tucson.

"What are we looking for?" shouted Chow into her radio mike, cutting through the roar of the engine.

"Hard to tell," admitted Holzgraf. "Cheap location, relatively new buildings, maybe some sparkly bushes, right?"

Chow nodded. They were both scanning the ground below, scouting for anything unusual. But all they saw were the rooftop air conditioning units and skylights on an endless array of tilt-up buildings.

"So much for north and west. Let's head south," said Holzgraf, kicking in a pedal turn. Aligning the chopper with Interstate 10, he flew southeast, past the Union Pacific yard, past Davis-Monthan, past all the historical old airplanes decorating the yard of the Pima Air and Space Museum.

They circled over an automobile junkyard and the municipal landfill on Los Reales Road, but all the buildings — sparse on the ground now — were old and tired.

Moving on, they passed over the Vista Montana housing development and a mobile home park overflowing with double-wides and RVs.

Turning east they flew over the Global Solar Energy plant and its vast acres of conventional solar panels.

"There's your solar power," said Chow. "And plenty of it. No research needed."

"Obsolete, ma'am. Yesterday's tech."

"You better hope."

"I do, I'm sure, very confident," said Holzgraf, not quite as sure and confident as he tried to sound. His obvious doubts made Chow giggle.

"Laugh if you want. Sooner or later, Ms. Chow, sooner or later, Darlington is going to step in, you'll see."

Chow pointed a finger at her head, signaling an idea. "If I had a lab and didn't want to be found, I'd set it up way out in the desert," she said. "Look at all the real estate." She swept an arm around to encompass the vast emptiness on the south side of the city.

Holzgraf veered southward.

"Jurnegan needs a road to supply his operation. Let's follow this one."
He glanced at the map open on her lap, tapped a line printed there.

"South Houghton," she confirmed, reading from the paper.

They flew over the Pima County fairgrounds and continued into the desert beyond.

"Nothing."

Holzgraf circled back to the east, crossing I-10, aiming toward a range of tall mountains. They were just north of Vail.

"Nothing here either."

"We're chasing our tails, you know. We don't have a clue," grumbled Chow.

Holzgraf turned the helicopter back to the north. They flew along for five minutes over desolate terrain. Here a ranch house, there a rusted-out truck, now and then a dilapidated old shack. Holzgraf's plan wasn't looking good.

Suddenly, Chow was pounding on the window.

"Whoa there. Hey, hey, hey!"

"What?"

"See that building? White. Looks like it was painted yesterday."

They were passing over a skeet shooting range. Beyond it, isolated on a narrow side road, an arched metal prefab structure was gleaming in the afternoon sunlight. It was set on a wide square of black asphalt and surrounded by a chain link fence. A large propane tank occupied one corner of the lot. A pile of dirt and a front loader were parked nearby. Behind the building, where the perimeter fence angled away, a collection of solar panels had been erected.

A garden plot became visible as they flew over the site. Bushes planted there were sparkling in the sunlight.

"I'll be damned, we found him!"

Holzgraf circled the chopper around the establishment. A white Mercedes and an old Land Rover were parked near the entrance.

"Maybe," said Chow. "Or maybe somebody's making plastic parts out of potatoes."

"Let's find out."

Holzgraf lowered the collective pitch. The helicopter began to descend.

Chow's stomach lurched. She gripped her seat with clenched fists.

"What are you doing?"

"Landing. Let's introduce ourselves."

Holzgraf had just enough space to squeeze the little helicopter in between the fence and the building. They sat there in the cabin while the rotors wound down and stopped.

"You would think, with an entrance like ours, someone would come running to check on us," said Chow after her heart stopped thumping.

"And look, the lab door, over there on the left, is wide open."

"Mmm. What's that on the ground just outside?"

"Yeah . . . . what?" Holzgraf wasn't sure what was wrong, but he had a queasy feeling.

"Better take a look," said Chow. She felt the same way.

They got out of the helicopter and started toward the open doorway. As they neared the building they slowed their pace. Long before they reached it, they could see that the lump on the ground was a human body.

"Oh no. Oh, no no no."

The figure was lying on the asphalt with arms outstretched. Holzgraf leaned over to check the face. An old man stared back at him with unseeing eyes. The cotton jacket he was wearing was torn to shreds, apparently from some sort of knife attack. Blood had pooled under his clothes.

Chow cupped a hand over her mouth.

Holzgraf felt the man's neck for a pulse. He stood up, wavering unsteadily.

"Whoever this is, he's dead."

Suddenly he turned aside, took two steps, dropped to his knees, and vomited.

"Gahhhh . . ."

Chow put an arm around his shoulder.

"You okay?"

Holzgraf waved her away. He remained on his knees for a while, collecting himself. Then he bounced to his feet, wiping his mouth on a sleeve.

"I'll be fine. Good to go."

Chow stared at him. "You don't look so fine, pardon me."

Holzgraf returned to stand over the body, steeling himself against the horror he was witnessing. He jabbed a finger toward the outstretched corpse. "This Jurnegan, you think?"

Chow shook her head. "I only met him once, years ago. He wanted to buy the bush Dad found. I don't think he would be this . . . old."

Holzgraf nodded absently. "Mmm. What's going on here? Mountain lion attack? A murder?"

Chow swiveled her head to check the surroundings. She fisted hands on hips. "I don't see any mountain lions."

"Right. Let's have a look at" — he tapped a small sign beside the open door that read *Advanced Solar Research* — "the man's lab."

"Be careful, rich kid."

Holzgraf led the way into the interior, a wide open space filled with workbenches, shelves, a hothouse, and a curious assembly of plastic tubes spread out across adjoining tables. Toward the back of the room bushes and shelves and hothouse windows were scattered around.

"This place is a mess."

Chow was examining the plastic tubes. Her foot slipped in a greasy spot. She looked down and discovered that the grease was blood. She could see a bloody trail stretching back to the hothouse. She leaned under the table to see where it led.

"Over here, over here. Oh Jesus," she squeaked.

Holzgraf moved to her side. A second body was lying under the table.

"Ugh."

"Don't throw up."

"I'm okay," he said. "It was just that first look — *oof!* — I never saw a body before. This guy, why underneath?"

"Trying to get away from someone?"

"Or something."

Chow looked closely at the crumpled shape. The face was turned toward her. Its mouth was open. "This is Jurnegan."

"Sure?"

"Oh yes."

Holzgraf marched outside and dialed 9-1-1.

"Hello. Hello? Hey, there, I have an emergency. Two dead men."

Pause.

"That's not an emergency? Okay, let me rephrase — I'm reporting very seriously injured people, then, how's that?"

Pause.

"Gerrit Holzgraf is my name. That's not important. And no, I don't know exactly where I am."

He waved to get Chow's attention.

"Where are we, Chow? GPS, on your phone!"

Chow opened an app on her smartphone and showed him the screen.

"Okay, we're southeast of Tucson, thirty-two-point-oh-nine north, one-hundred-ten-point-seventy-five or so west."

Pause.

"That's the GPS reading. I don't have a street name, the road here is gravel. I'm at a laboratory, Advanced Solar Research."

Pause.

"It could be an animal attack. The wounds look like claw marks."

Pause.

"Right. Got it. Thanks."

He ended the call and turned to Chow. "The dispatcher lady wants us to stick around. She's calling search and rescue and the sheriff."

Chow nodded. She walked slowly back to the helicopter and opened the cabin door. She was reaching for her floppy hat, but stopped with her hand poised in midair.

"Hey, you! Get over here, look at this."

The lumpy mass they termed a 'naked brain' was thumping urgently against the wall of its plastic container.

Holzgraf hurried over.

"What the — ?"

He picked up the box and stepped away from the helicopter. The lump was bouncing against the wall facing east. Holzgraf took a few steps and slowly turned around. The lump rotated around inside the plastic container to stay oriented and bumped repeatedly against whichever wall was facing east.

"East. It's looking at those hills."

Holzgraf turned eastward and started walking toward the perimeter of the Advanced Solar property. Chow followed a few steps behind.

They halted at the fence line. There the steel links were scratched and bent as if power tools had been let loose on them. The barbed wire strung along the top sagged.

"Look!"

Just beyond the fence, they could see the desert floor torn up in a yard-wide pattern that led away toward the eastern hills. A trail.

"There's your attacker. Some kind of animal," said Holzgraf.

Chow had other ideas. "I don't think our little blob cares about regular animals. Think what Jurnegan was doing in that lab. This thing wants to find some friends."

Holzgraf thought about that. Then he thought about cops and ambulances. Then he thought about trails in the desert.

"In a little while that trail there, it will be invisible."

"Probably."

Holzgraf returned to the lab and came back out with a couple of large Kevlar bags reinforced with straps and buckles.

"Come on."

He headed for the helicopter, motioning Chow to follow. By the time she climbed into the passenger seat, the rotors were already spinning.

"What about 9-1-1?"

"They don't need us," declared Holzgraf. "If we hang around till the cavalry arrives, they'll be nagging us all day long. Let's follow that trail."

The helicopter lifted off. It roared up and over Advanced Solar Research and flew slowly away into the empty desert beyond.

30

Late that morning, the Durangos received a call from Jurnegan. The good professor was becoming concerned about competition from NASA and wanted something done about it. Now, a few hours later, the brothers showed up at Advanced Solar Research in their Hummer and discovered their bosses' bodies lying where they fell. The lab was a shambles.

"Jesus Howling Christ, Ty," said Earl.

They surveyed the premises, noting the blood, the destruction, and the tipped-over bushes lying on the floor. Ty had few doubts about the cause of the carnage.

"It came from Outer Space, bro," he said, kicking a bush aside. "We saw those things crawling around."

Earl nodded. He agreed. "So, little brother, we are now unemployed."

"So we are. And after the police arrive, if they connect us, we're going to be suspects."

"I doubt it. We'd of shot 'em. Little tiny holes, not fucking gashes a yard long."

"What do you want to do?"

"Still got that guy's number?"

"The Russian spy?"

"Unh-huh."

Ty opened his wallet and extracted a business card. Earl took it and read off the name:

"Basil Temkhin, exotic minerals."

"That's him. So?"

"We could work for him. Let's grab some of these bushes. Insurance. The guy would go nuts to get his hands on them."

Ty looked around the parking lot. "Those little worms we saw couldn't have killed our boys. Whatever did the job must've been pretty big. And, hey, look here — the fence."

The two men strolled over to the fence, observed the damage to the chain links and the barbed wire.

"Trail out there. See it?"

"I do. I think that's our killer, making its escape. Temkhin would pay through the nose for that thing."

"If we catch it, we'll need to bag it. You know, with an actual bag."

Inside the lab a quick search turned up large Kevlar bags equipped with belts and buckles, same as the ones Holzgraf found.

"This work, you think? We run one bag inside the other?"

"Unless our baby is the size of an elephant."

"What about a crate?"

Another trip to the lab was rewarded with a heavy duty plastic box big enough for a large dog.

They climbed into their Hummer. Earl was about to turn the key when they heard sirens wailing.

"Uh-oh, here comes the law."

"How did they hear the news?"

"Maybe one of Jurnegan's Mexicans was here and got away."

"Now it's our turn. Let's ramble."

▼

An ambulance and two Chevrolet Tahoe SUVs emblazoned with Pima County Sheriff markings sped along the gravel road leading to Advanced Solar Research. The sirens went silent as the vehicles turned into the parking lot.

The Durangos and their Hummer were long gone.

Two deputies emerged and began a reconnaissance. Behind them, the EMTs opened up the rear doors of their ambulance, deployed a pair of stretcher trolleys, and stood by.

"Man, this place is hard to find," said the first officer, unsnapping his holster and loosening his pistol.

"I'll say. Over here, here's one of the victims reported," noted the second.

The two cops stared at the corpse.

"Could a big cat do this? Or a javelina?"

"That would be some cat. Or a very angry javelina."

"What, then . . ?"

The first officer peeked through the open door. He turned a powerful flashlight on the interior, swept it back and forth.

"Anybody home?" he called out to roust any murderer hiding in there.

The second officer joined the first. "Looks like the coast is clear."

He motioned the EMTs forward. "The report said two decedents. Where's number two? Somewhere inside here?"

"Let's find out. You first, I'll cover you."

"Right. Me first. Shit."

The deputies moved cautiously into the building.

PART FOUR

31

"See anything?"

Holzgraf had the little Robinson helicopter moving back and forth over a wide basin, a wash where water flowed in unusually wet years.

"No. Slow down, fly lower."

"Okay, slower. But if I fly any lower, we'll blow the trail away."

"Oh yeah."

"We know the trail is here, we saw it run right into the wash a quarter of a mile back."

"Right, so I lost it," said Chow, feeling grim. "So sue me."

"Nobody's suing anybody. Just keep your eyes open."

"All right, try over toward the edge, we'll get it back."

Holzgraf swung the ship toward the south rim of the wash.

"Ha! Got it!" Chow pointed proudly down at a faint disturbance in the rock-like *caliche* soil.

"Which way?" Holzgraf glanced toward the ground rolling underneath, but couldn't confirm Chow's observation.

"Up the hill, toward that crest."

Holzgraf turned the helicopter back toward the east.

"Now slow, easy, these marks come and go."

They followed the intermittent evidence of their quarry for a quarter of a mile.

"Whoa, up ahead!" Chow pointed toward the ridge top. "See that?"

Dust was rising ahead of them, blowing away on gusts of wind.

"That's our target!" shouted Chow. "Let's get after it!"

Holzgraf twisted the cyclic pitch grip and the helicopter shot forward. But suddenly the low-fuel indicator lit up, startling him.

"Fuck!"

His reaction scared Chow half to death.

"What? What's wrong?"

"Low fuel." He rapped a knuckle against a gauge on the instrument cluster. "I didn't check, we've been loitering. R22s have terrible fuel meters. Shit, we're way past our time limit."

"Time limit!?"

"I'm going to set her down."

"Here? In the middle of nowhere?" Chow's internal alarm bells were jangling.

Holzgraf scowled at her. "You do not want to autorotate in this machine. It's land now, easy peasy, or we crash in five minutes. Which do you prefer?"

Chow swallowed. She forced a sickly smile. "I'm thinking!"

Holzgraf cruised toward the ridge crest. Near the top he spotted a bare spot where bedrock precluded vegetation.

"Don't hit a cactus!" Chow braced herself.

Holzgraf brought the helicopter to a hover over the designated spot and slowly lowered the machine to the ground. As soon as the skids settled onto the rocky flat he killed the engine. The rotors whirled for a few seconds, gradually slowing down. Finally they stopped.

"Okay, we can get out now."

Chow cracked open her door, but didn't move.

"Accident prone? You? *Oh my God!*"

Holzgraf was hurt by the accusation. "Not really an accident. We're sitting here in one piece. The chopper is undamaged. And we've got our survival gear."

He handed her one of the packs.

"Let's go. Git!"

Chow plunked her feet down and stood up.

"How are we ever going to return the rental?" she wondered in a faraway voice. She glanced at her smartphone. "No service. We can't even call Triple-A."

"Worry about that later. Our goal is up the hill here."

Holzgraf shouldered his pack and skipped down off the rocky promontory into the wash. "Here's the trail."

But Chow didn't budge.

"You kidding? Whatever we were trailing, we lost it."

"Maybe not. Come on."

Chow jerked a thumb back toward civilization. "We should get out of here. Down on the ground, we're unprotected."

"So?"

"So . . . you know . . . if our whatsis goes all aggro, we're hamburger."

Holzgraf dropped his pack, reached inside, and withdrew a big black handgun. He held it up for inspection.

"This is a .40 caliber Gen-4 Glock 23. I think we'll be okay."

"Wow, concealed carry."

"This is Arizona, right?"

"Can you shoot as well as you fly?"

Holzgraf winced. "Ouch. I trained. I practice now and then."

"You are full of surprises."

Holzgraf put the gun away. "We're hot on the hunt. Don't tell me you don't care."

Chow considered the situation. She looked west, where the afternoon sun was already low in the sky.

"How far back to a street, or road, or houses?"

Holzgraf spread his arms wide. "Not sure. Miles. Five or so? Ten?"

Chow's lips twisted into doubt. "Long walk."

"'Fraid so."

She stared at the land they had traversed so effortlessly in the air. Hiking alone back over hill and dale did not appeal. This guy Holzgraf, he certainly knew how to get into trouble. Now he was smiling at her, his irresistible smile. She clapped her hands to mark a shaky decision, and joined him in the wash.

"We should probably stick together," she grumbled.

Holzgraf registered her chilly tone and started up along the trail without another word.

They spent fifteen minutes toiling up the wash to reach the crest. As Chow predicted, when they arrived their target was nowhere in sight. She looked back down the incline at their helicopter. In the distance the flimsy machine, screened by hairy chollas and tall cactuses, seemed tiny. She thought it looked like a jelly bean and couldn't imagine it carrying full-size human beings, even though she had been riding inside for more than two hours. While she was watching, the sun sank behind the western mountains. A cold breeze came across the slope, riffling her hair.

When she turned around, Holzgraf was already setting up a campsite.

She watched while he erected a small nylon tent, quickly and expertly installing flexible poles and an insulating fly.

"I hope you don't think I'm sharing that with you," she said.

"Not at all. Toss me your pack."

She walked over and handed it to him. He freed up an identical tent and set it up beside the first one. Then he pulled a crumpled windbreaker free and shook out the wrinkles.

"Here. Going to get cold."

She put on the windbreaker and zipped it up.

He opened a plastic bottle and poured a pink liquid into two plastic cups.

"What is that?"

"Rosé wine. Best thing on a picnic."

"This is a picnic?"

He ignored the barb. "Here's to adventure."

They clicked their cups together.

"Help me get some supper going."

"What have we got?"

"Well, soup, ramen — I knew you'd go for that — and veggie sausage things I saw at the mountaineering store."

He set up a camp stove. Chow filled a pot with water, poured in the freeze-dried ramen. Holzgraf lit the stove. The flame reflected off their faces, turning them blue. They sat down on rocky benches bulging out of the sand.

"Don't tell me you ran out of fuel on purpose."

"Why would I do that?" He refilled their cups.

"Lure me into the desert for a romantic interlude, such as we are now enjoying."

He laughed. "Triple-A is not going to get our helicopter back in the air. Serious family money is on the line here."

She raised her cup. "Here's to overtime pay, by the way. I'm still on the clock."

"Yeah, I'm good for it."

"What's your mother going to say about this little adventure?"

"Mavis is going to be annoyed. Or irritated, take your pick. An upper-class kind of cool disapproval, never actual anger. A turned-up nose and a lecture, at the least. If she's really stoked, she could delay my inheritance."

"She could do that?"

"Oh yes. Legally, she's my guardian."

"Must be nice to be rich," mumbled Chow, baffled by the mysterious ways of the upper classes.

"It has its charms."

They were slurping ramen and crunching sausages when they heard a roar coming up the slope, somewhere out of sight beyond the north rim of the wash. Headlights and an off-road lightbar lit up the saguaros, giving the impression of an alien army on the march.

"What's that?"

"Company. That whine, sounds like a Jeep in low-range."

The roar ceased. The headlights winked out. All was quiet, but not for long.

While they were drinking their third cup of wine two men appeared.

"Hi, there, campers," said one.

Holzgraf and Chow both stood up to greet them.

"Winter tenting, I call that brave," said the other.

The pair were dressed in military camo. They were carrying powerful flashlights. Holzgraf didn't think they looked much like vacationers out for fresh air.

"You guys hunters?" he asked. "What's in season?"

"Oh no," said the first man. "We lost our dog. He's up here roving around somewhere."

"We'd like to find him before the mountain lions do."

"Yeah, he's a big 'un, but not that big."

The two visitors exchanged knowing looks.

"How about yourselves?" said the older, leaner fellow.

"Long way from civilization up here," noted the younger, heavier one.

"We're just having fun," said Holzgraf with a nonchalant shrug and a glance toward Chow.

"Celebrating our anniversary," said Chow, quick to catch Holzgraf's cue.

"Really? We were wondering, maybe you've seen Dasher."

"Dasher?"

"Our dog. He was up this way. Big shaggy thing."

"Probably left a pretty good trail. He's a clumsy beast."

Holzgraf picked up his pack, bringing his Glock within reach. "Sorry, we haven't seen a thing. Did you spot anything, babe?"

Chow shook her head.

Holzgraf reached into his pack for the wine bottle. He raised it up.

"Can I offer you gentlemen a cup of wine?"

The two held up their hands.

"No thanks, we better turn in. Early start and all."

Holzgraf nodded sympathetically, still holding his pack. "Gotta find Dasher."

"That's right," said the older man. "Dasher."

"Happy anniversary, or whatever," said the younger one.

They waved and, following their flashlight beams, retreated back over the ridge crest.

Holzgraf and Chow sat facing their stove for a while in silence, slowly sipping the last of the wine, munching stale cookies.

"Our anniversary . . ." said Holzgraf, with an ironic smile. "That's a good one."

Chow giggled. "I couldn't think of anything else."

Holzgraf checked the stove. "We should kill this if we want hot coffee in the morning."

"Unh-huh, right."

Holzgraf closed the propane valve, choking off the little blue flame. He looked up at the stars and the Milky Way, brilliantly arrayed overhead. The waning moon had set hours ago. "Where, do you suppose, does good old Dasher come from?"

Chow followed his gaze. "Somewhere up there, right?"

"Think so. Gotta be. This isn't about perovskite anymore."

"Now we know why NASA is hanging around."

"Yup. And I would like to know a whole lot more. Maybe tomorrow."

He stood up. Over beyond the ridgeline he could see lights flickering and hear metal clanking, the sights and sounds of another campsite being prepped. He ducked into his tent. "Better get some sleep."

Chow crawled into her own tent, wriggled into a light sleeping bag, and curled up in a ball against the chill.

Twenty minutes later, Holzgraf was nodding off when the zipper on his tent door loudly unzipped. For a second he thought he was being attacked, but no, it was Chow.

She plunged inside and crouched down beside him. She was dragging her sleeping bag.

"Those two men. Who are they?" she breathed.

"Good question. I don't think they work for NASA."

"They know about the whatsis," she whispered. "Their Dasher is our mystery target — same thing."

"Think they killed Jurnegan?" Holzgraf found himself whispering too.

"There's an idea, but no. I think they would have shot him," she muttered, crawling into her bag. "Still got that gun?"

Holzgraf reached into a corner of the tent and hefted his Glock.

"Military dudes. Something about their casual bullshit, their clothes, the way they stood. Special forces."

"They seemed friendly."

"A little too friendly."

"And they knew we were trailing that thing, I could tell how they looked at each other."

"Wonder if they saw our ride."

"Probably. That would be a clue. No one goes camping in a helicopter."

Holzgraf grimaced. "Not unless you're very rich."

"Yeah, Holzgraf, *The Fucking Third.*"

"Hey, there, if you're so righteous, what are you doing in my tent?"

"I'm scared," she mumbled.

▼

On the far side of the ridge crest, headlights blazed, lighting up the night. An engine roared. Suddenly those headlights crested the ridge. The big Hummer behind them bucked over the top, heading straight for Holzgraf's and Chow's campsite. In five seconds it drove right into the tents, flattening both of them. Then it backed up and charged again, crunching packs flat, grinding the tents into the desert floor.

There was a pause while the passenger hopped out and gave the campsite a quick once-over. When he jumped back inside, the Hummer reversed over the ridge and moved slowly up the hillside. The headlights disappeared.

"How'd we do?" asked Earl Durango.

"They're flatter than Madonna on a high note," said Ty. "In a week or so the helicopter service will spot their ship, and everybody will be scratching their heads."

"On Dasher, on Dancer, on Donner and Blitzen," sang out Earl.

▼

But Holzgraf and Chow weren't as flat as the Durangos thought. Neither one of them could sleep, and nervous conversation slowly convinced them that their visitors meant to do harm. They sneaked out of Holzgraf's tent and worked their way across the wash, suppressing cries and curses when they ran into cactus spines. A freezing half hour went by before they spotted headlights and heard the big Hummer roaring over the ridge. They watched the attack from a distant knoll.

"Whew," said Chow, pulling her sleeping bag tight around her shoulders, like a shawl. "Look what they did!"

She leaned over against Holzgraf. The contact hit him like an electric shock. He hesitated, counted to three, then tentatively wrapped a steadying arm around her waist.

"Thank God we're easily spooked," he said.

32

By 7:00 AM next morning the stars had faded, and the sky was pale grey. Holzgraf was out of his ripped-up sleeping bag and scratching through the ruined campsite. By 7:30 AM the sun was peaking over the eastern mountains, and Chow was stirring.

"Morning," he said. "Good news and bad news. Our friendly visitors are gone, but they smashed our stove. No coffee."

"Urrrr," said Chow, attempting to fluff her hair. "I was dreaming about E.T."

They poked around, trying to salvage emergency supplies.

"Where is our little plastic box and the blob inside?"

"Our naked brain? If it has any sense it ran and hid last night."

"Come on, help me look."

Luckily, one of the packs had been punted across the wash by the Hummer's bumper instead of being flattened under its tires. They discovered an intact water bottle inside.

"If we're careful, we won't die of thirst," noted Chow.

"You're cheerful today," said Holzgraf.

"Mmm," she said, lifting the root ball's plastic container out of the pack. It was empty.

They scoured the area. After half an hour's search they discovered something that looked promising curled around the trunk of a teddy bear cholla. Holzgraf attempted to reach in under the branches and scoop it up.

"Ow, ow, ow!" he whinnied as spines dug in. He stuck his injured hand in his mouth and bounced around to ease the pain.

Chow laughed. "Let me try."

Holzgraf tossed her the little tub. "My pleasure."

She leaned down and called softly to the thing. "Yoo-hoo, little guy. Come here. We'll help you find your friends."

Holzgraf's jaw dropped when the thing uncurled from the cholla and rolled, slithered, and tumbled into its container. Chow slammed the top down to trap it.

"Christ," said Holzgraf. "It heard you."

"Weird. Very weird. And the more you think about it, the more weird it seems. Weirdness in a box. Our naked brain."

Holzgraf found some cordage and tied the container securely with double and triple knots.

"There . . . I hope. He handed her the rescued pack. "You carry it."

"Thanks a lot, boss."

"Now, let's roll. While you were sleeping I spotted the trail. Over this way . . ."

▼

They quickly crested the ridgeline near their camp. Beyond they could now see a succession of knobby hills rising out of deep folds, one behind the other, crenelated battlements guarding a cluster of towering peaks on the horizon. The challenging view sank their already low spirits.

"We've lost the trail. We should go back," griped Chow.

"No way," countered Holzgraf. "All employees of Darlington Energetix will now exert themselves toward a major scientific discovery. *Booyah!*"

He walked back and forth, eyes on the ground, looking for the trail. It wasn't far away.

"Got it," he announced, pointing down and then up the grade. "Yo, over here, let's go."

Accustomed to outdoor adventures, he set off at a quick pace. Chow made a show of dragging herself along in his wake.

They toiled up the incline, dancing around the chollas and creosote bushes, pausing now and then to pick up the uneven marks of their target's passage.

"What's that?" said Holzgraf, stopping suddenly. A fat pink and black lizard was slowly moving through the rocks and scrub just ahead of them.

Chow came up beside him. "Cool," she said, "*that* is a gila monster."

"Poisonous," he remembered.

"From their bite."

"So they're real. Not something we see around Pittsburgh."

"You almost never see one here either. This is rare."

He watched it move deliberately away under the low desert plants.

"It's so slow. How does it ever bite anything?"

"Got me. Maybe it has a surprise karate move."

"I hate surprises. Something to remember if and when we spot Dasher."

▼

An hour later they were laboring up a rocky chute carved into a steep slope by flash floods. They were nearing the top when the sound of an engine revving in the distance stopped them.

"Whoa. Careful now."

They crept forward slowly, keeping their heads low. Emerging from the rocky trench, they arrived on a local crag. To one side, the slope pitched down into a narrow valley. And far below, in the bottom of the valley, was the Hummer that attacked them the night before. Its wheels were buried in soft sand. One of their visitors was out in front with a shovel, trying to create a path. The other was revving the engine, rocking the Hummer back and forth. Neither of their efforts looked very effective.

"Well well. As fate would have it!" said Holzgraf.

Chow chuckled drily. "Rough justice, you ask me."

"Shouldn't we offer to help? Campers' Code of the Wild?" Holzgraf was trying for lighthearted sarcasm.

Chow, not even faintly amused, grabbed Holzgraf's shirt and pulled him away from the view. "Better get out of here while they still think we're dead."

▼

By noon they had hiked onto an upland plateau. Here the trail they were following zigzagged back and forth, dodging saguaros, crisscrossing itself.

"This is the third time we've been through here," grumped Chow, noticing their own tracks. "I think Dasher is confused."

"I'm confused, anyway," said Holzgraf.

They came around a low rise into a gentle swale, and there, in an area free from tall plants, was their quarry. Its six feet were thrust into the hard desert floor. A bundle of perovskite solar panels, like little leaves, formed a canopy above its inert body.

"Dasher!"

Holzgraf and Chow stopped short.

"Be careful, remember what Jurnegan looked like."

"Okay, but I think we're safe. It's recharging."

"That's what you hope it's doing. Maybe it's deciding how to attack."

"Or maybe it's lost and needs a new plan."

"If it does any planning."

"Maybe it could. It's not any kind of plant."

"But it's got those sparkly leaves."

"It's a creature."

"Or a robot."

"A robot . . . but sure as hell not from Mars. I read up, and the red planet is as dead as the professor."

Holzgraf took a step forward, waving his arms.

"Hey, Dasher, what's up?"

Chow tugged on his shirt again. "Stop that."

"Stop what? Let's find out if it's alive."

"Let's stay alive."

While they debated their best course of action, a steady thrumming noise slowly rose above the faint rustle of a light breeze. It beat down on them, growing louder and louder. Holzgraf raised a hand to shield his eyes and stared back toward Tucson. A white helicopter was approaching.

"See what I see? Look familiar?"

Chow squinted west. "What is it?"

"We've seen this ship before. NASA is here to steal the show."

The helicopter roared past and continued onward for a minute or so, then turned around and slowly worked its way back toward them. Soon it was hovering right overhead. It stayed poised there for another minute, then drifted sideways to an area free of botanical hazards. There it settled down. The engine remained running, and the rotors were still whirling, as two men jumped to the ground and marched toward Holzgraf, Chow, and the motionless Dasher.

"I don't think they know we're here," said Chow.

Holzgraf waved his baseball cap.

"Yo! NASA!" he shouted.

The two men were circling the creature / robot / plant. They stopped and peered toward the source of the greeting, clearly surprised to see other people nearby. Holzgraf walked toward them, waving his cap. Chow hesitated, then followed a few steps behind.

One of the men was an old codger. He was wearing a worn sheepskin jacket. The other was young and lean, clad in a black windbreaker. There was a handgun strapped to his jeans. He pushed dark sunglasses up onto his forehead and held up a hand, palm out.

"Halt where you are," he said.

Holzgraf and Chow kept walking. The man's right hand moved to the butt of his holstered pistol, popped the lockdown strap.

"Halt. This is a government operation, and you are trespassing."

Holzgraf and Chow stopped as ordered. The two NASA men turned toward Dasher. The older man unfolded a large Kevlar bag, reinforced with heavy straps, and handed it to the younger one. He in turn approached the sunbathing entity and prepared to bag it.

Suddenly the little crystal leaves all retracted into the thing's body. The nearest legs popped out of the ground and reared up. They sliced at the man, who dropped the bag and jumped back, one hand covering a forearm, where blood was showing.

"Fuck!"

The two men backed away, staring at Dasher. After a moment, the thing started moving cautiously toward them. They retreated toward the helicopter.

At that moment Chow felt something thumping and bumping in her beat-up pack. She reached in and withdrew the plastic box. The blob inside was bouncing around, attempting to escape. A thought occurred.

"Hey, you guys, want some help?" she shouted, all at once feeling strangely brave.

"Stay where you are!" said the younger man.

But Chow ignored the command. She untied the cords sealing the box and moved slowly toward the alien entity.

"Are you crazy?" yelped Holzgraf. He reached to grab her arm. She shook him off.

"Think *Oz!* If I'm right, Dasher is the Scarecrow. He just needs a brain."

"Jesus, Chow, the thing is moving, sensing, attacking. It already has a brain."

"Not the complete package. Just the lizard part."

Dasher stopped moving toward the helicopter and pivoted toward Chow. She stopped a few yards away.

"It's okay, I won't hurt you," she said.

Before the NASA men could intercept her, she bent to the ground and let the blob she was toting out of its box. It rolled and bounced across the ground to its cousin. When they touched, both objects dissolved into a pile of sand.

The younger NASA man ran toward Chow, shouting and cursing at her interference. But he stopped short when the pile of sand coalesced into a legless mound in the shape of a twelve-sided solid, a ball-like dodecahedron. The crystalline leaves were gone.

"What did you do? You idiot, you fucked it all up!"

Chow gestured toward the thing. "Oh really? I just increased its IQ by 200 points. Now it's going to be civilized, show proper etiquette in social situations."

"You fucking hope."

"Just try your bag, all right?" Chow helped the man tip the motionless lump into his Kevlar satchel. He ran the straps through their buckles and tightened them down.

Chow led him over to the helicopter "Got a first aid kit in there?" she asked.

The pilot offered a metal case with a big red cross sticker on top.

"Sit," she ordered, pointing to the open doorway. "Let me see that arm."

The man parked himself. Chow broke out an alcohol swab and ran it over his wound. Then she taped a butterfly bandage across the tear and wrapped a roll of gauze around it.

"Thanks," he said, flexing his fingers. "Now tell me, Nurse Nightingale, how it is you found our target before we did."

Chow looked at him. "Don't you remember me?"

"Sorry, I don't." His brow furrowed. "Oh wait, you — hah! — Harriet Chow. You sold me that perovskite crystal. At the show!"

"That's right, and you handed me a radio tracker with your name on it, Captain Lockwood."

A mischievous grin appeared on his face. "I did, didn't I?"

Holzgraf walked over, sensing that the tense standoff was over.

"And this is the gentleman who bought the rest of your stock, am I right?"

Holzgraf stuck out a hand. "Guy Holzgraf."

"Jim Lockwood."

The two men clasped hands.

"What's your interest in all this?" queried Lockwood, a hint of suspicion dangling from his words.

"Solar power. Perovskite is a promising material."

"Unh-huh. Perovskite on the run."

"Well, now that you mention it, we've revised some of our ideas."

"I'll bet." Lockwood stood up.

"How about NASA? What's your story?" wondered Holzgraf.

Lockwood pointedly ignored the question. "On our way here we passed over a tiny Robinson. Your chopper?"

"Yup."

"What happened?"

"He didn't check his fuel, that's what," said Chow, still sore about it. "He's accident prone."

Lockwood chuckled. "I dunno, you set her down in a tight spot. That takes skill."

"And now we're stranded," said Holzgraf. "Can you carry a couple of passengers?"

"That we can." Lockwood jumped into the helicopter cabin, and leaned down to offer Chow a hand. "Put your foot on the skid there, and step right up, Miss."

"It's Holly."

Chow eagerly took Lockwood's hand and allowed herself to be hauled on board.

Holzgraf followed. They all strapped themselves into the seats, jammed headsets over their ears.

When they were airborne, Lockwood made an introduction.

"This is my colleague, Chester Boggs."

The older man gave Holzgraf and Chow a little salute.

"He's a prospector, knows the desert, has a sixth sense for these bushes we've been finding."

"That's how you found Dasher?" asked Chow.

"Dasher?"

"The creature, or robot, whatever he is . . . or was."

"That's right, we've got a perimeter circling around Tucson, and the bushes seem to be spread out along it. Boggs just knows how to search."

Holzgraf and Chow eyed each other, silently agreeing that Lockwood knew nothing about Jurnegan's demise.

"Here's something," said Holzgraf. "On our way this morning we spotted a big Hummer down in the sand. Two men. Said they were looking for a dog called 'Dasher.' That's how we picked up the name. They did their level best to kill us last night."

"Two men?"

"Yeah. Special forces dudes."

"Think they knew what they were looking for?"

"Good bet."

Lockwood pondered the news. "You know, I may have crossed paths with them. We're not the only ones working on advanced solar power."

Holzgraf doubted the present NASA crew was working on anything like solar power. He looked out the window. Off in the distance he could see the valley where the Hummer got stuck. It was no longer there.

▼

The NASA Jet Ranger lowered itself onto a Horton Heliservice landing pad at the Tucson airport. Holzgraf and Chow stepped down onto the asphalt, ducked their heads getting out from under the whizzing rotor blades, and watched it take off.

Chow waved. Lockwood waved back.

Holzgraf noticed that he felt a little pang watching the low key social display and Chow's evident enthusiasm. It took him a few seconds to recognize the puzzling symptom of jealousy.

"Your handsome captain," he said.

She smiled. "He is pretty handsome."

"And you'd like to get to know him better, right?"

Chow squinted at him. He wasn't sure what the scrutiny meant.

"You're an idiot," she said.

Holzgraf considered the awkward working relationship he had established with the woman standing in front of him. "Here's a thought. We could call each other by our actual names. You know, Holly and Guy."

She laughed. "Okay, boss."

33

An oversized paper map of Tucson and its environs was pinned to a corkboard on the wall at Darlington Energetix. Holzgraf was staring at it, sticking pushpins into locations he knew had yielded up mysterious glittering bushes. There were just three: one pin west of Chow's home, a second just outside the KO Estates, and a speculative third in the eastern uplands where they recently tracked Dasher.

"Look here, Holly. Three points on my map."

"Unh-huh."

"I heard your captain mention that NASA had a perimeter circling Tucson. If I fit a circle over our points, it looks like this . . ."

He uncapped a whiteboard marker and drew a rough circle through the three points. It encompassed the city and its surroundings, centered east and south of downtown.

"I'll bet our NASA friends have a map just like this."

"Only with more points on it. Jim said that guy Boggs has found others."

"Jim?"

"Captain Lockwood."

"Right."

Chow dragged a finger along the circle, over uninhabited areas free of any pins. "We should have looked through the stuff at Jurnegan's place. All those bushes. He probably had good records for their original locations."

"I was too jumpy," said Holzgraf.

"Me too. I wish we had slowed down enough to take some of them."

"And mess up a crime scene?"

"Research options for Darlington. If nothing else, I could sell the leaves."

"We've still got a shot. Look, up here in the northeast, the circle crosses Redington Road. We could check that area without hiking all day."

Chow was doubtful. "Yeah, we should do it. As long as we don't run into Donner and Blitzen."

"I don't think Dasher came from any single bush. I think that guy was assembled from a lot of root balls like the one we found."

Holzgraf stood up and paced back and forth. "No one has ever seen anything like that thing. After all the years of wondering, all the sci-fi movies, the conspiracy theories, the fake-o UFO sightings . . . now, right now, something real shows up! In pieces! Scattered here and there, like they fell from the sky. Was that intentional? Alien mission design? Or an accident? Did a ship blow up?"

He slapped the prototype solar panel he had built. "What is NASA up to? That's what I want to know," he growled. His own plans and high hopes now seemed small and ordinary. "Exobiology — life doesn't have to work like it does on Earth."

"We could still check Jurnegan's lab, if you want," said Chow, reacting to Holzgraf's passionate outburst. She added "Drive there this time," with an ironic smile that quickly faded. An unpleasant problem suddenly hit home.

"But — oops — you called 9-1-1."

"The honest thing to do."

"Very noble. But police must be all over that place by now. Two men dead. What if they think we did it?"

▼

An hour later, a pair of Tucson Police Department SUVs charged into the parking lot right in front of Darlington Energetix. Tires chirped. Four uniformed police officers got out, slamming doors. They spread out, approaching the shop with caution, hands cupped over their sidearms. One of them pointed to the little sign above the office door. The other three acknowledged the correct identity of their destination. The first cop was getting ready to knock when the main bay door rolled up, revealing Chow. When she saw who the visitors were, she nearly fainted.

"Darlington Energetix?"

Chow managed a grunt and a nod.

"Gerrit Darlington Holzgraf, please."

She turned back inside. "Guy? Hey, boss — um — look who's here."

Holzgraf ambled forward to meet the police. "I'm Holzgraf. What's up?"

"You are under arrest for the murder of Professor Amos Jurnegan and Hubert Ingleside at their place of business, Advanced Solar Research."

"You're kidding."

"Put your hands behind your back, sir, I need to cuff you."

Holzgraf turned around and brought his wrists together.

"As you will find out, I didn't kill anybody. This is ridiculous," he said.

The arresting officer wasn't listening. "You have the right to remain silent," he recited, snapping on the cuffs. "Anything you say can and will be used against you in court. You have the right to an attorney. If you cannot afford an attorney, one will be appointed for you."

Chow watched with folded arms and a deep frown while two of the officers conducted Holzgraf into the back seat of the nearest SUV.

The third officer, a woman, addressed Chow. "Now you, miss. Are you Harriet Huifang Chow?"

Chow stiffened. "Yes, that's me."

"You are under arrest for murder and conspiracy to murder and as accessory to the murders of Professor Amos Jurnegan and Hubert Ingleside."

Chow turned her back without a word. The officer snapped on a pair of cuffs.

"You have the right to remain silent . . ."

The officer pushed Chow into the other SUV. Her partner returned to the shop, rolled the bay door down into place, making sure it was locked behind him.

The two police vehicles executed crisp one-point turnarounds and rolled out onto Grant Road.

34

Holzgraf's police escorts were silent while they navigated south through the city.

"Long trip," observed Holzgraf, craning his neck around for a glimpse of the following SUV with Chow inside.

The cops looked at each other, but said nothing. After several miles the driver turned into a wide lane and cruised slowly to the north gate of Davis-Monthan Air Force Base.

Holzgraf was already tense, and now he felt his chest constrict. Could the air base house a police station? Are you kidding? Nightmare thoughts tumbled through his head. He eyeballed the shoulder patches on his captors' uniforms. Maybe the men who had him in custody weren't cops at all. Maybe he was destined for a secret execution.

The driver handed a note to the guard at the gate. The man read it, quickly wrote up a pass, and handed it over, along with a map.

"Building 349. Right around the corner here, this side of the runway. Park in any spot marked 'visitor' and clip that pass to the rear view mirror."

The driver thanked the guard and motored slowly onto the base grounds. Half a minute later, the second police vehicle followed along behind.

▼

General Upshaw had a wry smile on his face as he stood up from his desk to greet four police officers and two accused murderers.

"We can dispense with the cuffs now, I think," he said.

The senior policeman was perplexed. "These two are under arrest, sir. The accusations are very serious."

Upshaw chuckled drily. "Leave them to me, this is a Federal case."

"Sir?"

"National security. That's all I can tell you."

"Yes, sir," said the cop with a dubious scowl.

"Believe me, my organization will know how to handle them. They'll get what they deserve, you can be sure of that."

"Okay, then. I have a sheet here, chain of custody. Can you sign it, please?"

Upshaw took the paper and scribbled his signature.

"The cuffs?"

"Oh, right." The senior officer motioned to his colleagues. Two of the cops came up behind Holzgraf and Chow and removed their restraints.

Upshaw handed the signed paper back. "And now, I think, you four are excused. Good job. Please convey my thanks to your supervisor for cooperating so effectively with us."

He made a point of shaking hands with all four officers, who then departed.

When they were gone, he turned his attention to the accused.

"Arrest — handcuffs — reading your rights — pretty scary experience, wouldn't you say?"

Holzgraf and Chow looked at each other, eyebrows raised.

"What's going on here? Like, what the fuck?" demanded Holzgraf.

"We didn't kill anybody," added Chow.

"So you say. And I accept your protest, provided . . . provided, that is, you agree to cooperate with us."

"Who the hell is *us?*"

"The Joint Powers Immigration Task Force. It's a small operation. My name's Maurice Upshaw and, I guess you'd say, I run it."

Holzgraf waggled a finger. "Upshaw? Wait a minute. *General Upshaw,* astronaut, space shuttle, Hubble missions, right?"

Upshaw acknowledged the recognition with a little nod.

"NASA. You're NASA. That helicopter. The thing you bagged."

Upshaw nodded again.

"Bagged with our help," noted Chow.

Upshaw smiled. "Yes, you two seem to have discovered the same things we're curious about."

"Except we were way ahead," insisted Chow.

Upshaw's smile broadened. "True. You have humbled the Task Force." He pressed a button on his desk and spoke into an intercom. "Jim? Come get your recruits."

▼

Captain Lockwood conducted Holzgraf and Chow into an office down the hall and sat them at a pair of desks. He handed them each a stack of paperwork.

"Read the agreement carefully and sign at the tags."

Holzgraf stared at the documents. The language suggested dire consequences at the slightest breach of trust.

"You can't put us in jail, we're American citizens," he said.

"This is totally bogus," agreed Chow.

Lockwood handed them pens. "The rest of us all signed the same contract," he said.

"You're swearing us to secrecy. What if we want to tell the world?"

"Then we turn you back over to the Tucson police. Murder charges."

"That would never hold up. My family has some really great lawyers," protested Holzgraf.

"Maybe not," allowed Lockwood, "but it sure would snarl up your life for a while."

"Good point," said Chow, "and I don't even have a family, or a lawyer, or a public defender." She stared intently at the small print, inwardly grappling with the issues.

Lockwood watched the two outsiders struggle with their consciences and fears. His hard-bitten attitude seemed to soften. "If it will make you feel better, once you sign, you're on the team."

Chow brightened. "Really? Your secret alien hunting squad?"

"I can neither confirm nor deny — until you sign."

Chow leafed through the pages, signing each protocol enthusiastically.

Holzgraf watched her progress. "Immigration, huh? Undocumented turnips . . . man, that's good." Grumbling and groaning, he put his name to the documents.

Lockwood collected the paper. Holzgraf and Chow put down their pens, stood, burst out laughing, and bumped fists.

Lockwood grinned. "Welcome to the Task Force," he said.

Chow impulsively wrapped her arms around him. The hug lasted two seconds; then she backed away with a red face. "This is so cool!" she exclaimed to cover up her embarrassment.

The door opened and General Upshaw joined them. Lockwood handed him the signed contracts.

"Now that we're on the same page — literally — I'd like some answers," said Upshaw. "You found the thing we recovered — whatever it is — and you tamed it. What I want to know, before we go any further, is — how?"

Chow flapped her arms in general confusion. "My father found one of these bushes years ago. Jurnegan tried to buy it. Dad wouldn't sell, and I'm pretty sure Jurnegan hired the people who stole it from us. Then we recently found another one. We think it was some kind of brain." She pointed at Holzgraf, who gave Upshaw a little salute.

"We both had read a science paper by that guy Jurnegan," said Holzgraf.

"How did you locate that thing running around in the hills out east?"

"Research. We tracked Jurnegan down."

"How? We know about the guy, but we couldn't find him." said Upshaw.

"Holly, here, and I, we thought the man's nutball obsession with secrecy indicated a lab hidden in the desert. We toured the area in a helicopter, and bingo."

"You're a pilot?" Upshaw was surprised.

"I am."

"But Jurnegan was dead when we got there." interjected Chow. "That thing killed him."

"So you called 9-1-1."

"I did."

Upshaw couldn't resist a good-natured jab. "How much to refuel that mousy little chopper sitting out there?"

Holzgraf sucked in his breath. "More than you think," he confessed. "But," he added, "well worth it."

Upshaw folded his arms. "We haven't checked that location yet, but we will. Good initiative, I have to say." His wide lips formed an ironic smile. "The difference between joining up and facing the law."

Signaling his new team members to remain in the room, Upshaw motioned for Lockwood to follow him outside. They consulted in the hallway.

"What do you think? They okay? Full membership, clearance?"

Lockwood shrugged. "They did beat us to the target. They found Jurnegan. They're enthusiastic."

"Not military, though. No idea of etiquette and tradecraft."

Lockwood chuckled. "What does it matter — look at Garibaldi and

Weatherall, to say nothing of old Chet, our mystery man."

Upshaw stroked his chin.

"All right then, show them the ropes."

Lockwood touched his brow in a little salute and started back into the room. Upshaw grabbed his sleeve.

"Hang on, Captain. You missed your appointment with Dr. Nyberg. That's two in a row now."

Lockwood made a face. "You're right. I don't need that guy anymore."

"Whoa, he told me six weeks." Upshaw's soft brown eyes were full of fatherly concern.

"Unh-huh," said Lockwood, clocking his supervisor's expression. "But you know, suddenly the mood swings are gone, the confusion too."

"The empathy factor? 'Loss of affect'? How about that?"

"Do I love my job? The team?" Lockwood pointed to his head. "Up here, I do." He pointed to his chest. "Down here, it's best to just kind of let go."

"Stay calm, you mean."

"That's the idea."

"Even keel, I get it." Upshaw awkwardly scratched an ear. "How long have we worked together?"

"Two years."

"I can rely on you?"

"Always. You know that. Hey, I feel good."

"You feel good," repeated Upshaw, trying to convince himself.

"Real good. Steely good."

35

Dr. Garibaldi, Dr. Weatherall, and Chester Boggs were standing at a window overlooking a gymnasium one story below them when Upshaw and Lockwood arrived to introduce the new team members.

"Roman, Nancy, Chet — meet our former competitors and now allies — Guy Holzgraf and Holly Chow."

Handshakes all around.

Garibaldi couldn't contain his morbid curiosity. He pointed at the window. On the other side, sitting in the middle of a recreational basketball court, was the creature they had chased up the mountainside. It was completely inert. Its legs were mere outlines grooved into the facets of an almost perfect dodecahedral body.

"Hello, Dasher," said Chow.

"That thing — Dasher?? — it makes my skin crawl," declared the government scientist. "That's just a cute name. What do you suppose we've got here? A creature? A robot? Is it male or female, or what the hell?'"

"I think a name has to have a gender. I think it's a robot-creature. A boy robot-creature," pronounced Chow.

"How about you? Holzgraf is it? What's your take?"

"Exotic plants?" offered Holzgraf, being cautious in the company of his new teammates.

Polite chuckles greeted this quaint notion.

"Yeah, that would be the biggest botanical news in a hundred years," he conceded, assessing the group reaction. "How about military tech? Did DARPA get a lucky break?"

Blank faces and silence.

"No? Of course not. Then these bushes came from . . . somewhere else. Somewhere *way far away.*"

Nods and murmurs. "Now you know why we're keeping it a secret," said Lockwood.

"I think the secret is out," said Chow. "We knew. Those guys in the Hummer knew."

"The Durango brothers," noted Upshaw. "We think they worked for Jurnegan."

"Watch out, they're dangerous," warned Holzgraf.

Lockwood made a face. "So? We're dangerous. And we have the advantage of Uncle Sam's blessing."

Garibaldi turned to Chow. "This thing was wild and aggressive, I'm told, and whatever you did cooled it off," he said.

"Unh-huh."

"What, exactly, did you do?"

"We found a bush out past the KO Estates."

"The Olson discovery," said Weatherall.

"That's right. There was an object attached to the roots, like a crystal potato, and under light it became a little critter. It could hear me talking. I think it could understand what I said. I think that's what the bushes use for a brain," she explained.

"But the thing could already move around on its legs, yes?"

"Oh boy. Maybe our little blob was a just a conscience or something, not a whole brain at all."

"Moral issues," speculated Weatherall.

"Could be."

Garibaldi wasn't satisfied. "But this creature, or robot — whatever it is — when it merged with your object, it just folded up. We haven't been able to get anywhere."

Holzgraf peered into the basketball court. "Why don't you bring in some lights?"

"We tried, you can see them standing over in the corner."

"Those things look like bedside lamps from Ikea," said Holzgraf, dismissing their efforts. "You need real power. And try orange light. These things prefer orange illumination — say about 2,000 Kelvin — that's the peak sensitivity for their kind of photosynthesis."

"How do you know that?"

"I ran tests. I'm a biologist. Energy production is my specialty."

"Really," sniffed Garibaldi, clearly unpersuaded.

But Weatherall was intrigued by the idea. "You know," she said, arm-waving the possibilities, "our origin candidate is a K-type star. It's small, produces half the energy of the sun, and the dominant color temperature of its feeble light is . . . orange."

▼

Lockwood called around and located a set of stage lights and their power supplies in the air base's documentary video studio. Holzgraf and Chow helped him set them up in an array surrounding the motionless Dasher.

"You ready out there, Holly?"

One of the side exits to the gym contained a small window. Holzgraf had punched through the glass and channeled power cords through it. Chow was standing in the hallway outside, waiting to connect them to a heavy duty cable that snaked away to an outlet near the building's breaker panel.

"Thumbs up, Jim," she called back.

The familiar use of first names produced a bitter taste in Holzgraf's mouth. He swallowed hard, but said nothing.

Lockwood punched a contact number into his smartphone. "Doctor Garibaldi? How do we look?"

Peering down from on high, Garibaldi raised his phone and waved. "Video is running. Now get out and lock the door."

Holzgraf was puzzled. "What's he doing up there?"

Lockwood shrugged. "He's jumpy around the bushes we found, and he's terrified of this thing."

Holzgraf eyed the enigmatic beast they were about to test. "Hmm, when I stop to think about it, I'm nervous too."

In the hallway, Chow snapped paddle plugs into the cable box. The stage lights began to glow softly. Holzgraf stationed himself at a Variac on the floor.

"Go for test," said Lockwood.

Holzgraf twisted the knob on the Variac. The stage lights blazed up, glaring bright blue.

"Doc says give it a minute," said Lockwood, indicating his phone.

A few leaves appeared on the dodecahedron.

"This might work if we were out in bright sunlight."

"Now back off to orange."

Holzgraf adjusted the Variac. Intense orange light filled the gym.

Weatherall stepped out of an elevator and crossed the hallway to watch the show. Nothing happened for another minute, but then long stems slowly sprouted from the creature's body. Dozens of leaves unfolded to drink in the energy.

The hair rose on Chow's forearms.

Lockwood whistled.

"Be damned," said Weatherall, slapping a knee. She hailed Garibaldi on her smartphone. "Roman? You getting this? K-type starlight! Origin hypothesis confirmed!"

They watched for ten minutes. The crystalline leaves weaved back and forth as if breathing, but Dasher did not stir.

36

"We are unemployed, bro," said Ty Durango.

"We surely are," agreed Earl. "Unless you want to rejoin Uncle Sam's version of the Foreign Fucking Legion, let's do something about it."

"Enough with the ragheads."

"More than enough."

Earl removed the Russian spy's business card from his wallet. He rapped it against a finger.

"What do we think?"

Ty raised his eyebrows. "You're talking about the guys who grabbed Crimea."

"Yup."

"They're thrashing Syria as we speak."

"Sure are."

"They're threatening Estonia and the whole fucking Baltic."

"Every day it's worse."

"Poland . . ."

"Can't sleep at night."

Ty smiled.

"But we're pals on the space station . . . give me the number."

Earl read it off. Ty dialed.

There was a brief exchange.

"Meeting at AJ's up at the north end of town. Man, I had trouble with the directions, the guy barely speaks English. Got our bushes?"

"One or two intact, and some fragments."

"He wants them."

"For enough money, he gets whatever he wants."

After a slow trip to the northern edge of Tucson, an area neither Durango had ever visited, Earl drove the brothers' Hummer around and around the parking lots near AJ's Fine Foods. The store was part of an upscale shopping center carved out of the Catalina mountain foothills, and there were two lots, one below the store and a second one higher up.

"Upper or lower lot?"

"Didn't say."

"Shit."

Earl parked in the upper and nearly empty lot. They waited for ten minutes before a white Lincoln Town Car cruised into view. It parked in a far corner, near the truck bays. A burly man with a black beard got out of the back seat. He was wearing a khaki windbreaker. He leaned against the car and lit a cigarette.

"That's him. Basil fucking Temkhin, Russian fucking spy," said Ty.

Earl nodded. "The Russian bear? Hah, he actually looks like a bear."

He restarted the Hummer and maneuvered alongside the Lincoln. Ty checked the pistol in his waistband.

The Durangos stepped onto the asphalt and approached the Russian.

"Hey, there, how ya doing?"

"Zdravstvuyte, gospoda! I am in good health. You are same, *da?"*

As the conversation began, Earl noticed the Lincoln driver's window roll down. An older man with white hair was sitting behind the wheel. His expressionless face, rough like a boxer's, was turned toward them. Earl nudged Ty.

"We're okay. We're doing okay."

"Khorosho! That is well, because I hear *plokhiye novosti* about Professor Jurnegan, who write excellent science paper."

"Yeah, bad accident."

"I wonder, what has become of his, ah, inventory?"

The Durangos grinned.

"Well, sir — *Mr. Temkhin* — we are here today to deliver some of it."

Ty fetched a stack of plastic tubs from the rear of the Hummer.

"Two intact bushes, plus bits and pieces. They're yours, if the price is right."

Temkhin peeled the lid off the topmost container and peered inside. He fingered the leaves. Then he picked up the bush and scraped dirt away from the roots, revealing a crystalline object the size of a baseball.

"Da, I like. How much?"

"Five thousand dollars," said Earl with positive assurance.

"Mmm. Take check?"

"Ha, ha, that's funny. Here we are in a parking lot, doing a Craigslist."

Temkhin grinned. "Of course not. Ha ha, joke, ha ha."

He snapped his fingers, and his driver thrust a large wallet out of the window. Temkhin took it, extracted a sheaf of bills, and handed them over. Earl made a count.

"We're good," he said.

"There. We do business. Bring me more, bring me *novosti.* I am all ears, and all ready to buy," declared Temkhin with an expansive smile.

They shook hands to seal their new relationship.

Earl drove the Hummer fifty yards across the empty lot and slowed to a stop. The Durangos watched in their rearview mirrors as Temkhin's driver emerged from the Lincoln and placed the plastic tubs in the trunk.

"That old bird doesn't walk so good," noted Ty.

"Looks like he's been over some rough roads."

"Probably dug a lot of the potholes."

37

A convoy of white Ford Explorers with the letters ITF stenciled on their doors drove east on a dirt track toward a GPS location determined by Holzgraf.

On the way from home base, Lockwood arranged to ride with Chow, making sure her boss was in one of the trailing SUVs.

"What about Holzgraf?" he asked.

"What about him?"

"Do you like the guy?"

Chow frowned at the oblique invasion into her private life. It took her a few moments to sum up her feelings. "He's all right, I suppose," she said, squirming evasively. "When he's not being too rich, or too glib, or too standoffish."

"Are you two seeing each other?"

"Oh my God, what? We just met last month."

"That's what people do though, right?"

She eyed the captain. "So they tell me."

"I think he's just shy around women. I'm pretty sure he likes you."

"So what?" She bit her lip. "He's a prince, and I'm a pauper."

The team soon arrived at Advanced Solar Research, where they encountered festoons of yellow *POLICE LINE DO NOT CROSS* tape. A lone Pima County sheriff's deputy was keeping watch on the facility.

General Upshaw got out of the leading car and approached the startled cop. He handed over a document. The cop read it twice. An animated discussion ensued. After a long lecture from Upshaw, the cop reluctantly removed some of the tape, allowing the convoy to enter the grounds.

"Officer Smiley over there isn't happy, but he got the message," said Upshaw to his team. "Let's look around."

The group fanned out across the area. Garibaldi wandered inside, found a desk, fished a notebook out of a drawer, and slowly leafed through it, studying the entries.

Boggs looked over his recent place of employment with a haunted expression on his wizened face.

Weatherall made a point of collecting bits and pieces of the crystalline plants trashed by Dasher. Then she stepped outside for a consoling cigarette.

Holzgraf and Chow looked on grimly in the background with the lacerated bodies of Jurnegan and Ingleside, now removed, weighing on their minds.

"That stain on the floor . . . dry now," said Chow. She tipped her head against Holzgraf's chest. "Ugh." Her abrupt familiarity startled him.

Lockwood finished a preliminary reconnaissance of the premises and took Holzgraf aside.

"How long have you known Holly?"

"Just about a month. From what I hear, we both met her that day at the show. Why?"

"You two an item?"

"No, she works for me, my little solar company."

"What do you think of her?"

"Um, I think she's a competent employee."

"You like her. You'd like to be an item, right?"

"Whoa there, buddy," said Holzgraf, thoroughly embarrassed. "Our relationship is strictly professional."

"Unh-huh. She likes you."

"How can you tell? She's tighter than a new shoe."

"She told me . . . indirectly."

"Can't date someone who works for you," protested Holzgraf, "it could raise a claim of sexual harassment."

"But wait, problem solved," insisted Lockwood. "You both work for us now. You need to make a move, ask her out."

"Or what? You'll beat me to it? What's this all about? Warning off a rival?"

"Just checking. When you need teamwork, it's important to understand the team."

"Oh, right, second that," said Holzgraf, with a touch of wounded irony in his voice.

Lockwood reacted with a cocked eyebrow and wandered off, leaving a small dent in Holzgraf's self esteem.

Outside, he discovered an intact bush in the little garden Jurnegan had planted. Boggs dug it out of the ground and carried it into the lab.

"Look here, everybody."

The team gathered around the find. Chow removed an empty plastic tub from a pile of debris on the floor and handed it to Lockwood.

"Here, Jim, shake the roots into this."

Lockwood took the bush from Boggs, held it over the tub, and worked the roots free of dirt.

"Whoa," said Garibaldi.

Exposed in the tangle was a crystalline rhomboid the size of a large cucumber.

"That looks a lot like the thing we found, right, Holly?" observed Holzgraf, pleased by the chance to address his companion by agreed-upon first name.

"Yeah," she said, nodding emphatically. "Be careful, people, just in case it's some kind of alien temper tantrum waiting to happen."

"Is this bush . . . alive?" wondered Garibaldi, keeping his distance.

Lockwood dropped the thing into the tub he was holding. "Let's check."

Holzgraf surveyed the lab setup, quickly identifying an industrial lamp and electrical controls.

"Bring that thing over here," he said.

Lockwood placed the tub on a lab bench near the lamp. Holzgraf flicked a switch. The lamp glowed. He rotated the Variac knob. The lamp brightened. Suddenly the bush's roots thrashed around, re-burying themselves in the pile of dirt at the bottom of the plastic container.

"Looks alive to me," said Boggs cheerfully.

Holzgraf reduced power until the bush was suffused in a soft orange glow. The leaves turned toward the source, spread themselves into a circular array.

"That's enough, kill it," ordered Upshaw.

The lights went out. The leaves collapsed.

Garibaldi held up Jurnegan's notebook. He tapped the cover. "The poor professor knew these bushes were exotic. But I don't think he quite understood that interstellar travel isn't the same as seeds floating by on the breeze. Minds are required. Planning and purpose. Minds that aren't too friendly, that we know. What was the plan? The purpose? That's what we don't know."

38

In the Davis-Monthan gymnasium, Dasher remained motionless.

The task force team was staring at it, nervously wrestling with a big decision. Air base carpenters, busy barricading the gym doors with wooden beams and steel bars, punctuated their discussion with the clatter of hammers and the zing of power tools.

"You want to introduce the root ball from the bush we just found into that room? Are you prepared for the consequences?" asked Weatherall.

"What if Dasher goes crazy?"

"What if he chews his way through a door?"

"What if he sprouts a ray gun?"

"Doesn't scare me," volunteered Boggs. "That thing ain't very big, and it ain't very strong. Our girl here, I watched her turn it into a pussycat."

Upshaw turned to Lockwood. "Jim? You're the one who got bit."

Lockwood considered the matter. "I'm in, as long as we keep well clear of those legs we saw."

Upshaw folded his arms. "If we do this, we're taking a risk. What's our upside?"

"We know mergers occur. We know metamorphosis results," said Garibaldi. "If we don't exploit the possibilities, we won't know what we've got here. We won't be doing our job."

Upshaw drew a deep breath. "True, our charter is explicit — to find out all about our visitors. Got your weapon, Jim?"

Lockwood nodded.

"Keep it handy. Roman? What's your idea?"

"We open one door, as far away from the thing as possible. We shove the new bush into the room, back out, bar the door again, and watch on video."

"From a safe distance," insisted Weatherall.

"Your hypothesis?"

"My working theory is, each root-thing has a different function, and each merger increases our captive's abilities and sophistication. I think Dasher wants to grow up. We'll see action, but not violence."

Upshaw took a good look at the hibernating critter, evaluating the team's chances. "Okay, children, let the video roll. If I'm wrong, I'll go in there and reason with that thing myself . . . ray gun or no ray gun."

Chester Boggs was elected to place the newly found bush inside the gym. Holzgraf rigged an intercom between the door and the viewing area above, where the rest of the team gathered to watch.

"We've got video coverage," said Garibaldi, with an eye on a monitor beside the window.

"Go for test," announced Lockwood. "You're the man, Chet."

Holzgraf opened the door, and Boggs scooted through. He placed the plastic tub containing the bush on the floor inside and gave it a mighty shove. It skidded out to the basketball court foul line. Boggs backed into the hallway, and Holzgraf slammed the door shut.

Carpenters immediately hammered the barricade back into place.

The team watched and waited, but nothing seemed to happen.

"Guy? Holly? Let's have some light."

Holly reconnected the power cables, and Holzgraf dialed in five thousand watts of orange light.

It didn't take long for leaves to appear on the dodecahedron.

"One minute thirty," said Weatherall, looking at a stopwatch.

Time passed and nothing more happened. The team was getting edgy. Then, imperceptibly at first, legs began to bud out of the thing. They stiffened, scratched at the floor.

Dasher stood up.

"Nine minutes," said Weatherall.

Very slowly and deliberately, the creature moved across the court to the plastic tub. A leg rose, snagged the rim, and flipped the tub on its side. The bush spilled out. The creature backed away and crouched down.

"Eleven Minutes."

The bush shook itself, scattering dirt every which way. A small blob separated from the exposed roots and tumbled across the court to the waiting creature. When blob and creature made contact, both dissolved into a pile of sand.

Team members mumbled and grumbled.

"Fifteen minutes."

Suddenly the sand whirled into motion. A larger version of Dasher materialized from the blur. Six longer legs. A wider body. A pair of bulbous eyes on long stalks. They moved this way and that, apparently trying to make sense of the situation.

"Seventeen minutes," said Weatherall, unconsciously retreating from the window. "God in Heaven."

Garibaldi's face turned white. He staggered backward and collapsed on a bench.

Upshaw rushed across the room. "Roman? You okay?"

The creature started moving, slowly exploring its prison cell. Approaching a door, its front legs rose. Little grippers appeared. They pushed and tugged on the exit's panic bar.

"Uh-oh, it wants out," said Weatherall.

Foiled by the barricade, the creature moved slowly along to the next door and methodically attempted to pry it open.

Lockwood toggled the intercom. "Guy, kill that light. Holly, Chet, all of you, get your asses up here!"

The creature's efforts stalled as the lights went out.

"Who's got a first aid kit?" demanded Upshaw. "Smelling salts? Water? Garibaldi is out."

▼

The team gathered at the far end of the gym, taking turns peering through the small reinforced glass window.

"Okay, Guy, some light, but not much," instructed Lockwood.

His voice carried away down the hall, and Holzgraf turned the Variac knob ten degrees. Faint light illuminated the creature, which sat on the floor with its legs folded underneath.

Garibaldi, having recovered from his fainting spell, but still pale as a ghost, shouldered his way to the forefront of the group for a good look.

"Whew," he said. "The feeling that came over me. Not as strong now, but still there."

"You don't have to hang around, Roman. Go home, get some sleep," advised Upshaw.

"No, no, I have to be here. This is important. Who else is bothered by this thing? Who else feels all creeped out?"

Garibaldi's colleagues looked at each other. Finally Weatherall broke the silence. "Me. Whenever I'm around these things I feel weird. Seeing this creature, or robot, knowing it's not from around here, it's a new experience. It challenges our sense of human superiority. No wonder I feel queasy."

"Possible, I suppose," granted Garibaldi. "Anyone else?"

Chow tentatively raised a hand. "Me too. I can't get over it."

Holzgraf joined the group. He nodded. "It comes and goes. It's worse when the lights are on."

Upshaw snorted. "You're my team. Are you telling me I've collected a bunch of chickenhearted wimps?"

Garibaldi swung around to face the general. "Come on, Mo, be honest. You're a tough old bird, so the effect is subject to your personal discipline, but you don't fool me."

"Okay, yes, I do notice a tiny twinge. Hanging around that thing we've got makes me feel strange. As it should — because it *is* strange."

Lockwood chuckled. "You guys! I feel fine."

"Boggs?" queried Garibaldi.

"I feel kind of funny. Ever since I hit my head."

Garibaldi spread his arms. "Right. Except for our intrepid captain, bless his military training, we all notice something. Who says it's because of stress? Or cowardice? Or wonderment, for that matter?"

"Roman . . ?"

"Or anything to do with our own psyches?"

Upshaw twirled his fingers around his temple. "You think our visitor is messing up our minds?"

"Yes I do," said Garibaldi stoutly.

"Come on, Doc. Mental woo-woo?"

Weatherall scowled. "I'm a skeptic or I'd be a terrible scientist. But look what we just witnessed. A creature that does not contain a shred of DNA is yet, by all external standards, alive. It exhibits behavior we have never heard of or imagined."

"Yeah," said Chow, "and it might have other kinds of claws to rip us up with."

"That's right," agreed Garibaldi, nodding vigorously. "The amazing show we've already seen could just be a trailer for the real movie. We need to study this, get to the bottom of it."

Upshaw stroked his chin. "All right, but how?"

"Radio? Tune through a lot of frequencies — maybe there's a signal we're missing," thought Holzgraf.

No one had a better idea. No one was convinced.

▼

Frustrated by their inability to understand developments, the team expressed mild curiosity about Holzgraf's solar project. So, at Garibaldi's request, the proprietor arranged a distracting tour of Darlington Energetix, complete with a take-out lunch.

When murmurs of admiration tailed off, when the tacos were gone and the beer glasses empty, Garibaldi turned to the real reason for their visit, his continuing worries about the mental powers of their botanical discoveries.

"Look, Mo isn't here to wave the caution flag, so let's think about the possibilities. We've got a creature sitting in the gym, and I'm convinced it's radiating its thoughts. What if those thoughts are hostile?"

"You mean, turn us into zombies?" worried Chow, genuinely upset by the prospect.

"Or slaves," said the scientist.

"Or, on the other hand, prevent us ignorant bozos from destroying ourselves," countered Weatherall.

"Or, hand us the secrets of the universe? That's the sci-fi take," said Holzgraf.

"Oh why not," scoffed Garibaldi, "hand matches to monkeys."

"Or maybe they're scouting a new home," thought Chow.

"The dying planet theory," said Weatherall.

"Or hatred of the imperfect, if they're robots," said Lockwood.

"What?"

"Creatures evolve, they compete to succeed. Robots, if that's what you're dealing with, they were created from scratch. Free of all that."

"What can we do about it?" complained Holzgraf. "We looked at radio, we got zip for results. We're out of ideas."

Lockwood stirred uneasily. "Human beings have a right to their own identities," he decided. "Dasher doesn't bother me — maybe I'm immune — but we have to act."

They all agreed. "Got to. Plan, anyone?"

Weatherall was pacing the room, muttering to herself. "How about this?

I know a guy at Stanford — Isaac Lunenberg, professor of neurobiology, top of his field. You want thoughts? That's what he studies. At the least, I'm sure he will have some advice."

▼

Showing a united front, they presented Weatherall's idea to their cautious leader.

Upshaw heard them out. He generated an ironic grin. "My loyal team, conspiring against me." The group did not grin back. He registered the rebellious mood and considered their proposal. "This means we alert an outsider to our little secret."

"You mean *another* outsider," said Holzgraf. "Is that a problem?"

"Our mandate doesn't forbid it. My discretion." He glared at Garibaldi, who glared back.

"Okay, Nan, make the call."

▼

Dr. Lunenberg was in the Stanford gym running on a treadmill when Weatherall's call came in.

"Ike? It's Nancy. Got a minute?"

Lunenberg touched a button, and the treadmill slowed to a stop.

"Hi, Nan. What's up?"

"I need some advice on a mental problem."

"You? Where are you? Rumors are floating."

"Tucson. Investigating . . . uh . . . something odd."

"Oh-ho, did someone down there just find Planet Vulcan again?"

"Better than that, but I can't go into details. Any chance I could fly you down here for a consultation?"

Lunenberg ran a towel over his shoulders, checked his watch.

"Sorry, no. I've got a double-blind experiment going, and two graduate classes. All tied up."

"Damn. What if I tell you we're looking at a possible case of — I know how this sounds — telepathy? Thought transference?"

"You're joking, right?"

"Nope. I'd like to put the idea to rest, and I need a pro to do it."

Lunenberg thought about the problem. He chuckled.

"Tell you what, the man for you is Bob Osborne. Great guy, you'll like him. He's a professor up at Sacramento State, solid citizen, no nonsense, and yet he's really into this kind of stuff."

Weatherall got a number from the information operator and placed another call. She reached Osborne at his desk.

"Osborne here. Hello?" He was using a speakerphone, and his voice sounded like it was coming out of a barrel.

"Hi, there, Doctor. My name's Nancy Weatherall, I'm an astronomer at Cal. Isaac Lunenberg gave me your name. I understand you're a neuroscientist with a strong interest in unusual brain activity."

Osborne was flipping a Rubik's Cube with one hand while he bounced a little rubber ball and collected a pile of jacks with the other. "Ike likes to joke, but now and then, yes, I dive down the rabbit hole."

"I've got a problem. We're conducting research on a sort of . . . uh, plant . . . that some of my colleagues think can project thoughts and influence us . . . well, telepathically."

"That is definitely unusual." Osborne put down his desk toys. "You're an astronomer? What are we talking about? Little green men?"

"I'm part of an, um, interdisciplinary study. Ike's a friend. And I can't tell you very much. I'm afraid our work is classified."

"Little green men for sure," concluded Osborne.

Weatherall squinched up her mouth, trying to figure out how to evade the sharp inquiry. "No, not green," she said at last. "Not necessarily astronomical. Or animal. Just peculiar."

Osborne wasn't convinced. "But we are talking about *them from there*, right?"

"Not sure where they come from."

"Look, I'd be there in a flash if you told me GE was going to donate a million dollars to my lab, but the truth is, I have enough trouble coping with the ordinary *human* mind. Especially the mind of my dean. He's not very sympathetic."

"I'm disappointed to hear that. I think you'd find the problem interesting, and we definitely need some help on this."

"Look, I dabble, but if you want a real authority on oddball mental life, I've got another idea."

"What? Who?"

"Someone who knows all about this sort of thing — first hand."

"What's his name?"

Osborne laughed. "It's a woman. She is your expert."

▼

Two hours and ten phone calls later, Weatherall joined her companions in Upshaw's office, where Garibaldi was monitoring their creature on his smartphone.

"Any change?"

Garibaldi looked up. "None. He hasn't moved."

"That's good, I guess. Where's the coffee?"

Upshaw pointed across the room. Weatherall filled a cup and sat down, relieved to take a break.

"Well — ?" All eyes turned toward her.

She sipped her coffee. "I burned up a lot of phone minutes, but I did manage to line up someone who will help us understand the telepathy angle, the anxiety our little pal produces."

"Your friend Lunenberg?"

"No, he dodged the bait."

"Who then?"

Weatherall exhaled. "A woman named Marianne Sarzeau."

"Where does she teach?"

"She doesn't. She's a cop. That is, when she's not on duty as a federal intelligence operative working for an agency called *The Full Spectrum Threat Assessment Program.*"

"Never heard of it," said Upshaw, brow furrowed, "and I've heard of everything."

"No you haven't, Mo. This group — those in the know call it FULTAP — it's a dark one. They do psychic surveillance."

"You're fucking kidding. The feds?"

"Her trade name is *Broomhandle.*"

"What in the world?"

Weatherall drummed her fingers on the table, uncertain about the best way to break some very unsettling news. Finally she blurted, "That's not even the funny part. I have to warn you . . . she's a witch."

39

Chester Boggs was looking over the merchandise in Trujillo's Nursery &
Dirt Emporium in the commercial blocks of Ajo Way, not far from Davis-
Monthan Air Force Base. Dr. Garibaldi was hoping to encourage the ITF
collection of exotic bush fragments, and Boggs was on a mission to purchase
irrigation equipment and potting soil.

Various types of dirt were on display in open bins. Boggs was tasting
them, one after another, forming an impression of their fertilizing potential,
when a couple of men drew up to his elbows.

"Hello, Chet," said the man on his left.

"How's life?" said the man on his right.

Boggs backed away from the soil samples.

"Earl, Ty, look who's here," he said, wiping his mouth.

"What's up, old man? What's going on over at the base?"

Boggs squinted at his interlocutors. "You heard about Professor
Jurnegan? Him and Mr. Ingleside both. Terrible thing."

"We saw what happened," said Earl with a nod. "Brutal."

"And we heard," said Ty, "that you've been working for NASA, or
whoever those government clowns are, with the idea of reporting back to
your former friends."

"They aren't clowns," said Boggs.

"No, I guess not. Not really. What are they up to?"

"Well, I don't know as I should tell you boys a thing."

Earl waved his arms around. "Jurnegan and Ingleside are dead. We're
running their operation now, and we'd like to renew the deal they made."

"Money?"

"Of course."

"For information?"

"That's it," said Earl.

"That's it exactly," said Ty.

Boggs folded his arms and appeared to fall asleep on his feet. When his
eyes failed to re-open after a few seconds, Ty touched his arm.

"Hey, Chet, hi-yo Silver!"

Boggs' eyes snapped wide. "Sorry, boys. Happens now and then since I hit my head."

"Concussion? You okay?"

"It's like I was away for a moment there," said Boggs. His eyes narrowed. A subtle change in personality seemed to come to the fore. "And I heard myself decide to help you."

"If the money's right?"

Boggs appraised the Durangos with what seemed like shrewd amusement. "Oh, yeah, if the money is right. Gotta be right. Damn right. What's your offer?"

"How about five thousand bucks for any bit of what we call 'actionable intelligence'? Info that will help us find more of these bushes, figure out what they're made of, keep us ahead of the government good guys."

"I can do that," said Boggs. "Gotta find all those things. Very important."

"We don't think they're really plants."

"No, not plants. Hah, no one knows what they really are."

PART FIVE

40

Holzgraf and Chow were detailed to pick up their psychic consultant at Tucson International Airport. They arrived an hour early, in time for lunch. They strolled through the north concourse, past the news stand, and settled into a booth at Carmina's Mexican Grille, where they ordered enchiladas and chili rellenos.

"Want a beer? Margarita?" asked Holzgraf.

"At lunch? No thanks," said Chow.

They stared at the crowds hustling by, avoiding eye contact, saying nothing. Just before the awkward interlude became intolerable, food arrived. Both were relieved to concentrate on their knives and forks. Finally Chow broke the silence with the burning question of the day:

"Who is this person we're meeting? Some old lady with a long nose? Black hat? Black cat?"

Holzgraf chuckled. "We'll be the first to find out."

Chow dabbed at her lips with her napkin and regarded the blond young man sitting across from her through wintery eyes. She sipped her iced tea. Then, out of nowhere:

"I'm Asian, you know. Both parents."

Holzgraf was jolted by the sudden change of subject. "Yeah? And I'm white. White bread. As white as anyone can get." He made a face. "And so, by the way, is Captain Lockwood."

"I know that, Mr. Holzgraf *The Third.*"

"Hey, I thought we agreed on first names."

"We did . . . . . . it's *Guy,* right?"

Holzgraf decided that his lunch companion was even stranger than Brenda Woolverton, his girlfriend back in ninth grade, and almost as strange as the creature they had discovered.

"All right — *Holly* — so your heritage is China. Mine's Germany, um, before all the trouble. What does it matter here and now?"

Chow tilted her head. "It doesn't. Just something to think about."

Marianne Sarzeau stepped out of SkyWest flight 3141 from Sacramento, after a tiring layover in Los Angeles, in the middle of the afternoon. She rolled her carry-on overnighter out into the concourse, searching for someone to greet her from, good God, where? *The Joint Powers Immigration Task Force,* an organization that she knew was as bogus as one of the counterfeit greenbacks she occasionally confiscated on her day job back in Applefield, California.

Finally the crowd thinned, and she noticed a good-looking young man holding up a sign that read, *Sarzeau ITF.* She waved.

"There she is," said Chow, waving back. She and Holzgraf were both surprised. Coming toward them was a woman in her thirties, fair hair pulled back in a ponytail, curves evident under a flannel shirt and jeans, intelligent dark eyes giving them a sharp once-over.

"She's young. She's cute," said Holzgraf.

"No hat, no cat," granted Chow, "but she's married, Weatherall told me."

"Hi, there, I'm Marianne," said their visitor in a silky voice.

"Welcome to Tucson," Holzgraf replied, folding up his sign.

"This gig better be good," said Sarzeau with a sardonic grin. "I'm a long way from home."

In Holzgraf's Jeep, Sarzeau broached the subject of her visit. "So, who's the mental one I'm supposed to check out?"

Holzgraf and Chow exchanged glances. "What the hell," said he, "you have to know."

"It's a creature," said Chow. "Or maybe a robot. We are pretty sure it wasn't born here."

Sarzeau nodded. "Not a native citizen of Planet Earth. Bob — Dr. Osborne, the guy who relayed the invite — hinted as much." She slapped her thighs. "Well, whooee."

▼

Sarzeau was introduced to the members of the Task Force at the window overlooking the barricaded gymnasium. Everyone was quick to shake her hand, doing their very best to conceal their astonishment at her youth and apparent normality.

"This is your mental wonder?" she asked, pointing at the inert creature on the basketball court below.

"This is it . . . or him, or her," said Lockwood.

"Our pal Dasher," said Chow. ⋅

"It's alive?"

Garibaldi stepped forward. "Not the way we are. Not a trace of DNA, but the components we found were definitely growing, as if they were bushes."

"Components?" Sarzeau was puzzled.

Garibaldi outlined an imaginary bush in the air. "We — and other groups — have found a number of metallic crystalline plantlike things out in the desert around here."

"And we even collected a few stretching back east, in Europe and beyond," added Lockwood.

"They grow, and they produce root balls, objects like metal potatoes. Those things blend together in bigger objects, and then we have . . . what you're looking at," finished Weatherall.

"And these things make you nervous."

"Especially this one. It's not obvious right now, but it has legs and sensors. Under bright light, it moves around."

Sarzeau nodded thoughtfully. "I take it you don't think your anxiety is caused by simply being around an alien, right? I mean, the idea itself is spooky enough for me."

Garibaldi looked at his team. "Opinion is divided. I'm in the something's-going-on faction. General Upshaw here is a skeptic."

"And you want me to figure it out?"

Cautious nods.

Boggs was standing behind the rest. He raised his voice to be heard over the chatter. "You don't look like a witch."

Sarzeau made a little curtsy in the old man's direction. "Thanks," she said, blushing. "A compliment."

Garibaldi winced. "Uhh, the team will actually decide, of course. But we'll be guided, somewhat anyway, by your, ahh, your special kind of expertise."

Sarzeau laughed. "Sorry to make you so uncomfortable. If it helps you feel better, Halloween is months away."

Weatherall giggled.

"Obviously, you're as worried about me as about that lump down there."

Upshaw grunted. "Let's give her the tour. But first, I need to conduct some business. He beckoned. "Miss?"

Sarzeau smiled demurely. "When I'm on the job, my name is Sarzeau. *Miss* works. Or better yet, *Marianne.* When I'm wrangling my kids, woof, then I'm Mrs. Wagstaff."

Upshaw sat Sarzeau down in his office and handed her the standard forms to sign. She took them and leafed through them.

"I can't sign anything," she said, finally.

Upshaw glowered at the mild-mannered challenge to his authority. "It's standard protocol, we've all made the commitment."

Sarzeau's eyes sparkled. "Look, I'm not just a local cop running down meth labs in the California foothills. I'm also a federal agent. I work for FULTAP. Nothing you show me can or will be kept secret from them."

"Tell you what, Miss — Marianne. Jim Lockwood, my associate, will show you around. But before we go much further, I need to make some calls."

"Try General Weaver," she replied. "He's my boss."

41

Lockwood took charge of Sarzeau and marched her across an alley to a building the ITF had recently turned into a laboratory. There he showed off their hothouse and its sparse collection of bush-like entities, gleaming under bright grow lights. Garibaldi and Weatherall tagged along.

"I'm not sure how you want to proceed, but we're very curious," said the eager scientist as they all donned Tyvek bunny suits and hair nets. "Do you feel anything, notice any . . . emanations?"

Sarzeau stared at the metallic objects. She moved around them, brushed a heavily gloved hand over the crystalline leaves, probed a finger into the soil beneath.

"They're rather pretty, aren't they?" she said.

"I suppose," acknowledged Weatherall.

"Like any well-formed being, there's a certain symmetry, an idea of something molded for fitness," grudged Garibaldi.

Sarzeau focused her attention on him, noted his pallor. "How about you? Do you feel creepy when you're near them?"

Garibaldi nodded vigorously, obviously ill at ease.

"Like right now?"

"Oh yes. Even now." He edged away from the alien garden.

"I should get closer." Sarzeau leaned into the largest bush, extending her well-protected arms in among the stems and leaves. After a few seconds she stepped away.

"Okay . . . It's faint, but your skeptical general won't be happy. I do notice something."

She peeled off a glove and held up her arm. The little blond hairs were standing on end.

"Brrr," she said.

▼

General Upshaw spent twenty minutes making phone call after phone call to track down the man in charge of FULTAP. He punched his way through obscure telephone trees, spoke with controlled calm to a succession of robots, pleaded utmost urgency to several human operators, and finally learned of an unlisted number in the mysterious 789 area code. He dialed.

General Weaver was returning home from dinner at a Georgia golf club when his secure smartphone rang.

"Administration," he said.

"General Weaver?"

"Yes."

"General Vernon Weaver?"

"Yes again."

"FULTAP, or whatever, right?"

"You found me. Who wants to know?"

"Maurice Upshaw here, thanks for taking my call. I need some information about one of your agents."

General Weaver's brow wrinkled. "Upshaw, eh? General Upshaw? I've heard of you . . . space shuttle, right?"

"The same. I'm currently running a group called the Joint Powers Immigration Task Force. NASA in bed with the Air Force. I've got a consultant on board who says she's one of yours, someone named Marianne Sarzeau. Is she really?"

Weaver chuckled. "Oh yes. Her father too. Don't be fooled by her youth and good looks. She is hard as nails, smart, a little bit reckless, and . . . she's an adept. A prime asset."

"An adept? You mean twitchery-witchery. There are such people?"

"Affirm. It's her abilities — hers and others' — that let us do what we do."

"And what do you do?"

"We're a specialized intelligence operation. Detailed off from DIA to see into the motives of our adversaries, check for hostile intentions."

"Unh-huh, psychic shit."

"That's the standard description," agreed Weaver, unoffended by the slur.

"Would you say this woman is sane?"

"Absolutely."

"She's trustworthy?"

"Completely."

"Knows her stuff?"

"There is no one else quite like her."

42

Sarzeau stood at the far end of the gymnasium, waiting for the barricade to be removed from the door.

"I can't actually open up until Mo gives us the high sign," said Lockwood. "Patience is a virtue."

"So they say. I've never tried it myself."

Eventually Upshaw appeared.

"All right, Sarzeau — Marianne — you pass the spy check. What are we doing here?"

"I need to go inside and touch that thing you've got locked up."

"Whoa, Nelly, that's taking your life in your hands. Two people are dead who got a little too close."

Garibaldi got in between the commander and his consultant. "But it hasn't moved in hours, even days, Mo. After absorbing Holly's so-called 'naked brain,' it's probably harmless."

"You hope." Upshaw was, as always, professionally dubious.

"We keep the light low, like now, and proceed with a necessary investigation," insisted Garibaldi. "What do you say?"

"Lockwood? Weatherall? Your opinion on this?" demanded Upshaw.

Lockwood nodded. "If we stand guard and prepare for a damn quick evac."

"Marianne has already had indications. The effect is real," insisted Weatherall. "We need to know what's going on."

"Get her a SWAT team helmet at least. And a Kevlar vest under her bunny suit" ordered Upshaw. "Jim, be ready with your persuader."

Holzgraf ran down a Kevlar vest. Chow requisitioned a motorcycle helmet from one of the base employees.

Carpenters were mustered.

Sarzeau climbed into her protective gear.

Lockwood flicked the safety off his standard issue Sig-Sauer pistol, laid his finger along the trigger guard.

Garibaldi checked his smartphone. "Overhead video is running."

The carpenters attacked the barricade with air tools and pulled it away from the gym door.

Holzgraf unlocked the door and cracked it open, bracing himself to slam it shut if need be.

Sarzeau slipped into the gym, shoes squeaking on the polished basketball court. She slowly approached the crouching entity, crouching herself as she drew near.

"I hear they call you Dasher," she said in a soft voice. "I won't hurt you as long as you don't hurt me. Deal?"

Dasher did not stir.

Sarzeau kneeled down, reached out her right arm, and pressed a gloved palm against the metallic body. She remained in that position for a long time.

"What is she doing?" growled Upshaw.

"Good question," said Chow. "She's as weird as Dasher."

After ten minutes, Sarzeau stood up and backed out of the gym.

Holzgraf slammed the door.

Carpenters hammered the barricade into place.

Sarzeau stripped off her helmet and vest and paper suit.

"Let's talk, but not here," she said. Her face was white.

"In my office, everyone," said Upshaw, pointing to the elevator.

▼

"Anyone got a voice recorder or video cam? We should probably get a record of this, while I'm fresh," said Sarzeau.

Garibaldi pressed a button on his smartphone. "We got the session from upstairs, so now I'm killing that." He opened up a small tripod, attached his phone, and set it on Upshaw's desk. "Here you go, talk here."

But Sarzeau suddenly toppled backward. Lockwood leaped forward and caught her just in time. He and Holzgraf dragged her to one of the office chairs and sat her down.

"Glass of water, somebody?" said Holzgraf.

Weatherall brought a brimming paper cup. "You okay?"

Sarzeau nodded weakly.

"Got a name, hon?"

"Marianne."

"Know where you are?"

"Tucson."

"Okay, drink up."

Sarzeau sipped a mouthful. She gargled. She sat up straight.

"Turn that phone on."

Garibaldi adjusted the aim of his smartphone, started the video app. "We're capturing, sound and picture — Sarzeau — plus date and time tags."

"Hello, I'm Marianne Sarzeau, it's March seventeen, I'm in Tucson, where I just now was in close physical contact with a being of some sort everyone here — the Immigration Task Force — is calling Dasher. This is my report.

"The thing I examined looks metallic, but I can confirm that it has a mind and a purpose."

"Whoa!"

"Incredible!"

"Hang on, hang on, let her talk."

Sarzeau took another sip of water. "It isn't exactly alive, like people, but it has thoughts, it has desires. It has been trying to convey them to you, which probably accounts for the creepy feelings.

"Its hope and plan is to get free and go looking for something. An artifact. Something it wants to hand over to you people. Something from home, wherever that is. It has some radio sense, I guess, and is using that to figure out the location of the thing it's hoping to find."

"Where is this artifact?"

"East. Not too far. Dasher got close once before, as I understand it, but couldn't get a good read. It — he — was incomplete. He needed to mature. Well, 'mature,' that's my way of putting it. I didn't actually hear any words, right?"

Lockwood and Boggs looked at each other.

"We were there," said Boggs.

"We need to go back," said Lockwood.

Sarzeau bobbed her head. She pointed. "That's my rap. Out east of here, there's something this little fella wants. A gift."

▼

Later, over burgers from McDonald's, the team pondered Sarzeau's disturbing account.

"A gift? Thank you, little alien, for being so generous." said Weatherall.

"Greeks from outer space," declared Upshaw.

"Bearing gifts," warned Chow.

"Beware the Jabberwock, my son . . ." mumbled Holzgraf.

Garibaldi finished his fries, downed a slug of root beer. He was of a contrary opinion. "I think we have to take a look. At the worst, no alien artifact can be left lying around. It might be dangerous. Explode in the face of some ignorant rockhound hunting up garnets. And maybe it is a gift, a diplomatic gesture. That doesn't seem far-fetched to me. It seems like a reasonable idea. An evolved, intelligent idea."

"I seem to remember how Europeans gave all the Native Americans little blue beads when they first met," said Sarzeau. "And then look what happened."

Upshaw nodded agreement. "We have to be careful. Before we dig up any damn gift, I'd like to know more about it."

Weatherall absently played with the remains of her lunch. "Should we call in the troops? Is it time? Send the marines into the hills?"

"No way," insisted Garibaldi, jealous of any opportunities slipping away.

Upshaw scowled in agreement. "We *are* the troops, Nan. We are going to handle this."

Sarzeau smiled a crooked smile. "With my help, you mean. There might be a way."

Everyone turned toward their psychic consultant.

"What way?"

"Wouldn't it be nice to know where your creature comes from? What it's like there? Who sent it? What it's supposed to find?"

Weatherall shook her head.

"Here's a little astronomy lesson, dear," she said. "The star we've identified as the origin of our discoveries is eleven lightyears away. If we radio them a note and they reply, it will take twenty-two years to read the answer."

"Assuming we can decode it," added Garibaldi.

Sarzeau grinned. "I don't use radio in my work."

"True, radio is yesterday's tech, and SETI is all about laser beams these days, but everything's limited by the speed of light," insisted the astronomer.

"No laser beams either."

"What then?" wondered Upshaw.

"Spells," said Sarzeau.

A cacophony of chatter erupted from the dumbfounded and incredulous Task Force.

"Hey, hey, hey, folks, you want answers, you have to accept my methods," insisted Sarzeau, mildly amused by the effect she was having.

Stony silence.

"Where's the bathroom? I need one. With a good mirror."

Upshaw pointed toward the corridor.

"Be right back."

After Sarzeau left the room, scornful glances passed back and forth.

"This is science?" snorted Garibaldi.

No one had an answer.

▼

In the bathroom, Sarzeau withdrew a small stone on a leather necklace from under her shirt; a talisman she had acquired from a dolmen in France some years ago. She reached into a pocket and curled her fingers around a small acorn that had mysteriously appeared on the steps outside her Applefield home a few weeks previously. She held both hands up high, gripping the objects in tight fists. She stared into the mirror above the sink.

"Whiskeyjack — !" she whispered.

Marianne Sarzeau came from a family of adepts, a long line of people possessed of unusual abilities, and the strangest and most unsettling to everyone — including her — was the power to communicate with beings from the spirit world who, when properly called, appeared in mirrors. *Virtual visitors* was the term scholarly books on the occult used to describe them. It started with her police chief, the ghost of a murdered human being traveling backward in time, but later that contact was replaced by an actual demon, a stupendous and fearsome monster. She shivered every time she performed her little summoning ritual.

At first, on this occasion, nothing happened. A minute or more passed. Then her hands began to tingle, and the mirror darkened.

"Marianne, we meet again. Both of us far from home."

The voice, strong and clear, was entirely a mental ripple in her head.

"Well, hello, there. How's Ogg?"

"He has been obliterated, and I continue."

"You are the best."

"Among the best, surely."

Staring at her from the depths of the mirror was a smoky apparition whose outlines shifted and swirled. A pair of glowing blue eyes held her in a hypnotic gaze.

Three years and two kids intervened between the present moment and her last contact, when the demon she called Whiskeyjack rescued her from the lust of a supernatural rival. She was still grateful. That is, when she could remain calm enough to acknowledge any feelings at all.

"Listen, old pal, thanks again for keeping me intact."

"My duty, indistinguishable from my pleasure. How may I be of service today?"

"Like this — a group of scientists I'm with have discovered a foreign presence here on Earth. We want to know where it came from. Maybe you live there. Or did a tour on vacation. How about it?"

"Was this presence conjured by someone?"

"No, they just found some stuff. Imagine metal bushes."

"I know nothing of such things. They are of your world, not mine."

"Damn, I was hoping."

"Do you still dream?"

"You mean the vivid technicolor nightmares?"

"Exactly."

"Now and then. They always scare the shit out of me."

"Be brave. Search the dreamworld. If your purpose is strong, if your mind is bold, that is where you will find answers to your questions."

43

"I need a bed," announced Sarzeau upon rejoining the ITF team.

"We've already booked you into a hotel downtown," said Upshaw. "Don't worry about it. We're done here anyway, so we won't keep you up."

"No, no, I need a bed right here, on the basketball court. I'm going to sleep beside Dasher tonight."

"Oh no you're not!" protested the general. "Are you crazy?"

"Or crazier than we think?" mused Garibaldi with a little smile.

"I'm serious. I need to dream . . . to dream of faraway places."

A chill settled over the group.

"Is this one of your so-called powers?" wondered Weatherall, suppressing a shiver.

"I have, on occasion, experienced vivid dreams that have a basis in reality," explained Sarzeau. "No guarantees. As you guys are quick to notice, what I do it ain't science."

"Not science," repeated Boggs, with an odd look in his eye.

"Nope. But if you think what I do is supernatural fakery, think again. Reality is more mysterious than you scientists have ever imagined. You have no idea."

The group absorbed Sarzeau's tart rebuke with shuffles and grumbles.

"We can't leave you alone in there, sound asleep," said Upshaw, pushing past the awkward moment. "It's dangerous. Who knows what could happen?"

"Turn the lights out, stand guard if you want."

Garibaldi was on Sarzeau's side. "We can make a cage. It might not survive a determined attack, but it would give us time to perform a rescue."

Upshaw paced the room. "Cost-benefit, where are we?" "You, Miss Adept Witch Person — what are the odds?"

Sarzeau shrugged. "Not good, but not zero either. I've already started to get acquainted with your guest. My take is, he's no threat. I'm not afraid."

"Me neither, but I'm not going in there."

Holzgraf raised his hand. "I'll buy some hardware cloth. We can bend it into a shelter. Double it up. Call your carpenters, get them to make a frame, and I'll be back in a flash.

Upshaw duly summoned the carpenters. A frame big enough to hold a sleeping bag and an air mattress was hammered together. An hour later Holzgraf returned with a roll of wire mesh and an electrically powered industrial stapler. Together he and the carpenters bent the metal fabric into a tent-like hollow and stapled it down to the frame. Lockwood and Boggs carried the result into the darkened gymnasium.

Sarzeau took off her shoes and her jeans, embarrassing the men, who made a point of looking away. She grabbed a sleeping bag offered by Chow and tiptoed into the room wearing just her T and panties under the requisite bunny suit.

Lockwood and Holzgraf followed. Lockwood had his Sig-Sauer in his hand. Holzgraf hoisted his Glock.

"You got a permit for that thing?" asked Lockwood.

"You bet."

"Can you use it?"

"I'm trained and I'm careful. I'll follow your lead."

"All right then. Going to be a long night."

"Yup."

Sarzeau watched them approach and take up stations on either side of her bag.

"Hey, you guys, get out of here."

"No way."

"It won't work with you around. Outside, both of you. Lock the door."

Lockwood picked up his phone, called Upshaw. "We're being excused. Got some guidance for your boys?"

Upshaw was staring down on the scene from the upstairs window. He blew out a puff of exasperation. "We've come this far. I'm not happy, but I think we have to bow to our visitor."

Lockwood put his gun away. "Okay, woman, you're on your own. Yell if you need us."

"Roger that," said Sarzeau.

The two men lowered the makeshift cage over her sleeping bag.

"G'night."

Once the men were out of the gym, Sarzeau readied herself for the night ahead. First, a prayer, she thought:

Now I lay me down to sleep;
I pray the Lord my soul to keep.
If I should die before I wake,
I pray the Lord my soul to take.

She laughed inwardly at her superstitions and her childish way of deflecting them. What she really needed was a focusing spell. Her old family spellbook contained hundreds of incantations for various purposes, all written in traditional rhyming couplets. She proceeded to recite one from memory in a soft voice:

Now fly me to the world of Dreams,
Where seldom is whate'er it seems.
I hereby leave the Earth behind
To journey far from my own kind.
May secrets strange embrace my soul;
But let no demons take their toll!

44

Eight hours later, morning sun was shining brightly over Tucson. Sunbeams poked into the Davis-Monthan gymnasium from a line of skylights high over the basketball court.

Chow found both Lockwood and Holzgraf asleep just outside the door.

"Hey, you two."

They jerked awake and jumped to their feet.

"Damn."

It took a few seconds to get themselves oriented. They were both puzzled and abashed by their failures on duty.

"How long were we out?" wondered Holzgraf.

"Got me," said Lockwood.

"How about our advisor lady in there?"

They peeked into the gym. Sarzeau was still asleep, but not inside the cage. Somehow during the night she had wriggled free, and was now snuggled up against the respectfully inert Dasher.

"Oh shit," said Holzgraf.

The three of them cracked open the gym door, stole inside, and attempted to wake her up.

"Marianne — ?"

"Hey, there — !"

"How you doing — ?"

No answer. Sarzeau did not respond.

Chow held the door open while Lockwood and Holzgraf carried her out into the hallway.

Upshaw arrived to frown upon developments. Carpenters arrived soon thereafter to hammer the barricade back into place.

In Upshaw's office, Sarzeau was eased onto the sofa. Air base EMTs were soon on their way. But when they arrived with their medical bags, ready with resuscitators and defibrillators, Sarzeau was sitting up. Her skin was almost translucently pale. She was in a daze.

"Look at me," commanded the first EMT. "Know where you are?"

"Uhhh . . ."

"What's your name?"

"Uhhh . . . still Marianne, I think."

"You think?"

She nodded. "I'm sure."

"That's good, that's great. How many fingers?" The EMT held up his hand balled into a fist.

"No fingers."

The EMTs stood back, looked to General Upshaw, who raised his eyebrows in an unspoken question.

"She'll live, sir," said the senior man.

"Give her a few minutes," said his partner. "She's just very sleepy."

Upshaw nodded, and the EMTs departed.

Sarzeau moaned and tilted her head down between her legs. "News flash — I've got a terrific hangover," she said.

Upshaw poured coffee from a dispenser and handed the cup to Weatherall. She held it under Sarzeau's nose.

"You okay, hon?"

Sarzeau sipped the coffee. She shuddered. "Sugar. Cream. Then I'm good," she said, looking around at an office full of long faces. "This is embarrassing. Where are my clothes?"

Chow produced her flannel shirt and jeans. Sarzeau stood and bounced around to jam her legs into the pants. Chow then handed over Sarzeau's tiny Beretta PX4 Storm.

"You pack?" asked Upshaw, mildly surprised.

"Always," she replied, strapping the holstered weapon around her ankle.

Garibaldi couldn't contain his curiosity. "You survived our little friend. Any . . . result? Did you dream?"

Sarzeau ignored the questions. "Who's got an English muffin? I'm starved."

Upshaw pushed a box of donuts across his desk. "Best we can do, but you're a cop, right?"

Sarzeau pointed an accusing finger at him. "Ooh, cop joke."

But she scarfed down a donut and started on another.

"Okay, boys and girls," she began with her mouth half full, "here's my story — dateline, dreamland . . ."

Garibaldi quickly arranged his smartphone to record Sarzeau's remarks.

Everyone moved a step closer.

"Got your camera running? Good, because nighttime memories don't last long. And just so you know from the get-go — usually when I dream, it's all about the spirit world, a scary place full of monsters. But this one was all about ordinary reality, you know — just very damned alien."

A chorus: "Tell us."

"Dasher is neutral. Friendly, now that he has all his parts. He's an emissary from a planet where the light is very bright. It washes everything like those mercury vapor lamps in parking lots . . ."

Weatherall interrupted. "What color light?"

"Orange, like a good sunset here."

"K-type starlight, I tell you. Bright you say?"

"Very."

"It only seems bright because the planet is close to the star. There are three planets we know of orbiting there. If the light is bright, that's the inner one. This nails our place of origin."

"I saw a room," continued Sarzeau. "It had like concrete walls, and it was chock-a-block with blinking lights and screens and buttons and dials.

"There was a table in the room. On the table was a little *box*. A cube about yay big" — she held her fingers apart to demonstrate.

"How big?" asked Garibaldi, suddenly paying close attention.

"Four inches, no more than six."

"Right, got it, a box. Go on, please . . ."

"Standing around the table were five people." She paused and shook her head. "No, they weren't really people exactly, but they were creatures. Or robots like Dasher, more likely. You know how we all look kind of the same?"

Chow and Upshaw, painfully aware of diversity issues, exchanged doubtful glances.

"Yes, including you, General, and you, Holly. But these guys, each one was different."

"How's that?"

"They were all glittery. But one of them didn't have a head. Just a squarish body with eyes sticking out front, and tongs for hands on arms like snakes. Another one was built out of metal spheres. It had a face like a Halloween pumpkin. One other dude was curvy and smooth, with an eye that wrapped all the way around its head. If, that is, the bulge I saw was actually a head."

"What were they doing, any idea?" asked Garibaldi.

"That's the easy part. No words, and I doubt they speak English, but I could sense their thoughts. They're waiting. They've been in that room waiting patiently for more than a hundred years."

"I'll bite," said Upshaw, "what are they waiting for?"

"Hard to tell," said Sarzeau. "There's another box. It's here somewhere. Here on Earth. They sent it along with the seeds for the bushes you already found. Now they're waiting for Dasher to help us locate the box. When we open it, the box will send a signal. They'll know about us."

"Good Lord," said Weatherall.

"Quantum entanglement," surmised Garibaldi. "If Ms. Sarzeau here isn't making this up . . . if we find such a box and we open it up, we will disturb a *q-bit*. At least, that's my bet."

"What's a q-bit?" wondered Sarzeau.

"Could be a photon or an electron," explained Garibaldi, excited by his idea. "Either way, it is still connected to its dancing partner, which our galactic pals created at the exact same instant in their matching box on that faraway table."

"A hundred years ago?"

"Sure, why not? Space and time don't erode their connection, or the hazy indeterminate state they share. But the moment we see the q-bit here, and thereby solidify its state, the q-bit in their box will solidify into a definite state too. We will be revealed."

"That's speculation, Roman. It could be a radio."

Garibaldi shook his head emphatically. "No tiny box four inches across could send an ordinary radio signal to another star. It just wouldn't be powerful enough."

"Okay, let's say there's a whatchamacallit q-bit in there. But it will still take them eleven years to get the message. We'll have time to think." said Upshaw.

"No, Mo, the q-bit on our end already took a hundred years to arrive. The news will travel instantaneously. Forget speed of light."

"This is possible?"

"This is quantum mechanics. Schrodinger's famous quantum cat, neither dead or alive until the box is opened, and then — *bing!* — spooky action at a distance. We do this stuff all the time in our own primitive way, but only between Florence, Italy, say, and Switzerland."

"Christ Almighty on His cross."

"One more thing before I forget," said Sarzeau, devouring her third donut, "in order to be sure the box doesn't open by accident, there's a code. It's a puzzle."

Later that morning Weatherall showed Sarzeau her diagram of the suspected impact zone encircling Tucson.

"This is where we found all the bushes. Where do you put that box?" she asked.

Sarzeau studied the map, then placed a finger on an empty area south and east of the city.

"Out that way," she said.

▼

Holzgraf and Chow drove Sarzeau back to the airport after lunch.

Chow was perplexed by the thought of her departure. "You should stick around. Now that we're hot onto that box, we're just getting started."

"Gotta go home. I've done all I can here."

"What's so important back home?"

Sarzeau was staring out the side window of Holzgraf's big Jeep. Her thoughts were far away.

"California weather, for one thing. Plus two kids for my lonely husband to wrangle."

"Kids," gushed Chow. "Wow, is your family all like you?"

"Tom? No, he's a regular guy. My daughter Rachel? Not sure yet. My son Gabriel, though, is a prodigy. Gotta watch that cute little fella every minute."

"What's he up to? Does he do spells and dream and stuff?"

"Now and then he can move things. With his mind. It's something to see."

This idea sobered Chow. "That is so weird."

"Very weird, even for me." Thinking about her son made her smile. "And to top it all off, I've got my radio show tomorrow night."

"You're kidding," said Chow, suddenly aware that their visitor's voice had a sonorous theatrical quality.

"Nope, I'm the Golden Girl of the Golden Hills on KVIG-FM. You can listen all the way down here, if you want, on the internet."

Holzgraf pulled up to the SkyWest gate. "Got your carry permit handy?"

Sarzeau waved a piece of paper. "Right here. It's Federal, and that always impresses the TSA."

She slipped out of the car, took a few steps, hesitated, then turned around and rapped on the passenger window. Chow lowered the glass, and Sarzeau leaned inside.

"Listen, I didn't say anything before, but I think you should know — there's something very strange about that old prospector."

"Chester Boggs?"

"Yeah, him. Stay alert."

"What is it? What's wrong?" Holzgraf was shocked by the insinuation.

"I don't have an answer, and I don't want to alarm you. Just, you know, eyes wide."

"Uhh, you are being awful damn mysterious."

"Oh, and there's something funny about Captain Lockwood as well."

"Whoa," said Chow, visibly stung. "what on Earth?"

Sarzeau touched a finger to her forehead. "I get the same vibe. Not sure what it means. Are you sweet on him?"

Chow shook her head. "What a question!"

"I could be wrong. My powers come and go. But maybe . . . is he gay?"

Chow reddened. "I don't believe it!"

Sarzeau's mouth curled into a wry smile. She shrugged. "Thanks for the ride. Be safe, you two, and if you can't be safe, be lucky."

Holzgraf and Chow watched their psychic consultant wheel her roll-around into the terminal.

"What was *that* all about?" exploded Holzgraf when she was out of sight. He was fighting off a sensation of vertigo, as if the familiar world had suddenly turned upside down.

"I think she's full of shit," pouted Chow.

45

Ty Durango was sitting at home in the grip of March Madness, watching the annual NCAA basketball tournament on TV. The University of Arizona Wildcats, Tucson's darlings, were in the Sweet Sixteen with a solid small ball offense and a fearsome defense. He was stoked about their chances.

His phone rang. An unknown number. He answered, but the caller had already hung up. Ty punched a contact on his list.

In an apartment about a mile away, Earl's phone rang.

"Yo, bro, I just got the call. Can you believe? Old Boggs. Something's up."

"Sure it wasn't some damn robocall?"

"How can I be sure?"

"I'll swing by," said Earl.

Boggs and the Durango brothers had previously agreed to meet once a week at the Home Depot on Broadway, not far from Davis-Monthan Air Force Base, with the proviso that anything urgent would be signaled by dialing Ty Durango's mobile phone and hanging up after the first ring. Explaining the procedure to the elderly prospector took the better part of an hour and left the brothers shaking their heads.

Earl motored across town to Ty's place, and the two of them headed for Home Depot, where they found Boggs in the garden shop, staring at plants.

"Yo, Chet, my man, what's cooking?" asked Earl.

Boggs scratched his beard. He folded his arms. "ITF think they've got a line on something up in the hills. Some kind of box."

"Not another bush?" probed Ty.

"Not as I can make out."

Earl squinted at the problematic old man. "What you call an *artifact*," he said.

"That's it, that's what they're calling it."

"Where'd you say?"

"I didn't, 'cause they — the ITF — we — don't know exactly. Somewhere out a ways east of here, in the Encantada Wilderness, south of the national park."

"We were up that way, chasing the thing from Jurnegan's lab."

"Right, so were Lockwood and me. The spot they're looking at is way beyond."

Ty kicked at a bag of potting soil. "Encantada Wilderness, that's rough country. Why there?"

"Someone told them scientists where, that's why."

"Who told them?"

"They hired a woman."

"Another scientist."

"No, she's a cop. But not no ordinary one. They say she's a witch."

"A fucking *witch?* Did you see her?"

"Oh sure I did. Doesn't look like a witch. Just a kid, you ask me. Cute as a button, though."

"A witch. How did she figure it out when the bookheads can't?"

"I believe they said she had a dream."

"Fuck me. A dream. And you expect us to act on this?"

"They're having a big powwow. But they'll get rolling, not a doubt in my mind, once they finish talking. Thing is, they're not the best trackers the world has ever seen. Be nice to have *someone* find whatever it is. Box or not."

▼

Basil Temkhin was waiting for the Durangos in the AJ's coffee shop in the Catalina foothills. When they arrived, he handed them each a tall latte. They sat down on stools at a little table to talk things over.

"Good coffee," said Earl, looking for a way to ease into the matter at hand.

Temkhin smiled broadly. "I love America! Look at all fine things on shelves." He extended his arms to celebrate the excellent cuts of meat on display in brushed stainless steel cases, the mind-numbing selection of aged cheeses, the bewildering variety of boxed goods, the perfectly shaped vegetables piled high in drip-irrigated bins, the entire store.

"Unh-huh," said Ty, "expensive shit here."

"In all of *Rossya,* nothing like this. Not in *Moskva,* not in *Petrograd,* not anywhere. Here, truly, you Americans are consumer society. I bow in admiration!"

Earl clocked a tough old man with white hair and a broken nose sitting on the other side of the shop. He nudged Ty, who nodded knowingly.

Temkhin's driver and, so it seemed, his bodyguard. The man looked like he was good at the job.

"Here's the situation," said Earl, pressing on. "We have info that the government operation has discovered an artifact up in the hills on the other side of town."

"What artifact?"

"Some kind of box, apparently."

"A box." Temkhin's body language expressed indifference.

"Yup."

"Bolshoy? Malenky?"

"Uhh, size? No idea. We were told it's a code box."

Temkhin straightened up in his chair. "Code? *Code box?* Now, I have interest." He grinned. "Purely for mineral properties, *da?*"

"The location is almost inaccessible," said Ty. "We will be working in competition with the government. It will be risky."

"So?"

"So," insisted Earl, "we want to be paid, no matter what. We bring you the box or we don't. Either way, fifty-thousand bucks."

Temkhin chuckled. "My boys, I pay. Bring box from another world? Hundred thousand!"

"It will have to be cash."

"Khorosho. On — what you say? — barrelhead," affirmed Temkhin.

46

Weatherall pinned a large paper map to the wall of Upshaw's office. A wide circle drawn in yellow hi-liner rimmed the City of Tucson. Red dots marked the original locations of every known bush.

Upshaw, Garibaldi, Lockwood, Boggs, Holzgraf, and Chow gathered around for a team briefing.

"Here's the impact radius in yellow. Statistically the seeds, or whatever they were, showered down preferentially around this circular perimeter, as you can see by the dots."

"Professor Jurnegan's journal entries helped us fill in the gaps," said Garibaldi.

"That's right," acknowledged Weatherall. "and the pattern is now well-defined."

"Why don't we see any bushes in the middle of the circle?" asked Chow.

"Good question. Roman?"

Garibaldi ran a finger across the diagram. "At first it looked like a fluke. But now we think the incoming craft, which has not been recovered, may have used some sort of active dispersal mechanism as it fell through the atmosphere. Either that, or our bushes can't grow on concrete in a city environment."

Upshaw scratched his head. "So, to the point — where is the craft and where is the artifact Ms. Sarzeau claims was deposited here?"

Boggs pointed a finger eastward. "That damn critter was running up that way when we found it. Must be near there."

Weatherall nodded. "I showed our, ahem, spiritual advisor, if that's the term, a version of this map. She reported the artifact's existence, and I wanted to see if she had gleaned any idea of its whereabouts."

"And — ?"

"Yes, apparently so. Same area Chet, here, just indicated. Quite a bit beyond where we found Dasher." Weatherall touched the map at a location south and east of the city.

Lockwood checked the area. "The Encantada Wilderness. Looks like rugged territory."

"Unh-huh," Weatherall agreed. "And the information came to her in a dream. *A dream."*

Grumbles from the group.

"Question is," continued Weatherall, "do we trust her dreams?"

"I don't trust anything," muttered Chow.

"We don't have to trust her, we have Dasher," said Garibaldi.

"If she's right about his role here."

Upshaw regarded the map as a challenge. "How high is that big mountain? What's it called, Encantada Peak? I don't have my glasses on."

Lockwood read a number off the map. "7900 feet. Not the highest around, but it's steep there."

Garibaldi inspected the location's tightly grouped contour lines. "Whatever the topography, I propose to recover that artifact, if it exists, with the help of our extraterrestrial acquisition."

Holzgraf was wary of the notion. "Set Dasher loose? What if he just runs away?"

"A chance we have to take." Insisted Garibaldi. "Why are we even debating? It is *unconscionable* to leave an alien artifact lying around when we don't know its characteristics." He ran his hands through his hair in exasperation. "Mo? What do you say?"

Upshaw strode away from the map, made a tour of his office pondering the problem, and plunked himself down at his desk. He shuffled some papers. Then, after a thoughtful interval, he came to a decision.

"I think . . . I think we need to see if Dasher takes an interest. Guy, I want you to light him up. Bright orange."

While the rest of the team gathered at the upstairs window looking down on the basketball court, Holzgraf descended to the hallway below. He plugged in the power cord and adjusted the Variac controller. Intense orange light filled the gym.

"Hey, look —"

While the team watched, the faces of the dodecahedron seemed to soften. Legs protruded. Dasher rose up. Eye stalks sprouted. They surveyed the room. Slowly he turned around and around in place. After a couple of rotations he seemed to get his bearings. He then crept across the floor to one of the exit doors. His front legs came off the floor. Claws appeared. They gripped the panic bar and joggled it.

"Which exit?" queried Upshaw.

Garibaldi pointed this way and that, trying to remember directions.

"East," announced Boggs. "That thing is aimed east, like I told you."

"Okay, boys and girls," said Upshaw. That's good enough for me. Let's go. Positive action. But first, Chet, let's glue a tag on Dasher so he can't get lost. Once we're done, that little monster is either going to wind up in Area 51 or the Smithsonian, take your pick."

47

An expedition wheeled out of Davis-Monthan Air Force Base, heading east on Golf Links Road.

Garibaldi led the way in an Air Force 4x4 pickup truck with Dasher tucked safely into a black Kevlar bag and tied down in the load bed. Boggs kept an eye on him from the passenger seat.

Following behind in a Ford Explorer were Upshaw and Weatherall, and behind them came Holzgraf in his four-door Jeep Wrangler Unlimited.

As they turned south a NASA helicopter with Lockwood and Chow inside caught up with the two vehicles. It cruised along above them for a mile or two before flying on ahead.

Boggs consulted a map on his smartphone, directing Garibaldi east onto Escalante Road and then south again on Old Spanish Trail.

"How far?" asked Garibaldi, uncertain of the topography.

"Miles to go," said Boggs.

Up ahead, the helicopter flew over Jurnegan's lab and on into high country. With every mile the hills became taller, the slopes steeper.

Chow spotted a narrow dirt road below. "Hey, we can drive up here."

"Old mining roads," said Lockwood. "They're all over the place. Get on the horn. Let's show them the way."

▼

Earl and Ty Durango sat in their Hummer within sight of the main entrance to the air base. They were waiting in the parking lot of the Circle K gas station for word from Chester Boggs, and to pass the time they were munching peanuts and sticks of beef jerky. Their radio was tuned to a talk show whose host was fulminating about the liberal tilt of American politics. His brutal remarks brought chuckles and snickers to the brothers, whose military experience gave them a comparatively tolerant point of view.

"We deport all the immigrants, and they'll just come back."

"Like homing pigeons."

"We build a wall, and they build tunnels."

"We are fucked."

"At least they can cook. Look at this crap we're eating."

Earl threw a partially gnawed corn dog out of his window.

A flight of A-10s took off, climbing right over them. The deafening sound of their engines interrupted all conversation. When they had roared off into the distance, Ty voiced a worry.

"What about this box we're after? Talk about your immigrants. What if ET is here already? And he isn't a cute little guy, but some five-eyed monster or what the hell?"

"Why just one? All those bushes Jurnegan had growing, why not a whole squad? A landing party, reconnaissance. Checking us out."

"Then what?"

"Then grab your gun, bro, grab your gun."

Ty's phone rang. He answered, but the caller had hung up.

"Boggs. They must be on their way. See anything?"

"What's that truck? And there goes an Explorer with 'ITF' on the side."

"Plus, looks like a Jeep is joining the parade."

Just then a white helicopter climbed out of the base. It passed overhead and swerved east, following the three vehicles along Golf Links Road.

"Hey, that's the NASA chopper."

Earl started the Hummer rolling.

"Hang back, don't let them see us."

48

When the ITF pickup truck reached Powerline Road, Boggs noticed that the Kevlar bag in the load bed was urgently rocking back and forth.

"Hey, stop, Doc. Dasher's getting restless."

Garibaldi pulled to the shoulder and parked. Upshaw and Holzgraf stopped just behind. The team members all got out and stared at the bag. Trapped inside, the alien entity was bobbing and lurching.

"I thought it took a lot of light to fire him up," said Weatherall.

"Must be reserve energy," thought Holzgraf, "like a battery."

The NASA helicopter appeared overhead, pivoted around, and landed in an open area on the far side of the road. Lockwood and Chow crossed over to investigate.

"What's up?"

Garibaldi pointed to the load bed of his truck where the Kevlar bag was bouncing up and down.

"Time to return our critter to the wild," he said.

"We don't know that, not for sure," countered Upshaw.

"Let's vote," said Lockwood.

"Jim?" Upshaw was disturbed by his assistant's appeal to democracy.

"That's why we're here, right? See where Dasher leads us. Seems to me he's on the scent."

Upshaw made a conciliatory salute. "All right. Six votes for you, six votes for me."

Garibaldi shook his head. "Come on, Mo, for God's sake." He turned to his companions. "Everybody, show of hands."

All the hands went up. Upshaw's brow clouded, and then he slowly raised his own hand.

"It's unanimous, twelve to zero," totaled Weatherall, earning herself a dirty look from the general.

Holzgraf climbed into the truck bed.

"Careful, Guy."

"I'm not worried."

"Wait a minute!" objected Chow. "You can't let him do this! If Dasher is feeling grouchy he could lose an arm."

"We decided," said Upshaw.

"The man is accident prone," she asserted. " Let me." She hitched herself up onto the tailgate.

Holzgraf made a face, raised his hands in mock surrender, then bent over and, preempting any further objections, quickly tugged the straps of Dasher's bag loose.

The dodecahedron rapidly developed six jointed legs and a pair of eye stalks. Before Lockwood could lower the tailgate, Dasher was out of the bag and over the side of the truck. He scuttled away across the road and into the desert beyond.

"Whoa! Tracker in place?" worried Upshaw.

"I glued it myself personally," replied Boggs.

"Start that sucker!"

Garibaldi was staring at a handheld radio direction finder with a tree-like antenna mounted on top.

"Got him! Going east."

Lockwood and Chow ran for the chopper. Garibaldi handed the tracker to Weatherall. "You ride with me now. Stay on that thing."

The team remounted their vehicles. The helicopter flew a quarter of a mile south, then settled into a hover.

"There, they found a trail."

The procession turned onto a dirt track under the chopper and slowly bumped, jolted, and slewed upward into increasingly hilly country.

"Still got him?"

Weatherall bit her lip. "Hard to aim this damn thing. He's off to our right, turning south."

Ahead of the team, Dasher was moving fast. His legs were a blur, throwing sand into the air with every step. He ran through a flat section of desert, dodging the cholla and creosote. Then he angled back eastward and skipped across a narrow road, where he barely missed being struck by the ITF truck.

"Holy shit," exclaimed Garibaldi, screeching to a halt. The rest of the team plowed up gravel and smashed bushes flat to avoid a collision. They all sat there without moving until the enormous cloud of dust raised by their evasive maneuvers dissipated.

▼

Half a mile away on a different dirt road, the Durangos were standing beside their Hummer, watching through binoculars.

"That thing they let loose. Like Boggs said, it's leading them to the magic box."

"We hope."

"Yeah, let's go. I don't see their eggbeater. I think those guys picked the wrong road."

They remounted their vehicle and continued uphill, turning this way and that around the many knobs and rock outcrops.

▼

In the ITF team's pickup truck, Weatherall waved the direction finder antenna back and forth.

"I lost him. No, there he is. Whoa, he stopped."

"You sure?"

"No. This toy is hit and miss."

"But you think so."

"Yes, right up ahead. Southeast."

Garibaldi pressed a button on a walkie-talkie. "Now hear this — Nan says our rabbit has stopped running."

"Where do you make him?"

"Couple hundred yards left. Follow me."

Garibaldi slowed to a crawl and vectored off into the weeds. The Explorer and Jeep followed.

"Okay, okay, we got him," said Weatherall, leaning close to the direction finder screen. "Left, left, a little further. Here he is!"

Garibaldi stopped the truck.

"I don't see anything."

"He's right here."

Everyone got out and started patrolling. Holzgraf took a few steps toward a tall saguaro, having spotted something shiny.

"Over here, folks."

He leaned down and picked up a small flat object, a couple of inches on a side: a circuit board, with a tiny lithium battery glued on the back and a short copper antenna sticking out. He held it up for all to see, where it glittered impressively in the afternoon sunshine.

"Damn," said Garibaldi.

"Our tracker. Who did the gluing anyway?"

"I think Boggs," said Garibaldi. "Someone should have checked his work."

"Someone should have, that's for sure."

Upshaw activated his walkie-talkie. "Jim? We lost our tag. What does our eye in the sky see?"

The NASA helicopter rose over the nearest ridge, turned over their heads and moved away uphill.

"No joy on Dasher, I'm afraid," said Lockwood.

Chow stared hard at the ground below.

"Wait, wait, we do see a trail," she announced. "It goes right by you guys. Follow us."

49

"There it goes!"

The Durangos were parked on a little-used dirt track that was nearly invisible under new growth. Both were off in the brush relieving themselves.

Ty pointed up a long slope.

"There! See? Zip up, bro, we got that runner."

Back inside the Hummer, Earl turned off the faint roadway and steered straight up the slope. The truck bucked and groaned, its engine whining with heroic effort.

Within minutes they were rolling along the trail left by the alien entity. After many more minutes they crested the local hilltop and there, crouching before them, was the otherworldly creature.

Earl skidded to a stop.

"Let's bag the bastard."

They grabbed nets and plastic bags out of their truck and advanced upon their quarry.

"You know, Boggs told us everyone is calling this thing 'Dasher'," said Earl.

"What you called your lost dog that night we waxed those campers."

"Yeah, that's funny, except we didn't wax them. They're part of the government op. And they're here. I spotted them back a ways."

A few more steps.

"At least we're not murderers."

"Not yet."

The alien creature was sitting under an umbrella of crystalline leaves, soaking up solar energy of the slightly wrong kind.

Earl licked his lips. "Here you are, Dasher. Good doggie!"

Ty cast a net over him. Earl stepped forward and attempted to pull a bag down over the thing.

But Dasher didn't cooperate. The crystalline leaves disappeared into his body. Claws like knives appeared on his legs. He thrashed, slicing through the net and shredding the plastic bag.

"Fuck!"

Earl fell over backwards. Ty retreated into a teddy bear cholla and howled in pain. He brought up his pistol.

Dasher spun around and around, then tore off down the far side of the hill and started up another. Ty never got a shot off.

Earl stood and scanned his wounds. Blood was dripping from multiple cuts on his hands and arms.

"Jesus Lord, would you look at me."

50

Upshaw's Air Force pickup truck soon proved inadequate to the Encantada landscape and was abandoned. Only Holzgraf's Jeep had the tires and torque to ascend the slopes the team now faced. Weatherall, Boggs, and Garibaldi gratefully joined him.

"Where's Upshaw?"

"Down the hill. That Explorer is useless in these conditions, no better than the truck."

"Christ, have we lost him?"

"The chopper picked him up. We'll rendezvous up on top somewhere."

"Oh great."

Holzgraf shifted into low range and coaxed the Jeep up the steep, almost invisible roadway. After a couple hundred yards they surmounted a local rise, and there to their left were the Durango brothers and their Hummer.

Ty waved them down.

"It's Earl. Your little pal Dasher cut him up pretty good."

"Got a first aid kit, Guy?" asked Weatherall.

"Under the seat."

Earl was propped up on the sill of the Hummer's open passenger door. Weatherall swabbed his wounds with alcohol and applied bandages and tape.

"The cuts are superficial. You'll live."

Earl nodded gratefully, at a loss for words.

Garibaldi was feeling less charitable. "Gentlemen, I warn you, this is a government operation. You're intruding on it. Your actions will be subject to prosecution."

As if to emphasize the government's view of the situation, the team helicopter roared overhead.

"Yeah, yeah," said Ty. "We know the score."

"Do you? Then turn around and go home."

Faced with a challenge, Earl seemed to recover his spirit. "Let's see who gets the brass ring-a-ding, pal. Then we can talk."

Garibaldi puckered his lips. "Do we have to shoot your tires flat?"

Ty laughed.

Holzgraf elbowed Garibaldi. "Uhh, no, no, Doc. They're impervious."

The scientist rolled his eyes. "Fuck it, then. Let's move on."

The team returned to Holzgraf's Jeep. Garibaldi couldn't resist a parting shot. "We've got your number!" he shouted. The Durangos gave the group a cheerful wave.

Holzgraf started slowly up the next incline.

"Insolent bastards," muttered Garibaldi.

"I know them — from Jurnegan's lab," said Boggs. "The Durango brothers. They are tough hombres. This is a contest. The box must be found."

Weatherall and Garibaldi gave the old man a funny look. Garibaldi put in a call to Lockwood, roaming above them.

"Be aware, we've got company. What do you see up there?"

"Not much." Lockwood's voice crackled over the intercom. "Tracks are visible. Up and east, you're on the beam as you are."

Holzgraf found another wisp of a road and centered the Jeep on it. He shifted into low-low gear and followed the track up the steepest pitch the team had yet encountered. The Jeep's engine was screaming, but the wheels were barely turning. Now and then they slipped, and the vehicle lurched sideways. Weatherall and Garibaldi gripped the arms of their seats with white faces and white knuckles.

The Durangos' Hummer followed for a few hundred yards, then veered away on a different path. Soon it was lost to sight around a rocky butte.

▼

After an agonizing climb, Holzgraf maneuvered his Jeep onto a small plateau standing out from the hills and buttes. He angled across it and stopped. The slope ahead was much too steep to negotiate in a vehicle. The group stumbled out to have a look around.

Holzgraf doubted the Durangos could have gotten much further. "Anyone spot that Hummer?"

Headshakes from his companions.

Just then the pounding rhythm of helicopter rotors turned their attention to the sky. In another moment the NASA ship appeared above the eastern slope. It circled over them, then settled down in a nearby flat spot. Hands went up to shield eyes as the machine blew a cloud of sand and dust over the group.

"Pfooie," said Weatherall, chewing grit.

The cabin door opened and Lockwood, Upshaw, and Chow dropped to the ground. They reached back inside and dragged half a dozen bulky duffel bags out of the ship and arranged them into a pile. Lockwood waved, and the helicopter took off. It banked away south, then west, back toward the air base. The passengers joined their colleagues. They were carrying packs and camping gear.

"There goes our ride," said Weatherall, dismayed by the steep terrain all around them and the prospect of trudging through it.

Lockwood and Chow handed out the packs. Upshaw pointed up the steep slope facing them.

"Up that way, boys and girls. We spotted Dasher's trail, but it's too rough to land a chopper. Now we hike."

Weatherall groaned.

Lockwood and Holzgraf shouldered the biggest packs, hoisted duffels, and set off, picking their way upward and easing the climb by switching back and forth across the incline.

"Come on, Nan, you can do it," said Chow, with an encouraging little punch on the astronomer's arm. She slung a pack across her back, grabbed one of the duffels, and followed the two men.

Upshaw handed a duffel to Garibaldi, picked up the last one remaining, and led the way among the less athletic members of the team.

"Life was easier in space," he remarked.

"I could use some oxygen right here on Earth," moaned Weatherall.

The ITF team slogged uphill for a mile or more before the late winter sun vanished below the western horizon. A hot dry day became cool, and as twilight faded, downright cold. The group busied itself erecting tents and cooking dinner.

"Who wants a hot dog?" asked Lockwood, playing chef.

"Who wants some of this amusing rosé? chimed Holzgraf, holding up a plastic bladder filled with pink liquid.

Murmurs of enthusiasm for both. The team was proud of itself. They had gained more than a thousand feet of altitude in challenging country.

Looking back west and downhill, the lights of Tucson sparkled in the clear dry air. They all found the view breathtaking.

All except Weatherall. "Look at those lights! And Tucson is supposed to be a dark sky city!"

Holzgraf was puzzled. "Dark sky? What do you call this?"

Garibaldi offered an explanation. "City lights reflect off moisture and particles in the atmosphere, wrecking astronomical observations. Tucson belongs to the International Dark Sky Association and has pledged to keep its lights dim and down."

"Oh yeah, they pledged." said Weatherall, full of scorn. "Kitt Peak is about thirty miles over that way, and it won't be long before all those telescopes will be useless."

Upshaw was quick to defend the city and the scientific bureaucracy. "Come on, Nan, they won't be useless."

"Degraded then, how's that?"

"Degraded. A fair description."

"Hey, eat up," urged Lockwood. "Dasher's trail leads up that grade right behind us. Big climb coming."

▼

Chow was perched on a rock away from the group to dodge the smoke from Weatherall's cigarettes. She was nursing a plastic cup of Holzgraf's rosé. Lockwood zigzagged through the scrub with a hot dog and a small bowl of instant mac-and-cheese.

"Here you go, fuel for tomorrow."

Chow accepted the offering with a nod. He sat down beside her.

"I'm looking northwest," she said, pointing. "Out beyond the city, those lights? I can't be sure, Marana or not?"

"That's home?"

"Yeah, I live on a pecan ranch."

"I grew up in Oracle, around behind the Catalinas," noted Lockwood.

"We're the only locals on the team, I guess, huh?"

"I don't feel local. I'm ex-Army. All these scientists, I feel like an outsider." He looked her over. "You too, I bet."

She recoiled. "You mean the Asian thing?"

"Not too many people with your background grew up here."

"Two-point-seven percent," she said, well aware of the details.

"But you've adapted."

"I cope. No problem."

"Outsiders have to define themselves on their own, right?"

Chow wondered what was running through her new teammate's mind. "I suppose."

"I feel the same way. You know, a few years ago, I fell down a cliff and hit my head. Afterwards, for a few minutes I couldn't even remember my own name. I felt outside myself."

"Wow, that's terrible." She leaned around and looked him closely in the eyes. "You're okay now, though, right?" She touched his forehead. "Knock-knock. Still Jim in there?"

"Well, my memory is sketchy. Just flashes from the past."

"Childhood stuff?"

"I remember becoming an Eagle Scout."

"Mom and Dad?"

"I've got photos."

"What fills up the space where the memories should be?"

"Observations. I'm a people watcher. That's how I know how to behave."

She sat back. "Uh-oh. You're watching me?"

"I think you're a good human being."

"Thanks, me too. But that sounds . . . "

"Sounds what?"

Chow thought it sounded kind of eerie. She fumbled for a tactful response.

"Um, really . . . unusual."

"Tell me."

51

To the human eye, a moonless night in the desert of Southern Arizona was plenty dark. The Milky Way blazed above the arid mountains of the Encantada Wilderness. The stars of Orion twinkled in the west. Jupiter was rising. Every now and then the quick blip of a meteor flashed overhead.

Weatherall was counting. She and Chow were admiring the heavens with after-dinner drinks and toasted marshmallows, courtesy of Holzgraf's camping know-how.

"That's seven now," she said.

"A shower?" asked Chow.

"No, just an ordinary night on Planet Earth. Modern life, most people have no idea what's up there."

"What about Dasher? Can you see where he came from?"

Weatherall scanned the sky. "Over there, just above the horizon, the constellation Taurus." She pointed to the west. "I can't actually see the star right now, it's a dim one. But in the fall, it will be around to our east, and that's when he arrived."

"Or his parts, anyway. What a long trip. Long and lonely."

"I like your friend, by the way," declared the astronomer, lowering her gaze to the here and now.

"Friend?"

"Guy Holzgraf. Don't tell me that's a surprise."

Chow was blushing, but it was too dark to tell. "I like him too."

"Good. I see you two angling around each other. It's ridiculous. Do something about it."

"Big step."

"Not that big. Not on the galactic scale of things."

Lockwood and Holzgraf were on the other side of the camp, peering downhill at a different set of lights.

"What do you think?" mused Lockwood. "Our pals with the Hummer?"

"Gotta be their campsite," said Holzgraf. "These are the guys who ran over our tents."

"Got your gun? Who knows?"

"Yeah — who?"

Soon the chilly air made it too uncomfortable to sit around the camp stove, and everyone retreated into their tents. All except Weatherall, who continued to stare at the sky, alone with her shooting stars.

▼

Later on, Holly Chow poked her head out of her tent. All was quiet except for old Boggs; she could hear him snoring away. But not everyone was asleep, she noticed. A lamp in Lockwood's little dome made the fabric glow. Up late reading?

She crawled outside and stood up. She was wearing a light wool shirt over pink panties. Bare legs made her shiver. Where was Weatherall? There, over on the edge of camp, now all bundled up with a blanket over her knees, facing south. The red end of a cigarette gave her location away.

Chow rubbed her legs to keep off the chill, bit her lip, and made a decision. When she was sure the coast was clear she daintily tiptoed across the campsite, eyes raised to pretend she was stargazing. As she neared Lockwood's tent a faintly audible voice made her pause. The man inside was mumbling. She couldn't make out the words, but it sounded like an ugly conversation with himself. It made her skin prickle.

▼

Holzgraf was dozing when the flap of his tent noisily unzipped. Not for the first time. His eyes flew open. He got himself up on one elbow and felt around for his Glock.

"What in hell?" he mumbled.

"Do you know what I did?" came a girlish whisper.

In the dim light he could just make out the shadowy form of another person.

"Holly?"

She was kneeling beside his sleeping bag. "I was over by Jim's tent just now."

"Unh-huh." Holzgraf tried to swallow the upsurge of jealousy that caught in his throat. "Why tell me?"

"I thought you'd be interested."

"Christ, woman, I was almost asleep."

"Want to know what happened?"

"Do I? Probably not."

"I heard him talking to himself."

"What?"

"He sounded angry. And he sounded kind of mechanical."

"Well, he's got a lot to worry about," said Holzgraf, interested to find himself vastly relieved by her news. "Mind on the mission, that's normal."

"Think so? What if I was planning to duck into his tent? See if he wanted some company?"

Holzgraf was shocked. "Did you?"

"I did not. But — I would have made a good case for myself."

"No doubt."

"I got to thinking about Marianne's warning, so I was eavesdropping. She had him nailed. That man is strange. I don't think he has feelings like the rest of us."

"Really? You were going to try and seduce him?"

"Would that bother you?"

Holzgraf winced.

"Should it?" he replied, in a voice thick enough to betray his feelings.

"I'll take that as a 'yes,'" she murmured. "Okay then, since you're wondering, here's how I would have made my pitch."

She removed her flimsy shirt. Nothing underneath. The starlight was faint, but Holzgraf was pretty sure he was staring at Chow's left nipple right in front of his nose.

"Good God, Chow."

She kicked off her panties. He became aware of a darker patch between dimly seen thighs.

"So what is it — I'm Plan B?"

"No, this is Plan A."

Chow tugged at a corner of Holzgraf's sleeping bag, poked a leg inside.

"Now wait a minute," he said. "I let you in here, how do I know you won't sue my ass for sexual assault and rape ten years down the line?"

Chow squirmed into the sleeping bag and snuggled down beside him.

"In ten years we'll be married, so I wouldn't worry about it."

PART SIX

52

In the early hours before dawn, Holly Chow, mindful of discretion and a very full bladder, climbed out of Holzgraf's tent, and wandered away to find a spot to pee.

After the sun was over the mountain, the rest of the group woke up and staggered out of their shelters to greet the new day.

Strong coffee and cellophane-wrapped pastries energized them all.

"Where's Holly?" asked Weatherall.

Holzgraf looked around. No sign of his lover. *His lover!* He was dazzled by the very term. But, he reminded himself, it was true. *Amazing!* And where the hell had she gone?

"Off relieving herself?" he guessed.

"Okay, troops, here's the plan," announced Upshaw. "Nan and I will stay here, guard the camp. The rest of you, find Dasher, and get that box we heard about."

"Yay, team," said Lockwood.

Upshaw smiled. "I'm not good at pep talks. The Durangos are out there. Maybe ahead of us. They must not win this race! Chow? When she turns up, we'll let her know what's going on. Look, your senior colleagues have had enough of the climbing. We await results. Have at it."

▼

A long and exhausting ascent brought the adventurous members of the Immigration Task Force to the crest of a steep hill, and then, following Dasher's trail, down into a narrow valley. There before them was Dasher himself. No eyes were visible. Crystalline leaves were nodding in the morning light. He was recharging his energy reserves once again.

"Whoa!" said Lockwood. "Take it easy, everyone." He toggled the transmitter on his radio. "Yo, general, be advised, target in sight."

Garibaldi edged forward. "Considering his potential, this guy looks pretty sleepy."

Holzgraf placed a cautionary hand on the man's sleeve. "Careful, Doc. Poison ivy doesn't move, and it's still itchy."

"Let's check," said Boggs. He strode boldly up to the thing.

Suddenly Dasher's leaves retracted. He swiveled around to face his visitors. His legs started digging in the hard desert soil, moving so fast they were as blurry as hummingbird wings.

"Hah! So much for the sleep theory," said Garibaldi.

Within minutes a pit appeared under Dasher's feet. And in the pit was a small metallic sphere about the size of a soccer ball.

Garibaldi moved to pick it up and jumped back as Dasher lifted menacing legs.

"Okaaay . . . your move, little guy." He raised his hands in mock surrender.

Tongs appeared on Dasher's front feet. He lifted the sphere out of the pit and, cradling the thing with his middle legs, lightly touched a button on the side.

Hissss . . .

The sphere cracked open. A puff of gas or steam escaped and drifted away in the thin mountain air. The upper half of the sphere fell to the ground.

"Holy crap," said Garibaldi. "An aeroshell!'

Exposed in the lower hemisphere was a tangle of fibrous material.

"With a dust bunny inside," said Holzgraf.

"Jesus, where's a camera?"

Lockwood took several pictures.

Boggs inched up close and reached out. Dasher deposited the spongy ball in his hands. "Thing feels like steel wool."

"May I?" said Garibaldi. "Over here, please."

Boggs dutifully handed the snarl to the scientist.

Everyone crowded around to look.

"Wait a minute. What's this?" Garibaldi pulled on a pair of rubber gloves and tugged at the metallic fibers. They fell away, gradually revealing a dull grey cube. "Someone get a baggie."

Lockwood handed him a plastic bag. Garibaldi spread it on the ground and placed the cube on top.

Dasher's eyestalks tilted to watch the action.

"The box," said Holzgraf. "I call it!"

"No details visible. Size approximately ten centimeters," noted Garibaldi. He produced a small radiation detector from his backpack, flipped switches, unclipped a wand from the side of the case, and pointed it at the cube. He watched a liquid crystal readout while counting to twenty.

"No radiation I can detect. At least it won't fry us."

"What about radio? How did Dasher find it?" wondered Holzgraf.

"Yeah, how?" Garibaldi dug into his pack and came up with a portable spectrum analyzer. He held it near the cube for a few seconds while turning a dial to adjust the frequency response.

"Nothing. Well, not much. There might be a faint signal in the upper end of the S-band. Four gigahertz. It comes and goes."

They all stared at the little cube. No one had ever seen or imagined such a thing. A chill ran up Holzgraf's spine. Here was a device of some mysterious purpose, and it was not made by human hands.

Just then Dasher rattled his legs. All eyes swiveled toward him. They watched in fascination as he started to vibrate, and they gasped in astonishment when, without further warning, he dissolved into a pile of sand.

"Holy shit!"

Lockwood scooped up a handful and let the crystalline particles run through his fingers.

"Get a sample," ordered Garibaldi.

Holzgraf filled a plastic bag with the stuff.

"Dasher's not going to wind up in the Smithsonian after all," said the scientist, shaking his head.

Lockwood wrapped the cube in the plastic bag it was sitting on. He shoved the bundle into his pack. "Let's get out of here."

The team worked its way back up and out of the little valley. At the top of the ridge they suddenly stopped. Waiting for them on the downhill slope were Earl and Ty Durango. They each had a hand on Holly Chow, whose face was pale with fear. Ty was waving a pistol around.

"Hand it over," commanded Earl.

"Or what?" said Garibaldi.

"Or we shoot your girl here."

"You're not going to shoot anybody," growled the scientist, ever defiant.

"Might not kill her. But she'll need a big helping of first aid."

Holzgraf was almost as pale as Chow. "Hey, Doc, take it easy."

"We are duly chartered by the Federal Government of the United States of America," sputtered Garibaldi, now in high dudgeon. "And we are not going to deliver the most important archeological find in the history of the human race to a couple of mercenary criminals."

"Oh no?"

Ty turned his pistol toward Chow's left temple. She cried out involuntarily.

Lockwood felt for the butt of his own sidearm, but he hesitated. "Maybe they're serious, Doctor. We can always track them down later."

"No, no, these are hired hands. They work for somebody."

"We can't stand here forever, gentlemen," warned Earl. "You give us the doo-hickey you've got there, we give you the girl."

Lockwood bent down on one knee, removed the parts of an AR-7 rifle from his pack and rapidly assembled it. He stood up with the weapon pointing at Ty Durango.

"Okay, shoot her," he shouted. "But if you do, you're dead men."

"Hey, hey, hey," yelped Holzgraf, thoroughly alarmed. He grabbed Lockwood's pack with the little grey cube inside, and before anyone on the team could react, he ran down the hillside to the Durangos' position.

"It's in there, in the pack. Take a look."

Earl opened the pack and hauled out the cube. He nodded approval.

"Now give us Ms. Chow. Let her go."

The Durangos beat a quick retreat, dragging Chow along.

"Can't do that, I'm afraid. Then you really *will* shoot us."

In no time they disappeared around a rocky promontory. Holzgraf and the others could still hear Chow pleading and whimpering for a few moments. But soon enough her voice faded into the distance.

Garibaldi could not contain his fury. "You idiot! You just gave away the store! The biggest store in the galaxy!"

Lockwood put a hand on the scientist's shoulder. "Calm down, Doctor. We'll stop them."

"How? How will we stop them? What if they kill her?" Holzgraf was as incensed as Garibaldi.

"Got to risk it. Got to protect that box."

"Fuck you both!"

Holzgraf dropped his own pack. He re-tied his hiking boots with double knots, jammed his hands into leather gloves, and sprinted away; running, skipping, leaping, and sliding down yesterday's path.

He bolted through the team campsite, where Upshaw and Weatherall were finishing cups of coffee, at top speed.

"Whoa! What's the hurry, kid?"

"They've got Holly!" he yelled over his shoulder without slowing down.

Indeed they did. The Durangos dragged Chow down the backside of a long ridge to their Hummer. There Ty shoved her into the rear seat. He dropped the pack containing the little extraterrestrial cube into her lap.

"You found it, you hold it. Any screwing around in there, we shoot you, understand?"

Chow nodded weakly, clutching the pack to her chest.

"And buckle up, for Christ's sake, going to be a bumpy ride."

On the next slope Holzgraf missed his footing and somersaulted ass over teakettle into spiny desert plants. He picked himself up, hardly noticing the pricks and stings he just earned.

Up above, Lockwood got on the radio to Upshaw. Upshaw got on the radio to Davis-Monthan, summoning the NASA helicopter and a pair of armed MP's.

Holzgraf continued running. Where was his Jeep? He was streaking through territory in a few short minutes that had taken long hours to climb. But he hadn't really noticed how far the team had been hiking, and he was near to panic. Another misstep plowed him into the hard desert ground like a baseball player sliding head first into third base.

"Ah, shit," he mumbled, spitting out dirt. He smacked his gloves together, glad of their protection, then tore off down the trail again.

Up an incline, down the side of ridge, around a rock pile, and there — finally! — his Jeep. With hands shaking almost uncontrollably he punched his remote to unlock the door, punched the remote start button to fire up the engine, and clambered inside. He was breathing hard. He was dripping with sweat. It took him several little moves to back around and face downhill. And then, when he got all four wheels onto the downslope, the low range gearing had him descending at a crawl.

"Come on! Come on! Go!"

He levered the transfer case out of low range, and the machine plunged downward, bumping and bouncing over rocks, skidding through the sand. He hit the brakes, ground to a halt, and pulled his seat belt as tight as he could. Then he let her roll again — and immediately ricocheted off a promising young saguaro, knocking it flat.

"Leave nothing but footprints," he warbled. "Right on!" He was giddy with the crazy joy of his reckless escapade.

As the terrain leveled out, he slowed and stopped. He could see that the track he was on would be joined by another one, mostly concealed behind a high ridge, just a few yards farther down the hill.

He killed the motor and cocked an ear to the sounds of the desert. Not much going on . . . a light breeze, a bird twittering, not sure what kind. Somewhere out of sight, the faraway jet engines of an Air National Guard training mission. But then he heard a low rumble. Aha! Here comes that fucking Hummer!

He couldn't see it. But the sound of its engine was getting louder and louder. He restarted the Jeep. Suddenly the Durangos burst into view just ahead of him, heading west and down, traveling fast.

The Jeep lurched forward. Holzgraf gripped the wheel with total determination, aimed at the Hummer's left rear quarter, and slammed the accelerator to the floor.

KA-BLANG!

The deafening impact stopped the Jeep cold and slewed the Hummer sideways. Its right rear tire smacked into a boulder. The force of the secondary jolt snapped the big SUV's nose around and sent it down into a gravelly ditch. Another boulder jacked the front wheels into the air. The Hummer pitched over onto its side, skidded a few yards, and toppled onto its roof. A rock-walled rivulet in the bottom of the ditch caught and cracked the windshield, rolled the machine onto its other side and then, miraculously, snapped it back onto its wheels, where it finally stopped.

Airbags exploded inside both vehicles. Dust filled the air.

Holzgraf, prepared for the smashup, was the first to recover. He leaped out of the Jeep, bounded down to the Hummer and yanked open the rear door.

"Holly! Grab my hand."

Chow was completely discombobulated by the wrenching collision. She fumbled with her seat belt, unhooked it, and rolled out of the Hummer into Holzgraf's arms. She managed a sloppy grin.

". . . accident prone . . ."

The Durangos were dazed by the unexpected crash. They pawed at the collapsing airbags, trying to work themselves free. By the time they understood what happened, Holzgraf, Chow, and their precious artifact were bouncing down the road toward civilization. Steam was rising from the Jeep's heavily damaged radiator.

53

The box.

Garibaldi measured it: 10.74 centimeters on each side, a perfect cube.

He weighed it: 153 grams, about one-third of a pound.

He scanned it: this time with precision lab gear borrowed from the Air National Guard. No ionizing radiation, and now, after being located by Dasher, no detectable radio frequency emissions.

He drew a conclusion: the thing was certainly mysterious, and he did not begin to understand it.

The box was sitting on a small table in the middle of a makeshift laboratory on the air base, in a shop requisitioned by Upshaw that, under other circumstances, was used to maintain and repair aircraft avionics.

"The witch and her dream — be damned, I thought she was a total fake," admitted Weatherall.

"She said there was a box, and what do you know?" said Chow.

"Thanks to these two, we've got it," said Lockwood.

Holzgraf smiled a crooked smile. A patchwork of band aids decorated the cuts on his arms. He tucked a hand around Chow's waist. She was wearing a neck collar. A prominent white bandage was taped to her forehead.

"How do we open it?"

"We don't," said Upshaw. "If that thing notifies an alien civilization of our existence, as we now suspect, we have to defer. Others will want to make the decision."

"Others?"

"Politicians. I don't know how it will work — NASA bigwigs? The State Department? Defense? The President? Above my pay grade."

Garibaldi delicately waved a hand over the cube's surface. "The Sarzeau woman said it would be locked with a code of some kind. A puzzle box."

"I don't see any buttons or controls. It's featureless," observed Weatherall. Both scientists were obviously lusting to investigate.

"Now, now, you guys. This is serious," warned Upshaw.

Garibaldi shrugged. "You're right, of course. We don't know what's going on. But committees are scared of their own shadows. If enough decision-makers get involved, we'll never open it."

Upshaw stood firm. "Two stalwart members of the AF Security Forces will rotate on guard. They will have your names. Work in pairs. Remote sensing, okay. But no destructive testing."

Garibaldi delivered an ironic salute. "Yes sir, Mo."

▼

In spite of their bumps and bruises, Holzgraf and Chow volunteered to stand watch. His first act was to roam along the shop's workbench until he found a remote-sensing thermometer gun.

"Garibaldi did some scanning, but he didn't take its temperature."

"Think it's got a fever?"

"No, but it could be dead. It's what? At least a hundred years old."

"And no battery replacement."

"Right."

He aimed the thermometer at the workbench and pressed the trigger. The digital readout flickered up and down, then stabilized.

"Seventy-three-point-five."

He then targeted the little cube.

"Seventy-three-point-seven-five."

"It's warmer than the room," said Chow. "Not dead."

"So it seems. See anything?"

Chow was squinting at the cube.

"Nope."

"Damn."

Chow shaded the object from the glare of the fluorescent tubes shining down overhead.

"Wait, maybe . . . something . . . I think. Kill the room lights."

Holzgraf did so.

"Oh my God!" exclaimed Chow. "Now look!"

She stood away from the cube as Holzgraf approached. In the near darkness they could both see the glimmering outlines of little squares appearing on each of the cube's faces. Their skin started to prickle. They backed away across the room. The flickering display faded.

Chow rubbed her arm to flatten the hairs back down. "Whoa, got me."

Holzgraf shivered. "Yeah, spooky."

After a tense moment, Holzgraf beckoned Chow. They tiptoed forward.

When they were within a yard or two, the flickering resumed.

"Uh-oh, it knows we're here."

"Careful now . . ."

"Hey, whatcha got there?" One of the airmen on guard could not suppress his curiosity. He opened the lab door, casually ambled into the room, and peered over their shoulders at the cube flashing away.

"What is that thing?"

"Sorry, can't discuss it. Classified," said Holzgraf.

"Oh, secret weapon, huh?"

"You know the story — 'neither confirm nor deny,'" said Chow. She pointed to the door. "Move! Back to your post."

The airman rolled his eyes and retreated.

▼

Garibaldi was relaxing over coffee in Upshaw's office when he heard the news. He dropped his cup in the waste basket and hurried down to the lab. Weatherall was right behind him.

There, Holzgraf and Chow demonstrated the cube's slightly elevated temperature and darkened the room again to show off the flickering square outlines.

"We'll take over, you kids can skedaddle," announced Garibaldi. "Go get some sleep."

Weatherall looked the two up and down. She smiled. "You can lick each other's wounds . . . figuratively speaking, of course."

54

In a paved turnout on South Houghton Road, just outside the heavily developed outer edges of Tucson, the Durango brothers were killing time in their beat-up Hummer.

"I liked that spot up in the foothills better. More people, civilized, keep our business businesslike."

"Yeah, Temkhin got nervous, wants to stay out of sight."

"Fifty grand, bro. That's what he owes us."

"You know it."

They had been waiting for quite a while, and the sun was high overhead when a long white Lincoln Town Car glided into the turnout. It parked fifty feet away, and Basil Temkhin emerged. He took a step toward the Hummer, lit a cigarette, and stood there.

"Here we go."

Ty checked his pistol. Earl reached into the rear and picked up a small duffel bag. They joined Temkhin in the middle of the pavement.

"*Gospoda!* How you are?" Big smile.

"We're good, Basil. You?"

"I am *khorosho*. What have for me? Important artifact, I hope."

"We do have an artifact."

Earl opened the duffel and displayed a metallic hemisphere. He nodded sagely. "Not from this Earth."

Temkhin's face fell. "A shell? Half shell? This is all?"

"It's an unusual alloy."

"It survived re-entry."

"Ha ha, maybe part of *Soyuz*. But I am waiting for true artifact. Evidence of cosmic civilization."

"Well, this is it. The alien creature dug it up."

"Give me creature."

"Can't do that. It turned into sand."

"Sand." Temkhin's voice hardened. "You say, sand?"

"Who would have believed, but we saw it, didn't we, bro?"

"Damn right."

Temkhin took a few steps back and forth, thinking over the situation. He took a last drag on his cigarette and threw it down.

"I give one thousand dollars for half shell," he decided.

The Durangos rocked back on their heels.

"No, no, pal, you owe us fifty-thousand," reminded Earl.

"I never made agreement."

"Oh yeah, up at AJ's. We work, we get paid. Look at our truck!" demanded Ty.

Temkhin cast a cool glance at the Hummer, unmoved by its wrinkled sheet metal and starred windshield.

"I pay for results."

"And hey, my man, you got 'em, you're holding 'em," growled Ty.

Temkhin sighed dramatically.

"I like you *malchiki,* so American to believe in hard work. Two thousand dollars." He made a gesture, and his rough-hewn old driver got out of the car holding a wallet.

"The fuck you say! Fifty!" snarled Earl. The skin of his face was white and tight. "A deal's a deal. We shook hands."

"Contract? You have paper? I don't think so."

Temkhin produced a wad of bills. Earl slapped them out of his hand. They floated onto the ground. A light breeze wafted most of them into traffic, where passing cars whirled them into paper tornadoes.

"I think our business is done," said Temkhin, with a touch of regret in his voice. "I wish you good health."

"No fucking way, you fucking spy," snapped Earl. He gave Temkhin a hard shove. The Russian staggered backward. His driver shuffled forward.

Temkhin rearranged his jacket. "This is no way to behave."

"Tell you what — fifty thousand! — or how about we turn you in?" said Ty.

"Do what?" Temkhin's face darkened.

"I'll just call the FBI," said Earl. "Send your lying ass to jail."

"You will not do so," countered the Russian.

"Oh no?"

The Durangos turned toward their Hummer. Temkhin's driver raised his hands. His fingers were laced around a nine-millimeter Tokarev pistol.

Blam!

He fired, and Ty slumped to the ground.

Blam!

He fired again, but Earl was already running around the Hummer. He reached inside and came out with an M4A1 military assault rifle. Crouching behind the left front wheel he raised the carbine above his head and held the trigger down.

Bap! Bap! Bap! Bap! Bap! Bap!

The gun chattered, and bullets sprayed every which way.

Temkhin's driver fell backward. Temkhin himself dove to the ground, crawled to the side, then picked himself up and retreated behind the Town Car, now peppered with bullet holes, its windows shattered. Gas was leaking from punctures in the fuel tank. Drips contacted the hot muffler.

Sizzle!

A fire spread along the Town Car's underbody as Earl paused to reload.

Temkhin gauged the pause, took a deep breath, and sprang to the rear of his burning limousine. He popped the trunk lid and hefted a wicked-looking rocket-propelled grenade launcher. He aimed it at the Hummer.

Whoooosh!

The rocket streaked across the turnout.

BOOM!

The rocket bored into the Hummer's sheet metal and exploded, blowing it into the air and dumping it on its side. The blast sent Earl flying. When the Hummer came down, it crushed Earl's feet, trapping him.

Temkhin limped onto the roadway and flagged down a UPS truck that was passing by.

The driver skidded to a stop and dialed 9-1-1.

55

In the ITF team's darkened temporary lab, Garibaldi was crouched on a stool beside their otherworldly cube. He was studying the flickering lights, trying to discern a pattern.

"Okay, on top. Let's call it Face One — I see a repetition. Nine squares arranged symmetrically on the surface, blinking one after another, starting with the, um, left corner."

"Left?"

Weatherall was sitting beside him, wearing a camping headlight, taking notes.

"I dunno, left, west, damn, how should we identify the parts?"

"Got a Sharpie?"

"Whoops, no destructive testing."

Weatherall rose from her chair and found a roll of plastic electrical tape on the workbench. She cut a little piece free.

"Is a sticker 'destructive testing,' do you think?"

Garibaldi pressed the tape against the cube.

"All right then, blinking starts at the marked corner and proceeds — not sure — looks random."

Weatherall scribbled on her notepad. "Next?"

Garibaldi peered at one of the side faces. "Blinking starts on the corner opposite the mark, but against the already described Face One. But on this side, call it Face Two, three corner squares are blinking simultaneously."

"How? That's ambiguous."

"I know, I know. Let's number the squares one through nine, going rows top to bottom."

"Okay, noted."

"So the blink starts at squares four, one, two. Then two, three, six, then six, nine, eight, then eight, seven, four, then square five alone . . . and then, it just repeats again and again. Not so random."

"Got it. A pattern."

Garibaldi went around the cube, methodically calling out the sequences. Weatherall wrote everything down. On Face Three, the squares flashed in alternating V-shapes , five squares at a time. On Face Four, it was alternating crosses and diagonals. Face Five blinked in marching pairs.

Garibaldi stuck his hands into latex gloves. "Okay, I'm clean, I'm picking up the cube. And on Face Six we see, starting directly opposite the Face One mark, individual squares firing in a clockwise pattern, followed by the center square . . ."

"No animal could ever figure this out," groaned Weatherall.

"Animal, hell, *I* can't figure it out. But I'm going to try."

"Don't you dare press any buttons, Roman."

"Just kidding."

56

Holzgraf and Chow were asleep in bed, locked together arm in arm.

He had taken up residence in the offices of his little research company shortly after opening for business. Hasty wood framing, unpainted drywall, and a plastic curtain separated his living quarters from the work area. A tiny kitchenette and a rudimentary bathroom completed the picture of rough and ready domesticity.

Suddenly his eyes flew open. He glanced at the bedside alarm clock. Late evening, not yet midnight. He squinted toward the skylight overhead. Dark out there. He struggled to free himself from Chow's embrace without waking her up.

He sat up slowly, gingerly flexing his very sore muscles and silently vowing to buy a double bed as soon as stores opened. He hung his legs over the side, reached for a shirt and pulled it on. He stuck his legs into his standard jeans and pushed his feet into a pair of hiking boots. He stood up.

"Where are you going?" came Chow's groggy voice.

"Can't sleep," he said, running a hand through his matted hair.

She yawned. "What's the problem? This is . . . mmm . . . very cozy."

Holzgraf yanked the bedroom curtain aside. He drew water and placed it on his two-burner stove to boil.

"I got to thinking about the team," he said. "The team . . . and temptation."

Chow sat up. She threw off the blanket and threw on her clothes. "You think someone will press the wrong button?"

"I do."

"Who?"

Holzgraf poured hot water over instant coffee grains. He handed a cup to Chow.

"Remember our spiritual advisor lady? She was sure those bushes had minds, persuasive powers. What if that little cube does too? Urge people to activate it? What if . . ?"

". . . one of us can't resist?"

"Yeah. I want to be around and make sure everything happens like it should."

"That guy Boggs. Marianne said he was weird. And" — Chow made a self-deprecating shrug — "she was right about Jim. He's weird too. So, if anyone, it would be Boggs, or maybe even our captain."

▼

Chow drove them across town in her Impreza. On the way she squeezed the steering wheel hard, gulped, and broached a concern.

"You told me your mother was kind of . . . judgmental."

"Stepmother. She's young enough to be my sister,"

"She's anglo?"

"Oh boy. More protestant than Martin Luther. Debutante, country club, charity balls, cultural causes, you name it. Pittsburgh royalty."

Chow stole a glance at her own dark eyes and round Asian face in the rear view mirror. "What is she going to think of me?"

Holzgraf laughed. He leaned over and kissed her on the cheek. "She is going to be outraged. You! Me! Dogs and cats living together! The shame of it! Her friends will never speak to her again."

Chow sank down in her seat. "No, come on, really?"

Holzgraf delicately touched the bruise on her forehead. "Here's the thing. The family has always insisted that Darlington Industries be run by an engineer. I'm first in the line to dodge that responsibility. But you *are* an engineer. Hydraulics, yet."

"The watery municipal kind, not oil and big diggers."

"Doesn't matter. You'd be surprised how closely sewage and hydraulic fluids resemble each other."

"Oh sure. I'll never show my face. We have to elope."

"Nonsense. Mavis is going to love you."

"How's that?"

"Your pedigree! Someday, *you* — madam engineer — *you* are going to run the company. Darlington's darling!"

"And you?"

"I'll be your wholly owned subsidiary."

57

Dr. Garibaldi couldn't sleep either. Earlier in the evening Lockwood and Boggs had relieved Weatherall and himself from their watch over the cube, the presumed box. He knew that, once those two timed out, the security forces would lock up for the night. And the cube was on his mind, unbidden, unwelcome, filling him with puzzle thoughts, interfering with much needed rest.

He rose from the couch where he was huddled up, shuffled into a bathroom in the hallway, peed, and brushed his teeth. He put on a T-shirt and chinos over running shoes and stealthily made his way downstairs, outside, along a brightly illuminated sidewalk, and into the building that housed the team's temporary lab.

Only one airman on guard this late.

Garibaldi unlocked the lab door.

"Excuse me, sir, we heard your group only works in pairs."

"That's right," — he checked the stripes on the airman's blouse — "*Sergeant.* Only in pairs. But my colleague had a long day, so tell you what — why don't you join me? Be the other half of the pair?"

"Really?"

"Why not? I could use the company."

Garibaldi pushed his way into the lab, followed closely by the airman, who looked mighty pleased to join the team.

"Got a flashlight, Sergeant?"

"Yessir, right here."

"Good. I'm going to need reference to my notes, and we won't see much on this little block here with the lights on."

"Shall I douse the lights, sir?"

"Please."

The airman hit a switch and the room went dark. As the two men approached the little cube, outlines of tiny squares started flickering over its surface.

"If you don't mind me asking, sir, what is this? What's going on?"

Garibaldi pointed at the cube. "This . . . this is a box. With a combination lock. We're trying to understand the combination."

"What kind of box? That Chinese woman wouldn't tell me anything."

Garibaldi gauged the young man standing before him, decided that he was a member in good standing of the millennial generation. "You play video games?"

"Yes, sir, I do. All the time. Well, when I'm not on duty."

"This is a like a video game. Think Rubik's Cube, but with a little computer inside."

"Got it. But . . . that doesn't explain —"

"— What it is? What we're doing?"

"No, sir, it does not."

"And you're pretty curious, am I right?"

"You bet I am."

"Well, it really *is* a game," Garibaldi avowed. "A war game. The Red Team has encoded this box, and the Blue Team is going to prove they've got their heads up their butts. We're going to decode it."

"You . . . you're on the Blue Team."

"That's right. Now, here are my notes. Let's see what we can see."

Garibaldi pulled on his latex gloves, pressed his lips together, and lifted the cube, being careful to balance it gently between fingertips on opposite corners. He slowly turned it over and over, examining each face with the reverence worthy of a holy relic. The little squares lighting up reflected off his glasses, giving his eyes a glittery intensity.

"I think we start with Face Six. What's the note say?"

"Face Six. Single squares around perimeter. Four, one, two, three, six, nine, eight, seven. Then center. Boy, complicated."

Garibaldi watched the lights chase each other around the edges of Face Six. Then, when the center square lit up, he pressed his thumb down on it. At his touch all nine squares lit up and stayed lit.

"Tah-dah!" said the airman, thrilled to be part of the action.

"Now, I think, Face Five."

The airman read the note. "Face Five, lights in pairs."

"Two at a time, yes, here we go." Garibaldi waited for the central square to glow, then jammed his thumb down. Again, all the squares lit up.

"Very good, very good. Face Two, please."

"Face Two, lights at the corners, three at a time."

"Unh-huh." Garibaldi waited for the central square to light, then pressed. As expected, all the squares then lit up.

"Halfway there. What's next?"

"Face Four. Squares in crosses."

"Right." Garibaldi turned the cube over looking for the face with the pattern. When he found it he waited patiently for the center square to light up. Once again the surrounding squares came to life at his touch.

"Pretty cool. Face Three is next on your list, sir," said the airman, eager to proceed.

"I remember now, V-shaped patterns." Garibaldi pressed the center square, watched the entire face light up. He sat back, knitted his fingers together behind his head, and stretched. "So far, so good," he said.

"You're doing great, sir, really great."

"Here's what I'm worried about — Face One. It's random, no pattern I can see. But it always starts at the marked corner, so . . ."

He readied a finger over the corner square.

"No, no, sir, pardon me, sir."

Garibaldi's finger hung in midair. "What?"

"Notice how the squares light up one after another, but then there's a pause before they go again. There's no pattern, but the last light is followed by a little pause. Didn't you notice? That's the one to punch."

"Oh, I didn't see that. Why not the first one, always the same?"

"I'm a gamer, sir. Trust me on this."

Garibaldi leaned in toward the cube. His face was inches away, his finger poised to finish the job.

"Whoa there, Doc!"

Holzgraf burst into the lab and rushed to Garibaldi's side.

"Put the cube down!"

"I can't," said Garibaldi. His eyes were glazed.

Holzgraf made a grab for the thing, but Garibaldi snatched it out of reach.

"We must notify. It is our duty."

"No it's not. Come on, give me that thing."

Garibaldi stood up and carried the cube into a far corner of the lab.

"Stay back. I don't want to go through the sequence again . . . it's tiring."

"Watch out, Guy, something's funny," warned Chow, arriving on the run and out of breath. "Nancy's on her way."

Holzgraf turned to the airman standing by. "You — arrest this guy, he's going to ruin everything."

"Geez, I'm not authorized to make actual arrests."

Holzgraf closed on Garibaldi. "Listen, Doc — you know the rules. We're not supposed to mess around."

"It is research," said the scientist. His voice had acquired a mechanical quality.

At that moment Weatherall appeared. She was wearing a flannel robe and bunny rabbit slippers.

"For God's sake, Roman, give us that cube."

"No. I'm in charge here."

"Don't be silly. You could be exposing the human race to disaster."

"I'm giving us the chance to take our place in the galaxy," he replied.

Holzgraf and Chow looked at each other in disbelief. Their colleague had obviously drifted over the edge.

"You have no idea what you're talking about," growled Weatherall. She strode forward, put out a hand to wrench the cube away. But just then the random pattern of lights on Face One settled on a final square.

Garibaldi raised a finger and brought it down on the spot. All the squares on all six faces blinked in unison.

Crack!

The cube unlocked. Its faces hinged outward.

Flash!

Something previously hidden inside the cube flared like a torch, casting eerie shadows on the walls and momentarily blinding everyone. Chow stumbled to the door and groped for the light switch. When the big fluorescents kicked in, they revealed Garibaldi slumped down against the wall with his legs splayed sideways. What had been a grey metal cube was now a cross-shaped set of flat plates draped across the scientist's lap.

The box — described by a woman with second sight, located by an extraterrestrial robot, and secured by enthusiastic amateurs — was *open*.

58

Upshaw mustered his team early in the morning. He was beside himself.

"All right, boys and girls, I've been on the phone all night. Here's where we stand. My superiors — there are so many — have not yet agreed on the future of the Immigrant Task Force. My guess is, we'll be disbanded. But they have to figure out where to store the remaining bushes and our formerly cubicle artifact."

"And who gets to study them," said Weatherall.

"Who and where and under what conditions of safety. You want in, I can probably make it happen."

"In spite of our screw-up?" marveled Holzgraf.

"I'm a persuasive kind of guy. But why I don't just fire your useless asses, I do not know. Getting sentimental in my advancing years."

Weatherall was sitting on an arm of the office settee. She moved to the coffee dispenser and poured herself a cup.

"How's Roman?"

Upshaw toyed with a pen on his desk. "He's still in a coma, over in the infirmary."

"Ooh," said Chow.

"Probably a good thing. It's obvious to me that the box itself affected him. Messed up his mind. He didn't plan to break the rules on his own."

"What do your superiors have to say about that?"

"His condition is his defense," asserted the general. "My bureaucratic instincts tell me he'll come out of this with his reputation — how's this sound? — 'battered but intact.'"

"With a headful of stories he can retail over beers later on."

"If he wakes up."

"Right — if."

Upshaw picked up a newspaper and handed it to Weatherall. "Here's something else. Our competitors. Have a look —"

TUCSON DRUG DEAL GOES BAD

Yesterday afternoon a firefight with automatic weapons broke out on South Houghton Road. Dozens of shots were fired. One man was killed, two others are hospitalized with critical wounds, and two vehicles are burned-out hulks. Tucson police speculate that a major drug deal skidded out of control when a dispute over money and inventory occurred.

The team passed the story around. Upshaw paused to let them read, then filled in some details.

"Newspapers! What they don't know and never figure out" — he shook his head — "Drug deal? The man killed was a Russian *spetsnaz* operative, no ID. He was apparently protecting a mineral trader by the name of Basil Temkhin from the tender mercies of our friends the Durango brothers, who are now hanging on for dear life in the Tucson hospital ICU."

"Temkhin!" said Chow. "I think I met him at the gem show. He could barely speak English." She made a fist. "I knew he was a spy."

Upshaw grimaced. "You were right. His real name, I've been told, is Semyon Voroshilov. He was here on a diplomatic passport, and he's already out of the country."

"Back home to mother Russia," guessed Lockwood.

"One supposes," said Upshaw with a deep and weary sigh.

▼

Two days later the Davis-Monthan duty nurse called Upshaw. Garibaldi's vital signs were changing. She reported that the infirmary's encephalograph was no longer just recording alpha waves and spindles. Instead, theta waves were now being seen. She also noted that his core body temperature was elevated from the admitting benchmark.

"Which means?" asked Upshaw, baffled by the technical terms.

"He's out of the coma. Slipped into deep sleep. Give him a few hours and you can say hello."

▼

When Garibaldi finally woke up, his mouth was dry. He ran his tongue over his teeth. The terrible taste made him gag. He had to strain to open his eyes, which felt like they were glued shut. When he was finally able to focus, he saw the rest of the ITF team standing at the foot of his bed.

"Hey, Roman. Welcome back," said Weatherall.

"Christ, I urble argle wubble."

"What was that?"

"Ahhh, urb, urb, sorry, fahh."

The team's faces registered alarm. But suddenly the scientist thrashed around and sat up. He tugged at the IV drip connected to his hand.

"Huh? Whass ith?" He smacked his gooey lips. "What am I doing here?"

He was starting to sound coherent. Exhales of relief from the team.

"You, uh, had an accident," offered Weatherall.

"Accidental exposure," said Chow.

"Whoa, radiation sickness? Am I dying?"

"No, no, you're going to be fine," assured Upshaw.

Garibaldi's expression became suspicious. "What kind of accident?"

Old man Boggs piped up: "You opened the box."

"Never! I would never do that."

"Well, yes, you did, Roman," grunted Upshaw. "You were hypnotized, I guess. And the strain knocked you colder than a beer in the arctic."

Garibaldi flopped back down on the bed. "Oh shit . . ! A crime against humanity, and I'm the guilty one."

"Suppose that stuff you told us about q-bits and quantum mumbo jumbo is true . . ." began Holzgraf.

"And it could be," interjected Weatherall. "We've seen a lot of stuff that ain't in the literature."

". . . and suppose that the robots who sent the box have already found out we opened it up," continued Holzgraf, trying for optimism. "Uh-oh, they now know we're smart enough to solve their little puzzle. But this isn't *Star Trek.* It will take them a hundred years to get here, cause us trouble, right?"

"If they even want to make the trip," added Weatherall.

"You're scared," mumbled Garibaldi. "You should be."

"I'm not going let myself be scared," promised Chow. "Maybe we'll get them to clean our floors, like one of those little Roomba gadgets."

"Attagirl," said Lockwood. He admired her spunk, but seemed to think she was whistling in the dark. The rest of the group paid their respects with encouraging words and drifted away, but Lockwood lingered behind. He waited until he was alone with the government scientist.

"Hey, Doc, looking good. Feeling better?"

"Mmm . . ."

"Up to a conversation?"

"Depends. Why?"

"Technical questions."

Garibaldi raised himself on an elbow, curiosity aroused. "I'll give it a whirl. Shoot."

"Nancy might be right — alien robots might not want to intrude on a planet already populated by intelligent beings. And Holly might be right — if they do come, they'll be our little slaves."

"Anything's possible."

"Right. But I have thought about this. The bushes and their trans-formations are — *at the very least* — a potential threat to humanity. You, Holly and Guy, their children, generations yet to come, very nice beings as the galaxy goes, all at risk. I have an idea on how to contain the threat, but I need a lot of help in the nuts-and-bolts department."

Garibaldi, hitherto in a twilight stage of awakening, sat up, wide-eyed.

"Captain Lockwood? Now you're a scientist?"

"No DNA in those things, right?"

"That's right. Absolutely correct."

"But there's an organizing principle, or they couldn't do what they do."

"We have no idea."

"I think it's electromagnetic," declared Lockwood.

"Possible. I suppose that's the alternative," mused Garibaldi, willing to be convinced. "And you, an ex-military officer without technical training, you've got a plan?"

"I do."

"Pardon my surprise. Care to tell me?"

"Pushback. What military types would call *counterforce.*"

59

"Where the hell is Lockwood?"

Upshaw had called a meeting, eager to impart breaking news, but Captain James Lockwood, his chief lieutenant, was nowhere to be found.

Upshaw looked over his partially assembled team. "Guy — take a look around. I checked the gate, and he's on the base. Somewhere."

"Sure, I'm on it."

"And see if Garibaldi is up and at 'em. Can't find him either. Where's my discipline? What kind of operation am I supposed to be running?"

Holzgraf searched the building, made inquiries, and eventually found Lockwood and Garibaldi huddled over a workbench in the team's temporary laboratory.

They were working on a crude assemblage of electronic gear. Two different computer motherboards, three switching power supplies, a solid state laser, a signal generator, comb filters, and more. Holzgraf, barely aware of hardware design, was astounded.

"What in the world — ?"

Lockwood was wearing safety goggles while he soldered a connection between the main heavy-duty transformer and one of the power blocks. He barely looked up.

"It's a . . . whatsis," said Garibaldi.

"Huh?"

"I don't really know. It's Jim's project."

"Jim?"

Lockwood finished connecting the joint he was working on. He raised his goggles.

"Guy, just the man I want to see. Almost done here, but I need a klystron and about two feet of wave guide. V-band. We ripped apart one of the A-10 radars, but it's not what we're looking for."

Holzgraf stared at the collection of parts on the bench. A wisp of smoking solder flux wafted upward from the contraption.

"What are you looking for . . . exactly?"

"We need to propagate a rising microwave signal alongside a descending one at different frequencies," explained Garibaldi. "Make a kind of radio

282

moiré pattern."

"I'm lost."

"And I need the klystron for the ascending signal," said Lockwood. "Put it beside the magnetron I scrounged here." He pointed at a jungle of wires and heavy-duty electrical components.

"Did you call the vendors? This is high-tech country, someone must have a klystron, or whatever you want."

"Done. Zero. I see oscillators in the catalogs, but we need a drift tube. And, I heard that your father runs a big industrial company back east."

"Dad passed away. My uncle runs the company."

"Oh. He must have suppliers, contacts."

"Probably. But you need to talk to Holly."

Holzgraf punched a number into his phone and called Chow. She showed up a few minutes later, heard the requirements, made some notes. The pair then excused themselves and wandered outside, where Holzgraf made another telephone call.

"Rudi? Guy."

"The prodigal son checks in," said his uncle. "We were beginning to wonder if you had disappeared off the face of the Earth. How's life with perovskite?"

"You remember."

"Of course. Your stepmother and I are very interested in your progress. You never call."

"No disrespect, just busy. I'm calling now. Tell Mavis that our little enterprise is on track."

"Knowing you, that sounds just a little too good to be true."

"You're right, I'm making that up. Tell her anyway. She shouldn't be worrying about me."

Uncle Rudi chuckled.

"Here's my problem. I need a klystron tube."

"A what?"

"Microwave equipment."

"We make hydraulics. Nothing more high-tech than synthetic oils."

"You've got purchasing agents. They'll know. I need this like yesterday."

"Give me the details."

Chow was walking around with her arms folded tight against her body to ward off the chill of a cool spring morning. Holzgraf grabbed her hand and placed his phone in it. He made talking gestures. She just stood there. He bent her arm and raised the phone to her head.

"Mr. Holzgraf?" she said in a small voice.

"Yes . . ."

"Okay, we need a klystron drift tube, operating in the V-band, 60 gigahertz. Plus two feet of V-band waveguide and a five kilowatt power supply we can run off standard 240 volts."

"Say again? I'm looking for a pencil."

Chow repeated the specs while Uncle Rudi wrote them down. She tossed the phone back to Holzgraf like a hot potato.

"Who was that?" The company CEO's voice contained more than a hint of curiosity.

"Business associate," said Holzgraf. He grinned at Chow. She made a sour face.

"A woman," said Uncle Rudi in a suspicious tone.

"She works for me. You know, Darlington Energetix."

"Does she now?" Uncle Rudi didn't sound convinced. "Listen, kiddo, what I'm hearing . . . if this is romance, remember — your stepmother controls your inheritance." His voice became iron-hard. "And know this, the family will require a pre-nup if it goes all the way."

Holzgraf's face reddened. "If I inherit, great. If not, too bad. Tell Mavis — that's a discussion for another day. I'm just growing the shop."

Uncle Rudi registered his nephew's indignation and backed off. "All right, I'll get on it."

"Thanks for understanding. This is urgent with a capital U. Have it expedited ASAP to I-T-F, at Davis-Monthan Air Force Base, Tucson."

"I-T-F, what's that?"

"Some friends . . . uh, joint project. They rent space here."

"On an air base?"

"The Air Force is looking to cut costs. Privatizing their real estate."

"The government . . ."

"Right, hopeless. Home soon." He looked fondly at Chow. "Lots to talk about when I get there."

60

Dr. Garibaldi knocked on Upshaw's office door and slipped inside. The general was busy signing purchase orders for a long list of electronic gear. He turned a measuring eye on the scientist, whose recovery seemed rapid and complete.

"Roman! How you feeling?"

"Morning, Mo. Headache's gone." A faint smile played around his face, crinkling his eyes.

"Glad to hear it. What's on your mind?"

"Jim wants to see us all down in the gym."

"What for?"

"He's been working day and night on a secret project. He claims it will neutralize those bushes."

Upshaw brought a hand down on the pile of requisition slips littering his desk. "Is that what all this paperwork is about?"

"Guess so."

Upshaw snorted. "Jim doesn't know the first thing about hardware."

"Nope, but he learns fast. And, of course, I helped him through the rough stuff."

"Is he actually onto something?"

"Hard to tell. He's got an idea, and it might work. I've been worried that we will find a lot more of these bushes when we start looking hard. Jim thinks we can take care of them and sleep at night."

The team gathered in the gymnasium.

Holzgraf and Chow arrived from Darlington Energetix, where they had just finished analyzing the byproducts of their perovskite crystal arrays. They were floating on air, because the results confirmed their suspicion — hydrocarbons — in abundance — fuel for the future.

Weatherall came from a trip to the Tucson Mall way up north on Oracle road. She was dressed in the lightweight shorts and knit top she had just purchased. She crushed a smoke on the sidewalk and joined the group.

Old man Boggs was off pursuing his former livelihood, digging up semi-precious stones in the hills, and it took an hour and a half for him to show up. He arrived with a beautiful amethyst geode to show his colleagues.

When everyone was on scene, Lockwood rolled a cart into the gym. On the upper shelf was a laptop computer tethered to two skeletal motherboards and a signal generator. Below that were heavy iron core transformers and power amps.

Garibaldi followed, rolling a large box on casters, the multi-kilowatt power supply ordered up by Holzgraf.

The group oohed and ahhed over the gear, but what impressed them most was the big cylindrical klystron tube resting on the cart like a cannon.

"Looks like we've got ourselves a ray gun," said Upshaw.

Garibaldi ran a power cord from the hallway and plugged it into the untidy pile of electronic parts. Lights twinkled on the enigmatic boxes and controls.

Lockwood made an exit and returned with three of the metallic bushes the team had acquired. He set them out in the center of the basketball court.

Upshaw raised a hand.

"Okay, team. Before we start, I have a few words to say," he announced, adopting a firm tone designed to grab attention away from Lockwood's apparatus.

"The bad news is, the Joint Powers Immigration Task Force is being disbanded."

Murmurs of sad disappointment; the team's worst fears confirmed.

"The State Department is wording up a confidential memorandum to inform world leaders about our little box." He was amused by the idea. "Who knows what will happen when they kick over the diplomatic anthill?"

"So the army is taking over?" queried Weatherall. Her grim tone suggested resignation, combined with a big dose of jealousy.

"Homeland will run things, at least on paper. But yes, our stout-hearted men in uniform will be the real organizers. Big-time logistics, intelligence ops, firepower if needed — that's what they're good at."

Gripes and groans.

"Don't look so glum. Our little group will march bravely on, merging into the big picture. A rose by any other name. We will continue to pursue our charter to find, capture, and sequester as many of these damn glittering bushes as we can."

"Hear, hear," said Weatherall with a silly smile, surprised at her own profound sense of relief.

"What about me?" asked Garibaldi, still aching with guilt over his unauthorized activities.

"You too, Roman. The higher-ups are in a forgiving mood."

Scattered clapping from Garibaldi's teammates.

"Ready for more news?"

Something about Upshaw's tone further darkened the team's mood.

"On we go, but not with me driving the truck. I'm returning to NASA Ames, where I will resume my distinguished career as a government bureaucrat."

Confused protests.

"I'm lucky they didn't bust my ass out of the agency."

Noises of sympathetic denial.

"Look on the bright side," he continued. "I won't be around to yell at you. I'll be signing your checks instead."

"Who then?" asked Weatherall.

Upshaw pointed. "Jim, here. He'll be administrator in charge, and the rest of you will be working for him."

Voices chorused loud approval. "Hey, Jim! Jim, my man! Go, Jim!"

"Based here?" wondered Lockwood, as surprised by the turn of events as everyone else.

"Until you feel there's another locus for these things."

Lockwood's face clouded over. "Not sure this is a good idea. Don't count on anything."

Upshaw nodded to the group. "So that's the plan. Let's see what your new leader has in mind for us . . ."

Lockwood shook off his obvious doubts and took up a position in front of the pile of electronics. He folded his arms.

"Okay, then, human beings. Holly, Nancy, Roman, Guy, and you too, General — you are biological organisms, complex, the result of literally billions of years of trial, error, and occasional success.

"The entities we have discovered are robots. Very likely created by highly evolved creatures who have since disappeared, if you believe our helpful, uhh, consultant, Ms. Sarzeau.

"Well, robots and biology don't necessarily mix. Biology advances by competition — it's often violent — and when intelligence triumphs, we're still stuck with our instincts. The dark side. Original sin."

The group was getting restless. No one had ever heard Lockwood speak in this manner, at once affectionate and detached, scholarly and practical.

"What is he talking about?" whispered Chow.

"This is a new Jim. His idea of leadership?" replied Holzgraf through the side of his mouth.

"Like most people, I have great fondness for biology," continued Lockwood, "not least because of the friends I've made with the rest of you, and by observing the deep affection that you have for each other."

He directed a little wave toward Chow and Holzgraf.

"But robots have no evolutionary history to overcome. They may well think the galaxy is better off without the burden of a murderous past."

"You're guessing," said Weatherall.

"They might be friendly," opined Boggs. "Just plants looking for good dirt."

"Who knows, anyway?" hoped Chow.

"You don't know," granted the team's newly-appointed director. "But I believe those robots are coming. Their technology is — obviously — far beyond anything dreamed of by men and women. When they arrive they will, as a result of their superiority, likely have weapons that can wipe humanity from the face of the Earth."

Upshaw scoffed at the idea. "How is that possible? Wars always leave survivors. The worst diseases, like Ebola, always burn themselves out."

"Good point, sir. Maybe you're right. But humanity is up against a real threat. So it wouldn't hurt to have the perfect weapon to fight back with . . ."

Lockwood gestured to the carts standing behind him.

"That's what this is."

"Are you serious?"

"Let's show 'em, Doc."

Garibaldi connected plugs, flipped switches. A low hum filled the air. Lockwood took up the klystron tube and fitted the wave guide on the end, making the thing look like an assault weapon crossed with a vacuum cleaner.

"Ready?"

Garibaldi checked status lights and meters.

"All set. Let her rip."

Lockwood swiveled around and aimed the klystron toward the bushes at center court. The laser sight clamped on the waveguide flickered over the leaves. He pressed a button.

Howl!

A high-pitched electronic squeal resonated through the gym. All three bushes collapsed into piles of sand.

Lockwood's witnesses gasped.

Lockwood himself bowed theatrically. "Here you have it — my little contribution to humanity's future," he said.

"The grains of sand — metallic crystals really — are like cells, but instead of DNA they have nano-computers that know how to talk to each other and arrange their shapes," he explained.

Old man Boggs shivered. He quietly backed away from the group.

Upshaw was having trouble seeing his assistant as a full-blown expert on anything, much less alien life forms. "How, Jim — how in hell did you figure this out?"

"I've been suspicious for a while. Dasher got me thinking hard."

"Unh-huh, and the electronic know-how?"

"That's Garibaldi. I had the idea to erase their programming, but Roman helped me build this." He raised the klystron and shook it. "Just a prototype."

Chow clapped her hands. "But we've got a hundred years to perfect it."

Lockwood frowned. The klystron drooped. "Afraid not," he said.

"What?" Garibaldi was surprised by the somber tone.

"See, they're here already. They are, among other things, *parasites.*"

"W-T-F — as we say in our texts," objected Holzgraf. "Parasites? You're kidding, right?"

Lockwood's mouth tightened. "I'll show you what I mean." He turned the klystron on the team and held the switch down.

Whizz!

He swept the beam over his colleagues, to no effect.

"Jesus, Jim," growled Upshaw, mightily annoyed by the cavalier breach of safety protocols.

"See, humans are unaffected," Lockwood noted. "You're all exactly who you think you are."

"Well of course!" spluttered Garibaldi.

"But old Boggs here, that's a different story." Lockwood aimed the klystron at the old prospector.

Boggs shuffled backwards, arms raised in protest. The laser sight appeared on his chest. Lockwood fired again.

Shriek!

Boggs staggered, stumbled, and, just like the bushes, decayed into a pile of sand. His clothes fell to the floor in a heap. Sparkling crystal grains flowed out of the shirt sleeves and pant legs.

Everyone was shocked into silence.

They all stood there for a long time, eyes wide, jaws hanging open, each of them trying to absorb the meaning of the stunning event. General Upshaw pulled himself together first. He moved over, gripped the shirt and shook it. Sandy material poured out. He held it up, now limp and empty.

"Jesus Christ Almighty God," he muttered.

Suddenly everyone was talking at once. Upshaw raised his hands to shut them up. "Boggs! The old man was one of them. How did you know?"

Lockwood shrugged. "He liked to eat dirt."

"Fuck."

Garibaldi toed one of Boggs' shoes and tipped it over, pouring more sand onto the gym floor. "There's nothing human left here."

"No, those particles — slowly, slowly, they eat away at living things."

The implications of this idea gnawed at Garibaldi.

"Could there be more? What if another craft landed in Siberia, say?" Or on Mars? Waiting for us when we get there."

Lockwood nodded. "More? Very likely. Those bushes — if you tangle with the big ones, anyway — can sting a lot worse than a cholla. But ashes to ashes and dust to dust, right?"

Chow's face lost all color. She gripped Holzgraf's arm. "Oh no, Guy, I know what's coming."

"What? What's coming?"

Lockwood was staring vacantly at some inner thought.

"You okay, Jim? What's wrong? You don't look well," said Weatherall.

"Here's another thing," the ex-army officer announced. "Robots don't have emotions, so they don't know the rules — no one should ever betray a friend. I certainly wouldn't."

Lockwood propped the klystron on top of the cart, made sure it was balanced there, and turned it on.

"No, Jim! Don't!" cried Chow.

Then he walked around to face the business end.

Squeeee . . .

Like the bushes and like Boggs, Captain James Lockwood dissolved into a pile of sand.

Horrified screams and howls of amazement.

Garibaldi sprang forward and pulled the plug, shutting down the demo.

"Christ — one of them — just like Boggs!" gasped the scientist.

They all stared at Lockwood's clothes on the floor.

Holzgraf and Chow hugged each other.

"One of them . . ."

"But that weapon . . . still on our side, I guess, huh?"

"Human feelings after all . . ."

"Honor among robots, you think?"

A thousand more questions flooded the minds of the Immigration Task Force. But they remained unspoken. A sensation of terrible awe was stealing over the surviving team members like a shadow. They lapsed into reverential silence.

After a long moment, Upshaw lifted one of Lockwood's collapsed pant legs. Sand poured out. He shuddered. He felt stupid. He looked stupid. He cleared his throat.

"Looks like . . . well, damn . . . looks like we need a change in plans."

▲ ▲ ▲

Author's note:
*If you're curious about Marianne Sarzeau, who made a brief appearance in these pages, read **Shadowcop**, **Broomhandle**, and **Whiskeyjack** — she's the principal character.*